Praise for the Liz Talbot Mystery Series

LOWCOUNTRY BOMBSHELL (#2)

"Is there anything more enticing than curling up with a thrilling whodunit that keeps you guessing until the very end? Susan Boyer delivers big time with a witty mystery that is fun, radiant, and impossible to put down. I LOVE THIS BOOK!"

— Darynda Jones,
New York Times Bestselling Author

"*Lowcountry Bombshell* is that rare combination of suspense, humor, seduction, and mayhem, an absolute must-read not only for mystery enthusiasts but for anyone who loves a fast-paced, well-written story!"

— Cassandra King,
Author of *The Same Sweet Girls* and *Moonrise*,
inspired by Daphne du Maurier's *Rebecca*

"Another sharp, sassy, intriguing mystery...filled with unique southernisms, gracious charm, and a cast of eccentric characters... *Lowcountry Bombshell* is a cozy feeling, hard boiled PI novel with a little romance thrown in. The best of three genres all mixed together."

— Nancy McFarlane,
Fiction Addiction Reviewer

LOWCOUNTRY BOIL (#1)

"Imaginative, empathetic, genuine, and fun, *Lowcountry Boil* is a lowcountry delight."

— Carolyn Hart,
Author of *What the Cat Saw*

Lowcountry
BOMBSHELL

**The Liz Talbot Mystery Series
by Susan M. Boyer**

LOWCOUNTRY BOIL (#1)
LOWCOUNTRY BOMBSHELL (#2)
LOWCOUNTRY BONEYARD (#3)
(April 2015)

Lowcountry
BOMBSHELL

A Liz Talbot Mystery

Susan M. Boyer

HENERY PRESS

LOWCOUNTRY BOMBSHELL
A Liz Talbot Mystery
Part of the Henery Press Mystery Collection

First Edition
Trade paperback edition | September 2013

Henery Press
www.henerypress.com

This is a work of fiction. Any references to historical events, real people, or real locales are used fictitiously. Other names, characters, places, and incidents are the product of the author's imagination, and any resemblance to actual events or locales or persons, living or dead, is entirely coincidental.

ISBN-13: 978-1-938383-56-4

Printed in the United States of America

*This one is for my parents, Wayne & Claudette Jones,
who inspired my love of fast, red cars.*

ACKNOWLEDGMENTS

First, foremost, and always, thank you, Jim Boyer. I could not write my stories and chase my dreams without your unlimited love and support. Thank you to each and every member of my wonderful family for your patience with my crazy schedule.

Thank you, Donald Spoto, for the detailed research that went into your fascinating biography of Marilyn Monroe. To Jenna Glatzer, for the feast of visuals and memorabilia in The Marilyn Monroe Treasures. These books informed my understanding of the person behind the icon.

Thank you Jonathan, the waiter at Anson Restaurant in Charleston, SC, whose tie-clip caught my eye, and who graciously agreed to appear as himself in a cameo in this book. Thank you to everyone on the other end of the phone at the Hampton Inn in Mount Pleasant, SC, and various places all over Charleston County who answered strange questions and saved me a second or third trip.

Thank you, Stephany Evans, literary agent extraordinaire, Jacqueline Murphy, Becky Vinter, and everyone at FinePrint Literary Management. To Kathie Bennett, possibly the world's most creative publicist, Susan Zurenda, and everyone at Magic Time Literary Agency. To Rowe Copeland, The Book Concierge, without whose spreadsheets and schedules things would go the quickest route to torment.

Thank you, Kristin Weber. I count myself exceedingly fortunate that you are my first reader. To my sister, Sabrina Niggel, my mother, Claudette Jones, John and Marcia Migacz, Jan Rubens, and Bob and Vicki Strother, all of whom helped me find the mistakes I could no longer see.

A very special thank you to Jill Hendrix, owner of Fiction Addiction book store, for your advice, help, and creative solutions that have helped me numerous times along this journey.

To Darynda Jones, Cassandra King, and Nancy McFarlane, thank you, thank you, thank you!

Thank you to all my friends at Romance Writers of America, Sisters in Crime, Mystery Writers of America, and the South Carolina Writers' Workshop.

Thank you to all my Hen House sisters for your friendship and support—and let us not forget the roosters. And last, but never least, my heartfelt thanks to Kendel Flaum, Art Molinares, and everyone at Henery Press.

ONE

The dead are not troubled by the passage of time. I know this be-cause my best girlfriend, Colleen, died when we were seventeen. She hasn't aged a day in fourteen years. I turned thirty-one last February and commenced researching wrinkle creams.

My familiarity with the departed accounts for why, on that steamy Wednesday in late July, I entertained the notion that the blonde on my front porch was the ghost of Marilyn Monroe.

The doorbell rang at ten that morning. Rhett barked his fool head off upstairs where I'd stashed him. My golden retriever was unaccustomed to being on lockdown, but I'm a private investigator by trade and was expecting a new client.

Out of habit, I peeked through the sidelight by the front door. The woman on the porch was dressed in white capris with a white blouse knotted at her waist. There was no mistaking the platinum-blonde hair, calendar-girl figure, and beauty mark. Clearly, I hadn't guzzled enough coffee and needed a closer look.

I opened the door. Hot, moist air washed into the foyer.

"Hi," she said. "Are you Liz Talbot?" Her voice was smoky and breathless. It brought to mind Little Bo Peep, if Bo were trying to seduce you. She looked crisp and fresh, in utter defiance of the weather.

"Yes." I nodded slowly. "I was expecting Calista McQueen?"

"That's me," she said.

I tilted my head and looked at her sideways, as if the view might be different from another angle. I could feel my face squishing up in one of those looks Mamma has warned me countless times will cause wrinkles. All that money I'd spent on high-dollar cream would be wasted if I wasn't careful.

The woman on my porch sighed and fixed me with a double-barreled stare. "I'm not her. I'm not related to her, and I'm not one of those tribute artists, either."

"Of course. My goodness, I'm so sorry," I said. "The resemblance is just—"

"Startling, I know." She glanced around the deep porch. Her gaze drifted from the swing, to the hammock, and settled on the Adirondack chairs. "Did you want to meet out here?"

"No, please." I jerked the door open wider and scooted out of the way. "Come in. It's so hot out there I'm afraid my manners must have melted."

"Thanks." She turned and scanned the yard, then crossed into the foyer.

I swept my arm towards the room to her right. "Why don't we talk in here?"

She undulated into what now serves as my office. Like a giant Hoover, her presence sucked my self-confidence right out.

I followed, yanking the clip out of my hair and fluffing as I went. I could hear Phoebe, my hair stylist, ranting now. *Three freakin' hours to get that multi-toned blonde and you cram it into a freakin' clip.* When the temperature and humidity approach triple digits, all this hair causes my brain stem to overheat. At least I was dressed nicely in a cobalt blue shift that matched my eyes. It's hard to go wrong with Ann Taylor Loft.

Calista stopped in front of the fireplace on the far side of the room. She waited, posing the way models do at the end of the runway. "You have a lovely home."

"Thanks," I said. "It was my grandmother's."

Gram had liked to entertain, and her living room was large enough for fifty of her closest friends to gather for mint juleps. I had divided it into sections with my home office, the only office for the Stella Maris branch of Talbot and Andrews Investigations, occupying the left half.

My walnut desk and two guest chairs stood in front of a wall of bookcases that wrapped around the far left corner and flanked the windows on both sides of the fireplace. The opposite side of the room held a big green velvet sofa with wooden trim and a row of fringe around the bottom. It had been Gram's favorite piece. The sofa faced the wall of windows, with a set of chairs on each side to complete the conversation area.

I debated whether to sit behind the desk or on the soft furniture. I'd never met with a new client at home. Since I'd moved back to Stella Maris in April, I'd been holding initial meetings on neutral territory—a restaurant, maybe, or the park. But Calista had balked at that idea. I could see now why she was shy of public places.

I gestured toward the sofa. "Have a seat." While I grabbed a pad and pen from the desk, she arranged herself on the end of the sofa closest to the door. I settled into a tropical-print wingback on her right. Calista looked at the ceiling.

I willed Rhett to stop barking. "Don't mind him," I said. "He doesn't care to be left out. He's accustomed to having the run of the house and yard."

"You should let him come down. I had a dog once..."

"Thanks, but I think we'll be less distracted if he stays upstairs. He'll be quiet when he realizes I'm not letting him out."

Mamma would have been mortified at how long I just sat there staring at Calista McQueen. I kept thinking I'd find something that differentiated her from the movie star, but the woman next to me was Marilyn's doppelganger. I was acquainted with all manner of oddities, but a doppelganger—that was a new one. She must have been used to the staring because she just sat there with perfect posture, letting me get it out of my system.

Finally, I closed my eyes, shook my head to clear it, and located my professionalism. "How can I help you, Ms. McQueen?"

"Please," she said, "call me Calista."

I nodded. "I'm Liz."

She moistened her lips. "I'd like you to keep me alive."

"If someone's threatened you, we need to call the police."

"No one has threatened me."

I squinted at her. "Then why are you in fear for your life?"

"This is a long story," she said. "Could I please have a glass of water?"

"Of course." I jumped up. "Where *are* my manners? I just made some fresh tea..."

"Oh, that'd be swell."

"Lemon, mint, or both?"

"Mint, please," she said. "Thank you, ever so."

I scrambled to the kitchen. While I waited for the tap water to run hot, I heard Mamma's voice in my head lamenting my lapse in hospitality. I scrubbed my hands and slathered them with sanitizer. No sense running the risk of making us both sick. Bacteria are forever on the offensive, but they thrive in hot weather. Some people think roaches would be the only thing left after a nuclear apocalypse, but I'm convinced bacteria would not only survive, they'd kill off the roaches. Certain members of my immediate family make great sport of trying to trace what they refer to as my "nervous habit" to some incident in my childhood, or genetic mutation. This is ridiculous. I simply have a healthy regard for personal hygiene.

I fixed two glasses of tea, took a deep breath, and let it out slowly. Then, I headed back to the living room silently chanting, don't stare, don't stare, don't stare...

I set the glasses on coasters on the mahogany end table between us and returned to the wingback. "Please," I said. "Start at the beginning."

She took a sip of her tea. "My, that's good." She stared at the glass for a moment. When she looked up at me, her eyes shimmered. "This will sound absurd."

"You've come to the right place. I have an appreciation for the absurd."

The edges of her mouth crept up. She fixed her gaze on something far away, outside the row of floor-to-ceiling windows.

"I was born June first, nineteen seventy-six, at nine-thirty a.m., in Los Angeles General Hospital. My birthday was the fiftieth anniversary of hers. To the minute."

I reached for my tea glass but didn't take my eyes off Calista.

She paused for a moment. "My mother named me Norma Jeane. On my birth certificate, it says a man named Mortensen is my father, but I've never met him and I doubt that's his true name. When I was two weeks old, my mother put me in foster care. With very few exceptions, the first eighteen years of my life followed the same pattern as Marilyn's."

I set down my glass and picked up my pad and pen. "Wasn't her last name Baker?"

"She was baptized Norma Jeane Baker, same as me. Her mother's first husband was John Baker, but he was out of the picture long before Norma Jeane was conceived." Calista shrugged. "Martin Edward Mortensen was her mother's most recent husband when Norma Jeane was born, so he's on the birth certificate. It was pretty much the same with me, or at least, that's what they told me. Not the same Martin Edward Mortensen, of course."

I focused on keeping my expression neutral. "Go on."

"Sometimes my mother would pick me up on Saturdays from whatever foster home or orphanage I happened to be living in and take me places. To the movies, mostly, and out to lunch. I lived with her a couple of times, but it never worked out." Calista blinked. "My mother insisted I was the reincarnation of Marilyn Monroe, though I think her friend Grace put that idea in her head to begin with, probably before I was even born, when the doctor told Mother her approximate due date.

"You see, Mother's maiden name is Monroe. She lives in Los Angeles, and they've always been fascinated by Marilyn. Mother is very impressionable. Grace is...ambitious. They were very close, Mother and Grace. Aunt Grace. That's what she had me call her."

"Uh-huh." I felt my eyebrows creep up.

"I think they tried to make my life just like Marilyn's, the foster care, living with relatives, the orphanage. All of it."

"But they couldn't have known how much you'd grow up to look like Marilyn."

"No." Calista slowly shook her head. "At first I think the date ignited Grace's imagination. She was always into numerology, Tarot cards, horoscopes, all of that. As I got older and actually resembled Marilyn, she became more and more obsessed. The strangest thing of all is I don't look as much like her as it seems. *My* hair is naturally this color, Marilyn's wasn't. The head of Columbia studios arranged for electrolysis to raise her hairline, and to have her hair bleached with peroxide and ammonia. Another studio type she had an affair with took her to the orthodontist and had her overbite corrected. Her agent had work done on her nose and her jaw. I've never had any of that done. I look like she looked when they got through with her."

I caught myself staring at her with a tilted head, straightened and smiled. Best not to advertise how I thought she might be making this up. "When did you change your name?"

"I was barely sixteen when I married Jimmy, my first husband. He was five years older, and working at Lockheed. I'd been living with Grace and her family for a while. Grace's husband showed a little too much interest in me. Mother was in some kind of clinic halfway house when she wasn't at Grace's. I'd been dating Jimmy, and Grace arranged for me to marry him. It was either that or go back to the orphanage, since she said they were moving and I couldn't go with them. I had no choice. It was exactly like that with her, with Norma Jeane."

What kind of crazy people invested that much effort into making a child's life a perfect reflection of someone else's?

Calista continued. "Except *her* first husband didn't want her to be a model, and didn't want her to be in the movies. All mine wanted was for me to be a star. He kept setting up photo shoots, sending pictures of me to agents. Mother and Grace prompted him to do it. They nagged him about it. They signed me up for acting classes. They were obsessed with Hollywood, all the glamour. I was their ticket in." She closed her eyes and shuddered. After a moment, her eyes popped open, large and emphatic. "The last thing I wanted to be was a movie star. The summer I turned eighteen, I left California. I got as far away from Hollywood as I could. I divorced Jimmy and I changed my name. I never wanted to see any of them again."

"What made you choose Calista McQueen?" An irrelevant question. I was rattled, no doubt about it. I'd heard some crazy things in my line of work, but this freakish saga stretched the limits of plausible to new dimensions. And yet, her appearance testified to the truth of it.

"I picked Calista because I like the way it sounds. I chose McQueen because I was making my getaway. I always liked that movie, you know? *The Getaway*, with Steve McQueen and Ali McGraw? It's old, but I love old movies. I just don't want to be in them."

"So you left California in, what, nineteen-ninety-four?"

She nodded. "Yes, that's right."

"But you haven't been in Stella Maris since nineteen-ninety-four." Our small town was on an island near Charleston, South Carolina. You might hide from an ex-husband here, but you couldn't hide from your neighbors.

"No, I just moved here a few weeks ago, when my house was finished," she said.

There'd been only one new home built in Stella Maris in the last year. It sat on the shore of the small bay between North Point, where I lived, and Devlin's Point. The contractor, Michael Devlin, and I had a complicated relationship. There'd been a time when I wanted nothing more than to share my life with him, but too much had happened, or perhaps not enough.

The house stood less than a mile down the beach from mine, and Michael had taken me through it a couple of times. It was state-of-the-art hurricane proof. The concrete walls were nearly a foot thick.

I'd watched a crew test the steel shutters one afternoon. The sleek, contemporary home turned into a fortress with the flip of a switch. It wasn't huge, maybe twenty-five hundred square feet, but on a prime, three-acre, oceanfront lot, the house was worth several million dollars.

"Nice house," I said.

"Thanks." She didn't volunteer any information about the house just then, like where she'd come by that kind of money, or how she ended up on Stella Maris. "I lived in Charleston—West Ashley—for nearly sixteen years."

"What did you do there?" I asked.

"I worked in a bank. Of course, I dyed my hair brown and wore it flat. I wore these funny little glasses with no prescription and too much makeup. That's the one thing I enjoyed in the acting classes Mother and Grace made me take, becoming someone else. That's come in handy.

"Anyway, I went to school at night at the College of Charleston. I wanted to be a journalist, but I decided to stay in banking. I thought the money would be better. It's a good thing I did, because one of us needed to have a decent paycheck."

"Us?"

She turned from the window to look at me. "My second husband, Joe, was a baseball player."

"Of course."

It occurred to me that this could be a practical joke. My sister, Merry, and my brother, Blake, were both artists in the field. I didn't know much about Marilyn Monroe's life story. But I knew she'd been married to Joe DiMaggio, and I knew he'd been a famous baseball player for the New York Yankees.

"I met Joe when I was a senior at College of Charleston. He had played for the Charleston Riverdogs. They're a class-A farm team for the New York Yankees. A friend set us up on a blind date."

I couldn't help myself. "Is that how they met? Marilyn and Joe DiMaggio? Blind date?"

"Yes," Calista said. "Well, he asked to be introduced to her. It was—"

"Pretty much the same?"

"Yes. I was twenty-five, and he was thirty-nine. Only a knee injury had kept my Joey out of the majors. By the time I met him he was coaching the Riverdogs." She sipped her tea, set down the glass, and turned back to the window. "Of all the ways I wanted my story to be different from hers, I wished this one thing could have been the same. I always wished Joey could have made it big. He had the bat. His average was nearly four hundred."

"That's incredible," I said, as if I knew a solitary thing about batting averages.

She swiveled her gaze back to me. "I always wondered if it was my fault."

"If what was your fault?"

"Like, if by making things different, not becoming a movie star, you know? If that messed everything up for Joey. Maybe that's even what got him killed." A tear escaped her eye. She brushed it away and looked down at her lap.

The second husband was killed? I was still adjusting to the information that he'd been a baseball player. I took a cleansing breath. We sat there for a minute listening to a couple of birds chirping in the magnolia tree outside the windows. I didn't know how acquainted this improbable tale was with reality, but I knew that she was either a skilled actress, or she was grieving someone she loved. I recognized heartbreak.

"What happened to Joe?"

"He was killed by a carjacker one night after a game a couple of years ago. He must have made Joe get out of the car at Brittlebank Park. That's where they found him the next morning, shot in the head. The police told me he wasn't killed in the car, but on the bank of the Ashley River. They speculated that the killer planned to throw Joey into the river, but something spooked him and he left in a hurry. They never caught the lousy son of a bitch who did it."

"Wait. Somebody robbed and killed your husband across the street from the police department and was never caught?"

She raised her hand in solemn oath. "For eleven bucks and change and a short ride in a lousy fifty-year-old Cadillac convertible."

"How did you know how much money he had? If the carjacker took it?"

"Joey told me. He called before he left the field house. He was going to stop and buy a lottery ticket." She waved her hand dismissively. "He was always buying those damned things. I wanted him to hurry home. It was after eleven. I'd missed the game. I had a migraine. He was going to stop at an ATM, and then by the mini-mart near our neighborhood. He needed thirty bucks for the ticket, and he only had eleven dollars and some change."

"A thirty-dollar lottery ticket?" I asked.

"He always played the same numbers. My birthday, his, the day we met, our first date, the day we got engaged, and the day we got married. He bought a ten-draw ticket, with power play. Thirty dollars every five weeks."

"So, he never made it to the ATM?" I had no idea what her second husband's death had to do with why she needed protection, but I was enthralled.

She shook her head. "No, they checked the camera. At first they thought he'd been robbed at the ATM. But he put the top down, and some guy hopped into the car with him as he was leaving the ballpark. A couple of the guys on the team saw it happen, but they just thought the scum was a friend or something. They didn't think anything about it until they heard Joey'd been killed."

I didn't say anything, just waited for her to go on.

"The killer took Joey's wallet and the watch I gave him for our anniversary. They found the car later that day, abandoned behind a warehouse near the Cooper River Bridge."

"I'm so sorry for your loss," I said.

"Thank you," she said. "I know you must be wondering what all of this has to do with why I'm here."

I pressed my lips into a tight smile and tilted my head in a half nod.

"I just don't know what matters and what doesn't. Do you know what I mean?"

"Sure," I said. Usually I had the opposite problem. People left things out that got them, or me, or both of us in trouble.

Calista was staring out the windows at yesterday again. After a few minutes I asked her, "What have you been doing since Joe died?"

"Dabbling," she said.

I picked up my pen, suddenly conscious of the fact I hadn't taken a single note. I searched for what to write down. "Dabbling in...?"

"Oh, this and that. I've traveled some. At first I just went from one place to another. I spent almost a year in Maine before I came back. It was too painful, being in that house where we shared a life. I sold it, had everything boxed up and moved without ever going back inside."

Lots of questions popped into my head, but I let her talk.

"I stayed in a condo at Wild Dunes, you know, on the Isle of Palms, while they were building my house. I don't think I could ever leave the Lowcountry for good. I figured Stella Maris was close enough to all my Joey memories without being too close."

I nodded, as if she was making perfect sense. After a minute or two, I prompted her, "You must have done very well in banking."

"Oh no, I could have, if we'd moved to a city that was a banking center, like maybe New York, or even Charlotte. For a while, anyway. Now, banking isn't really the field to be in, is it?"

I shook my head in commiseration. I doodled on the pad for a minute, then looked up at her. "All of that traveling must have been expensive. And your house..."

"Ahh." She held up an index finger and took a sip of her tea. "You're wondering about the money. Not everything is about money, you know. But you should know about it, if for no other reason than you can quickly eliminate it as a motive."

She rubbed her lips together and sighed. "I've paid a series of attorneys a lot of money to keep this quiet. I need to know that you'll be discreet."

"I can't conceal a crime, or evidence relevant to a crime."

"I haven't broken any laws. And if there's an investigation, it will be into my death, in which case you can tell anything you need to tell from the rooftop."

"Okay then, you have my word."

"The night Joe died, he didn't know it, but he'd already won the biggest single-winner Powerball jackpot in history. Seven hundred million dollars."

I'd just taken a big gulp of tea and narrowly avoided snorting it through my nose. As it was, some of it went down the wrong way and sent me into a coughing fit. Calista jumped up and patted me on the back.

"That kind of money does tend to choke people up," she said.

I wheezed and sputtered for a minute and finally regained my composure. "So, he won with a ticket he'd already bought?"

"The last draw on the last ticket he bought. He was killed on a Thursday, but he'd won the drawing the night before. He never even checked the numbers. Joey, he wasn't thinking, 'Maybe I won.' He was thinking, 'I need to buy a new ticket.' It was just something he did. He bet on us, you know?"

"You're afraid someone will kill you for the money?"

She sat back down on the sofa and crossed her legs. "I doubt that will be it," she said. "The only people who know about the money have nothing to gain from my death. I've seen to that."

"Who are your heirs?" I asked.

"I've created a foundation and several trusts that will continue to support the charities I contribute to now. A homeless shelter, an orphanage, a children's hospital, mental illness research, several others, but no one benefits personally."

I combed my fingers through my hair just above my temples and stopped when my fingers touched in the middle. I held my head for a moment. "If not for the money, then why would someone want to kill you?"

"I'm sure I don't know," she said. "But unless you stop them, someone will kill me, and they'll do a fine job of making it look like suicide."

"And you know this...how?"

She uncrossed her legs and leaned forward, enunciating precisely, as if I were dimwitted. "Because that's what happened to her. I'm thirty-six years old. Today is July twenty-fifth. Unless you help me, I will be dead in ten days, on August fourth."

"I see," I said, but I so did not see at all.

From the other side of the room came Colleen's laugh. It's a distinctive laugh. I've often told her it reminded me of a donkey crossbred with a pig: *braay, snort-snort, braay.* She bray-snorted exuberantly from her perch on my desk. As always, my friend looked fantastic for someone who'd been dead fourteen years. Her pale skin was luminous, her long, curly red hair molten. Big green eyes sparkled with mischief. Thankfully, no one could hear her except me. But she was a distraction I did not need just then. I sent her my most threatening scowl.

Calista drew back with a stunned look on her face.

I faked a sneeze. "Excuse me."

"Take the case, already," Colleen said. "It's not like you're overbooked right now."

Colleen often offered me unsolicited advice. She professes to be a guardian spirit, as opposed to a guardian angel. According to Colleen, guardian spirits are sent back to earth with smaller-scale missions. Her mission is to guard Stella Maris. I'm her sole human contact. Sometimes she needs my help. Sometimes she thinks I need hers. The jury's still out.

I squared my shoulders, smiled at Calista, and commenced asking the same questions I asked every new client, even the ones who appeared completely stable.

"Calista," I said. "Are you taking any illegal drugs?"

She drew her hand to her face as if I'd slapped her. "That's the last thing I would ever, ever do. And just so you know, I don't drink hard liquor, either."

"No, no..." Of all the stupid things for me to say. Of course she'd be sensitive to drug use. Marilyn had died of an overdose. "What I meant to say is there are three questions I always ask new clients. It's just a formality, really. Nothing personal."

She lowered her hand. "Okay."

"So—no liquor, no drugs, got it." I took a deep breath and leaned closer to Calista, taking her hand. "Do you own any firearms?"

"Yes, actually, I have a pearl-handled revolver." She leaned in towards me. "For protection."

I nodded. "Good to know. And... now remember, this is a routine question which I always ask, right?"

"Sure," she said. She looked at me with such complete, childlike trust, I had to wonder if she trusted everyone she met so easily.

I was now holding both her hands in mine, and our faces were maybe a foot apart. "Have you ever been treated for mental illness?"

"Several times," she said. "But not with much success." She smiled this little enigmatic smile that left me wondering if she was joking or not. It gave me pause.

But I was fascinated by this woman's story. And, it's like Colleen said, my dance card wasn't full just then. I'd wrapped up the latest in a swarm of cases from new clients in old Charleston the day before. "I'll need to copy a photo ID." I patted her hand. "I'll get the contract."

TWO

I closed the front door behind Calista, slid to a window, and peered through the slats in the plantation shutter while Colleen watched through the window on the opposite side of the door. Calista walked down the wide steps to the driveway. She climbed into what must have been Joe's old Cadillac. It was a cherry-red convertible, the kind with the big fins, meticulously restored. Apparently, Calista had been unable to part with it. The blonde made quite a picture in the vintage car. We watched as she looped around the wide circle, then headed down the long, palm-tree-lined drive.

Out of habit, I checked the tag: 50CSOUL. I made a mental note to ask her what that meant. I had a lot more questions for Calista, but I needed to gather my thoughts and make a list. We'd made another appointment for Friday morning after she'd given me my standard retainer of five thousand dollars.

"Did she really move in a few weeks ago?" I asked.

"Yep."

"Damnation. I haven't even taken her a casserole yet." I pulled back from the window and raised my left eyebrow at Colleen. "What do you know about this?"

She faded out of the foyer and reappeared perched on the railing at the top of the stairs. Since she'd died, Colleen favored sundresses. The one she wore today was green with little white flowers. She slid down the banister and dismounted gracefully onto the dark hardwood floor.

"Would you stop fooling around?" I asked.

"I don't know anything you don't. And I'm sorry, but I can't help you with this one." She drifted into the office.

"Then why exactly are you here?" I followed her. Colleen had dropped by only twice since we'd finished work on the case involving Gram's death and a scheme to build a high-dollar resort on our pristine island home. Before that, I hadn't laid eyes on her since the day we'd buried her.

Colleen flashed me a facial shrug. "Nothing in the rules that says I can't drop by for a visit. No one is threatening the island just now, so I have some free time."

"Whatever." I blew wisps of hair from my face. I retrieved my pad and pen from the coffee table and sat down at my desk. "Typically, the person who wants a body dead is someone close to them. But she doesn't seem to have anyone."

Colleen stretched out on the sofa and propped her head on her hands. "If she told you everything."

"I'll have lunch with Blake at the Cracked Pot and talk to Moon Unit, see what she knows about our new neighbor." Moon Unit Glendawn owned the town diner and functioned as our chief information officer. My brother, Blake, was the chief of police.

Colleen stared at the ceiling. "Shouldn't you be guarding her if you're going to keep her alive?"

"You heard her—she doesn't think anyone will try to harm her until August fourth. I have until then to figure out who has motive."

"And you're willing to bet her life on that?"

"I just got this case. I'm going to do some investigating before I decide if she needs protection twenty-four-seven. Tonight I'll find out what Michael knows about her," I said. "It's odd. I know he met with her while he was building the house. But he never mentioned she was a dead ringer for a dead movie star."

"Looks like that would have come up," Colleen said. "About Michael, how's Nate?"

I didn't look up from my notes. Michael and I had known each other all our lives. He was my brother, Blake's, best friend. I'd tagged after them since I was five. Michael and I had dated in college, and would no doubt have married years ago, except for the intervention of my scheming cousin, Marci. She'd lied and seduced her way into a marriage with Michael that had recently ended. As Mamma would have put it, Marci had been called elsewhere.

"Nate's fine." Nate Andrews was my partner and my best living friend. We'd started our practice, Talbot and Andrews, in Greenville, in the South Carolina Upstate. He suffered the great misfortune of having my ex-husband, Scott the Scoundrel, for a brother.

"He still in Greenville?"

"Why do you ask me questions when you know full well the answers?"

"Okay, *why* did you let him go back to Greenville in April?"

"Oh, I don't know. Maybe because he said, 'Liz, I'm going back to Greenville,' and kidnapping is against the law?" When all hell broke loose on the island and I'd moved home, Nate came charging down to watch my back. Around that same time, I'd noticed how big the hole in my life was when he was in Greenville and I was in Stella Maris.

"I'm sure there are things you could have said that would have incented him to stay."

"You think I should have thrown myself at him?" Plenty of women threw themselves at Nate. He's handsome enough to have been carved by Michelangelo, with all the trimmings statues lack—blond hair, blue eyes, tanned.

Being separated made me more aware of his many fine qualities. It felt mutual. Okay, it was definitely mutual. There were enough sparks flying around to ignite the whole town. Had one of us taken a single step in the other's direction, we might have crossed into new territory in our relationship. This all happened at the same time Michael waltzed back into my life. The water was too murky to dive straight in, is what I'm saying.

Colleen rolled her eyes elaborately. "If throwing yourself at him was what it took, yeah. But trust me, you're the only person in the great state of South Carolina who missed that Nate is crazy about you. Life's short. You shouldn't waste time chasing the wrong man."

"I'm not chasing Michael. I'm not even dating Michael."

"Didn't you say you were seeing him tonight?"

"It's not a date. We're two old friends getting reacquainted. Lookit, this is what Nate wanted."

"Nate wants you to date Michael?"

"It's *not* a date. Nate wants me to be sure I've resolved all my Michael issues."

Nate was painfully aware of the torch I'd carried for Michael Devlin for ten years. Michael had stormed back into my life with marriage and babies on his mind. I learned too late that pining for Michael was just a habit—one I easily kicked. But Nate was unconvinced of my certitude in the matter. He went back to Greenville. And now, Nate occupied my mind a great deal.

"Are you having dinner alone with Michael? Because if you are, it's a date."

"I don't have time for this conversation." I pulled a new file out of the drawer and made a label. "In case you didn't hear, I have a new client who might be murdered in ten days."

"A lot of people thought Marilyn Monroe was murdered," Colleen said.

"Yeah," I said slowly. "And a lot of people think the British royal family is a cell of shape-shifting, reptilian aliens from the constellation Draco."

"True," Colleen allowed.

"On the outside chance what happened to her is relevant, could you talk to her. I mean, since you have time on your hands and all?"

"We've covered this," she said. "Calista isn't part of my assignment." Colleen was tight-lipped about most things related to eternity, claimed it was part of the rules.

I looked up from Calista's contract. "So you say."

"Whether she died accidentally, was murdered, or," Colleen sighed, "committed suicide, she died before her time. She's probably on assignment somewhere herself."

Colleen had committed suicide when we were seventeen. She'd tried to make it look like an accident, but everyone who cared to face the truth knew that she knew better than to drink tequila and go for a dip in Breach Inlet.

"Better let Rhett out of your bedroom. He was chewing on one of your Kate Spade sandals when I went to quiet him down."

"You went to quiet him down? Can Rhett see you? Not my blue sandals." I jumped up and ran for the stairs.

"See you later," Colleen said. And she was gone.

THREE

The doorbells jangled a welcome as I stepped inside the Cracked Pot. Somehow, Moon Unit had achieved a light and airy, yet cozy ambiance. The mix of an old-fashioned counter lined with swivel stools, an eclectic group of tables, tropical plants, and a wall-sized collage of island residents provided the perfect setting for one of our town's primary hangouts.

I scanned the dining room for my brother and found him in the back booth.

He looked up from his cheeseburger as I approached. I slid in across from him and waved to Moon Unit.

Blake was the stuff single women closing in on thirty dream about. Early thirties, fit, tanned, never been married, and has a job. His medium-brown hair was perhaps a little longer than your typical law enforcement style. Like Merry and me, he had inherited our mamma's cobalt blue eyes.

"What are you into today," he asked in his big brother voice. Blake was only one year older than me, but he subscribed to the notion that this gave him sacred rights and responsibilities concerning my welfare. It was sweet, on days when it didn't drive me crazy.

"Not much."

Sometimes Blake was happier not knowing the details of my cases. To say that he was not pleased with my career choice would be an understatement. He didn't like it one bit when I lived in

Greenville. His angst had doubled since I moved home. He didn't care for having a private investigator—any private investigator—on his island. We'd worked out an arrangement. If I ran across something he needed to know about, I found a way to tell him without violating my client's trust. If I needed backup, I called him, although sometimes not soon enough to suit him. Because our small town's law enforcement budget did not allow him to have dedicated detectives, if he needed one, which was rare, he would bring me in as a consultant. So far, so good.

"You finish that S.O.B. divorce case?"

I nodded. "Thank heavens." Clients from old-money Charleston, many of whom lived south of Broad Street—S.O.B.—on the peninsula, made up most of my growing client base. They liked hiring an investigator who was once removed from their world, but spoke the same language and knew the unwritten rules.

Moon Unit arrived with my iced tea. "Hey Sweetie." Moon Unit Glendawn and I had been friends forever. We graduated from Stella Maris High the same year. Her wavy, honey-colored hair was pulled high into a ponytail, her hazel eyes warm.

"Hey Moon."

"What chu want for lunch?" She didn't bother with a menu. I knew what was on it. And she knew that I took that list as more of a suggestion—sort of an inventory of what was available in the kitchen.

"You know that Southwestern chicken salad you had last week on special?"

"Uh-huh." She scribbled on her pad.

"Could you make me one of those, only add some avocado, hold the corn, and bring me some salsa on the side instead of the dressing?"

"Sure thing."

"And no corn chips."

"Got it." She spun off before I could modify her recipe further.

Blake shook his head and picked up his cheeseburger.

"Have you met the woman who just moved into that new house in the bay?" I pulled out my hand sanitizer.

"The McQueen woman? Drives that fifty-nine Eldorado Biarritz?"

"Yeah."

"She came in Monday to report a B and E."

"Say what?"

"Yeah—wanted to talk to me. Wouldn't talk to Clay or Sam. Even Nell." He shrugged. "It was a slow day. She's new in town. Thought it'd be good for public relations."

"What was taken?" I asked.

"That's the screwy part," Blake said. "Nothing was taken, but she says someone broke in and left a bottle of sleeping pills on her bedside table."

"Sleeping pills?" Hells bells. There was something she left out?

"Yeah, they were capsules, labeled Nembutal. Warren says you can't even get that stuff in capsules legally anymore, in this country. The liquid is used in hospitals, and hell, they use the stuff for lethal injections."

Warren Harper was our town physician, and, when necessary, the coroner.

"Were they in a prescription bottle?"

Blake nodded and raised his eyebrows as he finished chewing a bite of cheeseburger. "Yeah, but get this. The doctor on the label doesn't exist. Somebody went to a lot of trouble to dummy-up a prescription label."

"Have you had the drug tested?"

"Oh, yeah. My CSI lab got right on it."

"Sarcasm does not become you."

"Listen. That woman has a screw loose. Five will get you ten there's nothing in those capsules but powdered sugar."

"Was there evidence of a break in?"

"None. My opinion? She typed that thing up herself."

"But why would she do that?"

"Who knows? Maybe she just wanted an excuse to talk to somebody—get some attention."

Coming from Blake, this position didn't surprise me. Women had done all manner of kooky things to get his attention.

"I don't think so," I said. "She hired me this morning. Paid my retainer. She thinks someone is going to try to kill her."

Blake set down his tea glass. "Five thousand dollars?"

"Yep."

"That's a lot of money to pay for a joke."

"Did anything strike you about the way she looks?"

"I'm used to all that crap."

I wrinkled my face at him.

"Blue stripe in her hair, fourteen piercings, tattoos. I hardly even notice that mess anymore."

I smiled and nodded. "Me either."

What did this woman really look like? Had she worn a Marilyn costume when she came to see me? Or was she tired of going around looking like a pinup poster, so she'd gone to see Blake incognito?

Likely, she'd worn the same getup to meet with Michael, which was why he hadn't mentioned he was building a house for a dead movie star.

Moon Unit delivered my lunch. "Here you go." She drug out 'go' into five syllables. "Can I get you anything else?"

"Not right now, thank you, Moon," I said. "Hey, have you met Calista McQueen?"

"Mousey little thing that drives that big red convertible?"

Blake and I looked at each other.

"Sure," Moon said. "She comes in a couple-three times a week. I declare, that girl needs to get in to see Phoebe. I bet you with some highlights and different makeup she'd be a looker."

"I bet you're right," I said. "Have you talked to her much?"

Moon Unit raised a perfectly arched eyebrow. "Well, sure. I talk to all my customers."

Blake rolled his eyes and looked over his shoulder. Moon Unit saying she talked to all her customers was like Paula Deen saying she put a little butter in all her recipes.

"What exactly was that look for?" Moon demanded.

"Not a thing." Blake dug back into his cheeseburger.

"Michael just finished her house, down from the Pirates' Den," I said. Usually, if you gave Moon Unit a prompt, she'd take it and run. Her parents, John and Alma Glendawn, owned the Pirates' Den, a popular restaurant and bar.

"Yeah, Mamma and Daddy sold her that three acres. She gave her word it would be built to environmentally friendly standards, and, you know, they knew Michael was going to build it and they trusted him. They still have more than a hundred acres. What were they ever going to do with all that land?"

Moon Unit, and everyone else on the island, sang a different tune if the topic was commercial development. We loved our small beach town just as it was.

We were not in need of condos, time shares, or resorts of any kind. Land was usually a very serious topic. Several bodies had piled up in the war over protecting the land on Stella Maris back in April.

"Moon, does she come in by herself?" I asked.

"Always. Bless her heart, I don't think I've ever seen the poor little thing with anybody else. We need to introduce her around. I don't think she knows a soul except me, Michael, Mamma and Daddy, and Robert Pearson."

"Robert?" I asked.

"Well, yeah. He handled the closing on the land. She asked me about attorneys and I gave her his name. I don't know if he handles other business for her or not." Moon laid a ticket on the table. "Y'all holler if you need more tea."

Blake flashed me a stern look. "There is not one mousey thing about the woman *I* met who drives a red Cadillac. What have you not told me?"

I sat back in the booth. "When she came to see me, she looked just like Marilyn Monroe."

"How do you know we're all talking about the same woman?"

"Same name, same Cadillac."

"I told you she was crazy. Maybe some kind of con artist. Apparently, she has nothing better to do with her time than play dress up. She's just trying to get attention. End of story."

"We'll see." I had a bad feeling Calista's story was about to take an even more bizarre turn.

As soon as I started the car after lunch, I pressed the voice command button. "Shuffle, artist, Kenny Chesney." "Sherry's Living in Paradise" floated through the speakers. I rolled down the windows. I could deal with the heat. Like Sherry, the salty air soothed my soul.

FOUR

Back at the house, I got busy building Calista's case file. I entered everything she'd told me into the standard interview form Nate and I used.

"The following interview was conducted by Elizabeth S. Talbot, of Talbot & Andrews Investigations, on Wednesday, July 25, 2012, at Stella Maris, SC. On this date..."

The form is a clone of the FBI's FD 302, chosen for its popularity with judges and attorneys, who become familiar with the form in law school. I can't prove it, but I hold the belief that they consider anything typed in this particular format to have a better pedigree than ordinary case notes. I printed out the form, dated and signed the page, and placed it in the folder I'd created earlier along with Calista's contract.

Next, I started creating electronic profiles for Calista and everyone who touched her life in any significant way. For every case, I construct a basic time line for a subject's life, then fill in the blanks using a variety of public databases and paid subscription services. I like having the whole of a person's life in front of me—you never know what might turn out to be important. Each fact could be a piece to the puzzle.

Not many years ago, this step would've taken days and involved mailed requests for documents, trips to courthouses, and library visits. These days, in most cases, a PI could accomplish basic vetting in a few hours on the Internet.

Calista was my first profile. I would've bet a case of my favorite pinot noir that in short order I would discover I'd spent my morning with either a con artist or a delusional woman. I would've lost that bet. Everything Calista told me about her background checked out—from her birthdate and time, to her history with the foster care system, to her marriage to James Edward Davis. Even to when she legally changed her name from Norma Jeane Mortensen Davis to Calista Faith McQueen, moved to West Ashley, and married a ballplayer named Jose Raphael Fernandez. I felt something cold with little feet crawl up my spine. It was creepy how much the first eighteen years of Calista's life paralleled the other Norma Jeane's.

Jose's early life was not the near-perfect parallel to the baseball icon's that Calista's had been to Marilyn's. After a little digging, it was clear that beyond his chosen variation of his name and his profession, Joe's background bore no similarities whatsoever to Joe DiMaggio's. This came as a great relief. The crazy was limited in scope, and that's always easier to deal with. Jose was an only child. His family was of Cuban descent, but had lived in Florida for three generations. His parents had died in a car accident in 1997.

I was most intrigued by Calista's mother, whose name had been Gwen Monroe when Calista—Norma Jeane—was born. The surname Monroe gave me pause. Was this the seed from which the obsession had sprung? Gwen changed her name to Gladys the following week, the same day a woman named Donna Clark at the same address had changed her name to Grace McKee. To go to the trouble of changing their names, these women must have been heavily invested in the whole recreating Marilyn fantasy.

I found no trace of a man named Mortensen in Gwen's history. Likely that was just a name she and Donna gave the hospital for the birth certificate to begin building their reincarnation fantasy. As far as I could determine, neither of them had ever been married. Here were the con artists—not Calista, as Blake had suggested. She was their victim. Dressing in outlandish costumes suddenly seemed tame as quirks go. If I'd been raised by crazies like that I might have a few screws loose, too.

My iPhone quacked like a duck, which meant a client was on the line. I glanced at the screen and answered. "Hey, Calista."

"Liz, can you come with me to Charleston?" Calista's voice sounded thick, like she'd been crying.

"Right now?"

"Yes. Please. Harmony's dead."

"I'm sorry—Harmony?"

"My life coach. Her assistant just found her. She's been shot. Please."

A life coach? "Did the assistant call 911?"

"I'm sure she must have. She called me because I had an appointment this afternoon. She didn't want me to arrive at a crime scene."

"That sounds like good sense to me. I'm sorry for your loss, but there's nothing you or I can do, and the police won't appreciate our being there."

"I'm quite sure they will want to talk to me. I'd like you to be there."

"Why would they want to talk to you?"

"Because I'm the one who got her killed."

"I'm on my way." I grabbed my iPhone and my favorite summer Kate Spade tote.

FIVE

I pulled my hybrid Escape into Calista's drive expecting her to be waiting. She wasn't. I studied the white concrete dome in front of me. It looked out of place next to the palm trees and live oaks, as if it had landed here from someplace on the other side of the galaxy. Wide border beds with lavish gardens surrounded the whole affair. Massive walls of concrete reached out from either side like giant arms enclosing two sets of steps with a fountain between them.

The opening in the concrete wall between the sections was about six feet wide. When I stepped through it, I was in a small courtyard. Glass block formed the front edge of the fountain, and the gurgle of water soothed me. It was like stepping into a temple. A feeling of peace washed over me. I climbed the steps on my right to the partially sheltered porch surrounding the house, rang the bell, and waited.

Elenore Harper opened the door. Here was a surprise. Elenore was the first wife of Warren Harper, the town doctor. She had a reputation for being flakey. She'd abandoned Warren and their three children when the kids were little. Elenore was a rare breed of woman on Stella Maris—one who didn't bother with such things as makeup and hair color, and owned only sensible shoes. "Ms. McQueen is expecting you." She stepped aside without so much as a hint she knew me from Adam's house cat.

"Hey, Elenore, how're you doin'?" I offered my brightest smile.

"Ms. McQueen is in the living room. This way."

She started down the white-tiled foyer.

"So, you work for Ms. McQueen?"

"Yes." She did not look back at me.

"Are you her secretary?"

"I manage the house." Her voice crackled with ice.

That seemed a little vague. I figured it meant she was the maid, not that there was anything wrong with that. The foyer opened into a large living space that combined the living room and dining room and was open to the kitchen. The décor was white-on-white, with stainless steel accents.

Calista was curled into a nook of an over-stuffed white sectional. A brown-haired gentleman sat next to her, applying a compress to her forehead and petting her arm. My first impression was that if he took off his shirt, he'd look like he walked off a Chippendale's billboard.

Elenore announced me. "Miss Talbot has arrived." Then she slipped away.

"Hey, Calista. Are you ready?"

Calista sat up and slid her feet into a pair of flats. "Liz, come meet Niles Ignacio. He's my yoga instructor. Niles, this is Liz Talbot. She's helping me out with a problem."

"Nice to meet you," I said.

Niles stood and took my outstretched hand. "The pleasure is mine." He moved with extraordinary grace. All that yoga, I guessed. He held onto my hand just a little too long. I retrieved it. Something flickered in his brown eyes. I fought the urge to reach for my hand sanitizer.

Calista stood. "Thank you, Niles. You've been a life-saver."

Niles ran his hand slowly from Calista's shoulder down her arm. "Darling, are you sure you want to go into Charleston today? Perhaps a nap would be in your best interests."

He was awfully chummy for a yoga instructor. And neither of them were dressed for yoga. I wondered exactly what he meant by "nap." "Calista? We don't have to do this today. I'm sure the

Charleston detectives will come here to interview you if you have information related to their case."

"No," Calista said. "I want to speak to them today. It's terribly important. Niles, let yourself out. I'll see you tomorrow at one."

Niles clasped her elbow. "Calista, dear-heart, really, you shouldn't push yourself."

"Nonsense. I'm not sick, just shook up a little. And who wouldn't be?" Calista pulled her arm free and picked up her purse. She smiled gently at Niles.

"I'm rattled myself." Niles placed his now free hand on his chest. "Poor Harmony. Who would do such a thing?"

"She was such a gentle spirit." Calista's eyes misted.

I hated to sound uncaring about poor Harmony, but Niles was a new character in Calista's orbit, and I needed to start vetting him quickly. "I didn't realize we had a yoga studio on Stella Maris," I said.

"We don't," said Calista. "Niles comes all the way over from Mt. Pleasant to give me private lessons."

"How sweet of him," I said, thinking I'd bet private yoga lessons were pricey, or lucrative, depending on which end of the transaction your downward dog stretched.

"He's just a doll," said Calista.

He looked like somebody's toy, I'd give her that much. I wondered if he was hers. "We'd best go if we're going," I said.

Calista passed me on her way to the door. "Do you mind driving?"

"I insist."

Niles followed us out to the Escape. He hovered over Calista as she slid into the passenger seat, lodging one protest after another. He was still carrying on as I turned the car around and drove down the driveway.

I turned left onto Ocean Boulevard, making my way towards the ferry dock. "He's very attentive."

"Niles? Yes. He worries about my stress level."

"How long have you known him?"

"Since just after I moved back to South Carolina. I've been practicing yoga for years. When I moved to Wild Dunes eighteen months ago, I started taking classes at Serenity in Mount Pleasant. I'd been there a few months when Niles came to work there. He was always my favorite instructor. After a while he started giving me private lessons. He's a good friend."

I wondered if Calista had any friends she didn't pay. "Is he from here?"

"I don't think so. He moved down from Vermont."

Ocean Boulevard dead-ended at Main Street. I turned right. This section of Main was residential, with brick sidewalks shaded by live oaks draped in Spanish moss.

"I wish it was cool enough to roll the windows down," Calista said.

"Me, too. But the exterior thermostat says ninety-eight. I think we'll leave the windows up and the AC on if you don't mind."

I bore right into the traffic circle that bordered the park in the middle of town.

Calista said, "I've loved this little town since I first laid eyes on it. It's like the postcard for small towns. Bigger than Mayberry—you know what it reminds me of?"

"What?" I glanced down the picturesque row of shops on Palmetto Boulevard as we rounded the circle.

"Bedford Falls."

"Bedford Falls?" I turned right and continued down Main.

"You know, from the movie, *It's a Wonderful Life*. Lots of people watch that movie at Christmas. I watch it all the time. I'd like to live in that town. This is the closest thing I've ever found. Except there's no snow here. Everything is so green. It's perfect."

"Yes, it is. Calista, if you had an appointment with Harmony this afternoon, why was Niles at your house? Neither of you were dressed for yoga."

"He came by to drop off some essential oils. Lavender,

chamomile, and sweet marjoram to help me relax. Niles helps me manage my stress level. Yesterday at our session, I was very stressed."

"How much have you told him?"

"Nothing about the money. Nothing about my history. All he knows is that I'm a widow who traveled a bit and now lives on Stella Maris. I got the call from Harmony's assistant while he was there. He was just doing what any friend would do. Comforting me."

"So you and he are not involved romantically?"

"Oh my, no. Niles is gay."

"Really?" I'd read him wrong, and that unsettled me. I would've sworn he was exuding pheromones at both Calista and me.

"Yes. He's confided in me about his boyfriend. They fight a lot. I think his boyfriend is very jealous."

"So what does he think you're stressed about, if he doesn't know you're in fear for your life?"

Calista shrugged. "What is anyone stressed about? When he asks, I just say my investments, or mention something vague about family."

"Does he ask you a lot of questions?"

"You mean like you do?"

"I'm a private investigator. You are paying me good money to ask questions. You are paying him for personal fitness training and what-all. You'll notice I haven't said 'Namaste' once."

"I see your point." Ordinary conversation sounded like bedroom talk coming from Calista.

"So, does he ask you a lot of questions?"

"Not that I've noticed," she said, her voice oozing sensuality.

"Have you always talked like that?"

"Like what?"

"Like...like Marilyn. All breathless and..." I parked to wait for the cars coming off the ferry.

"Yes. I've always spoken like this. Just like you've probably always had that lovely drawl."

"Drawl? I don't have a drawl. I mean I can turn it on when I want to, don't get me wrong. But I don't normally speak with a drawl."

Calista giggled. "Of course you do. What's interesting though, is that I've read she didn't talk like this, not normally. Only for the camera."

"You've read up on her?"

"Wouldn't you?"

"I suppose I would, in your shoes. So, you don't think she committed suicide, or died of an accidental overdose?"

"No. I think her biographer, Donald Spoto, got it mostly right. Or maybe he knew the whole truth, but knew he couldn't prove it."

"And what did he think?"

"Marilyn was getting ready to remarry Joe DiMaggio. She was happy. Making plans for the future. Do you know she was being fitted for her wedding gown just a few days before her death?"

"No, I've never heard that."

Calista nodded emphatically. "She'd made arrangements for a small reception at her home."

"Interesting. But how did she die, according to the biographer?"

"She hadn't slept well that Friday night, August third. She had several meetings on Saturday with her psychoanalyst, Ralph Greenson. She was in the process of terminating his services and the housekeeper's as well. Both of them manipulated her terribly. The housekeeper reported to Greenson. He arranged for Marilyn to hire her."

I drove onto the ferry and parked behind a minivan. "That's odd. For a psychoanalyst to hire a housekeeper for a patient."

"Precisely. Anyway, either he gave her Nembutal that day, or she took it on her own because it was a very stressful situation. She was moving on with her life. Cutting ties with the people who had been controlling her for the last year, people she'd trusted. They weren't happy about that one bit."

"So she took some Nembutal during the day on Saturday?" I was remembering what Blake had told me about Nembutal.

"Yes. And then later that night, either the good doctor instructed the housekeeper to give her an enema with a big dose of chloral hydrate, or the housekeeper did it on her own. That stopped Marilyn's body from metabolizing the Nembutal, and it killed her. Of course it's possible the chloral hydrate alone would have killed her. She had twice as much of that in her system as the Nembutal."

"I'm sorry, did you say the housekeeper gave her an enema? She was killed with an enema?"

"Exactly. Marilyn was accustomed to using them for health and dietetic purposes. Lots of actresses did back then. But that night, hers had a dose of chloral hydrate in it. And she never woke up."

"You're saying she was murdered?"

"You should draw your own conclusion. It might have been an accident. It could have been that she took the Nembutal without Greenson knowing, and later he decided she needed the chloral hydrate enema to help her sleep. But *she* knew she'd taken the Nembutal, so it's hard to imagine she would agree to an enema with chloral hydrate. Read her biography—the one by Spoto. Chapter twenty-two is fascinating. Many books have been written about her, but his is exceptionally well documented. Not gossipy at all."

"You believe people close to her killed her and made it look like she either accidentally, or purposefully, took too many pills?"

"That's what I believe, yes. And I further believe that's what will happen to me unless you prevent it."

"Who in your life is manipulating you?"

"No one. I never let anyone get that close. Not anymore. With me, I think it will be people who feel like I let them down."

I was thinking how the people closest to her were on her payroll, which seemed yet another parallel to Marilyn, but as I had other questions on my mind, and in light of Harmony's recent passing, I didn't mention it. "We're not going to let that happen. I understand you found a bottle labeled Nembutal by your bed."

"Yes. I would have told you about that on Friday. I thought I'd already overwhelmed you this morning."

I smiled, thinking how that was a valid concern. "Any ideas who would do such a thing?"

"None that make sense."

"Tell me the ones that don't make sense."

"Mother, Grace, or Jimmy. Maybe the three of them working together. It wasn't just the pills."

"Something else was left by your bed?"

"No, I mean, other strange things have happened. Sometimes I hear a dog barking inside my house. It only happens when I'm alone. I don't have a dog, but I did when I was a little girl. It was a stray I brought home and named Tippy. I was amazed my foster family let me keep him. He followed me everywhere. One of our neighbors got mad because he thought Tippy barked too much. The heartless SOB shot Tippy with his shotgun."

"*Ohmygosh.* That's heinous."

"Yes, it was devastating," Calista said. "The same thing happened to the first Norma Jeane. But I bet she picked the name Tippy. I wanted to name my dog Taffy. Grace said it was silly to name a dog after candy. She insisted on Tippy."

I absorbed that for a moment. "What other strange things have happened?"

"Things disappear from where I typically keep them, then turn up somewhere else a day or so later. A plastic surgeon's office called three times to confirm appointments I never made. There is a long list. The most appalling thing is that I found an enema kit in my private bathroom three days ago."

I must have looked as horrified as I felt.

Calista nodded. "It totally freaked me out, too. I went running to Mrs. Harper and asked her where it came from. She said I put it on her shopping list, so she picked it up. I never did that. But she showed me the list. It was added to the bottom. Even I think it looks like my handwriting. But it isn't."

I could feel my eyes growing bigger. "Did you save this list?"

"Yes. I'll get it for you."

I cocked my head at her. "Someone is trying to gaslight you."

"I know. That's why I didn't tell your brother about everything. He'd think I'm crazy, and that's exactly what they want. I started not to report the pills, but I thought it might be a good idea to have it on the record that I don't take that sort of thing."

I sighed, remembering how Blake thought she was crazy anyway. "So tell me about the costumes."

"What's to tell? If I go out looking like this, people stare a lot. Some days I don't mind. It's what I look like. Sometimes I just want to mix in." She shrugged. "Some days it's just fun to play dress-up and pretend to be someone else."

I decide not to mention how that sounded a lot like acting to me. "Can't you just try a new hairstyle? Cut it, or grow it out?"

"I could. But I like it like this. Most days."

I shook my head. "Here's a tip. If you want to mix in on Stella Maris, skip the look with all the body art."

She grinned. "That one blends in better in the city. I was really just having fun with your brother. He's kinda cute. I know he didn't take me seriously. But I accomplished what I needed to. There's a permanent record of my report."

We stayed in the car on the ferry ride from Stella Maris to Isle of Palms. Technically, I was supposed to turn the engine off as soon as I parked the car. But the middle deck, which was air conditioned, looked crowded. As hot as it was, the ferry crew let me slide. I took the opportunity to sanitize my hands and pull out a wipe for the steering wheel, gear shifter and turn signal. "Exactly what does a life coach do?"

"They help you reach your full potential. I bet she could have helped you overcome your fear of germs."

I looked at Calista sideways. "A healthy fear of germs keeps you healthy. Give me a minute. It's not a good idea to show up unannounced at a crime scene."

I called Sonny Ravenel, an old family friend, who was also a Charleston city police detective. Luckily, he'd caught Harmony's case. He was at Harmony's storefront, in the four-hundred block of King Street. Not cheap real estate, I'd bet. He agreed to meet us at Kudu, a nearby coffee shop.

I put down my phone and turned to Calista. "How did Harmony go about helping you reach your full potential?"

"She was helping me find my balance. But she wasn't just a life coach."

"Really? What else was she?"

"She was a gifted feng shui consultant. She helped me design my home."

"Did she consult with Michael?"

"No. She and I met privately. I told Michael and my interior designer what I wanted."

"When did you see her last?"

"Last Thursday. That was for follow-up on my accountability goals. My appointment today was for clairvoyant counseling."

"So, she was a clairvoyant feng shui expert and life coach?"

"Don't criticize what you don't understand."

"Who said that?" I was sure I'd heard the quote before.

"I just did."

"No, I mean, never mind." I took a deep cleansing breath. "Why do you think you are responsible for her death?"

"During my last several readings, she's been trying to warn me about a man in my life who means me harm. I think she was close to figuring out who's going to try to kill me. But he killed her before she could see him clearly enough to identify him. He knew she was on to him."

Sonny Ravenel was one of Blake's oldest friends. He shared my brother's skepticism when it came to the supernatural. He was not going to like any of this. "Calista, did you discuss with Harmony your fears about someone trying to kill you?"

"Of course. How could she help me if I wasn't open with her?"

"Did you tell her everything?"

"You mean did I tell her about the money? No. I'm not stupid."

I covered my face with my hands, caught myself, lowered my arms, and crossed them. "What exactly did she tell you about this man she thought was a threat?"

"She said he was someone from my past who thought I owed him a lot of money. I suspect she was talking about my first husband, Jimmy. He always wanted me to make him rich."

"Did you go in disguise when you met with her, or did she see you looking like Marilyn Monroe?"

"I didn't wear a disguise, really. But I did wear my hair in a headband, and I didn't wear makeup. It's funny. If you look at candid shots of her, not the publicity photos, the resemblance is more striking, if that's even possible. But most people have the publicity photos as a reference. Harmony did say she thought I looked just like Marilyn."

"Did Harmony know about Jim—about all the parallels in your life to Marilyn's?"

"Well, I didn't tell her everything, I guess." Calista propped her elbow on the door and rested her head on her hand. "I should have been completely honest."

For a few moments we both watched the marina at Isle of Palms grow closer. I struggled to wrap my brain around everything Calista said, wishing I'd thought to record our conversation as I drove. I could hardly take notes. Who knew we didn't get through all the crazy that morning?

I tried to use a gentle voice. "Assuming for a moment that Harmony possessed all the talents you believe she did, did she tell you a single thing you didn't already know or suspect?"

Calista was quiet for a moment. "It was more that she confirmed my fears, independently."

"Did you tell anyone what she said?"

Calista raised her head. "Not a soul."

"Then even if she was really on to something, if no one knew, why would anyone have killed her on your account?"

"That's a very good point," Calista said. "Do you think he bugged her therapy sanctuary?"

"If the most likely suspect is your ex-husband, Jim, you tell me. Does he have the skills to install listening devices? And keep in mind, he'd likely have to break and enter to do that without her catching him."

"No." Calista shook her head. "The Jimmy I knew wouldn't have a clue how to do that. I guess he could've hired someone. But it's unlikely he'd have that kind of money. Sounds expensive."

I drove off the ferry, through the parking lot, and turned at 41st Avenue. "When is the last time you had contact with Jim Davis?"

"I haven't been in touch with anyone from California since I left eighteen years ago. I did have a trust set up to care for my mother. She's been in and out of mental health facilities. But she doesn't know where I am, or even my name. Neither does he."

We drove in silence for a while, tooling across the Isle of Palms Connector and down Highway 17. The twin, upside down v's that formed the supports for the Arthur Ravenel Jr. Bridge, the latest version of the Cooper River Bridge, grew gradually closer. It wasn't until we were on it that Calista spoke again. "People change. Maybe Jimmy has more street smarts than he used to have. Maybe he's found me after all these years."

"I'll check into Jim Davis. That should be easy enough." I didn't subscribe to some of Calista's notions, but she was, after all, paying me for my time. "You didn't mention Niles this morning."

"Why would I? He's my yoga instructor. Is he important? Do you want the name of my hair dresser?"

I smiled. "No. You live on Stella Maris. Unless you're still driving into Charleston to get your hair done, Phoebe DiTomei does your hair."

Calista smiled back. "Yes, she does."

"But I do need a more complete list of everyone you come in regular contact with. Especially anyone who has access to your home, like Niles and Elenore."

"I imagine you know more about Elenore than I do."

"Fair enough. But I didn't know Elenore was your housekeeper."

"I'll make a list." Calista pulled a notebook and pen from her purse.

"I need names and jobs of everyone from your gardener to your financial planner. If you're in a book club, or play bridge, I want to know with whom."

"Got it."

"Now, when we talk to Sonny, go easy on the metaphysical subject matter. He will find out all about Harmony's business and the various services she offered during the course of his investigation. You don't need to go into all that in detail."

"I shouldn't tell him the whole truth?"

I sighed. Damnation. What the hell was I thinking? "I guess you'd better." I was so not looking forward to this conversation.

SIX

Kudu boasts a perfect courtyard, with ivy-covered brick walls and a fountain, but it was way too hot to sit outside. Sonny and I often met at Kudu because it was mainly a student hangout. I liked the energy. He liked the pastries and the fact that other Charleston detectives didn't frequent the place. We both loved the coffee. The fact that it was also convenient to today's crime scene was coincidence.

We found Sonny tucked into the nook in the back left corner. He was already into a tall coffee and a ham and cheese croissant. My mouth watered. It purely wasn't fair he could eat those things and stay so lean.

Sonny was a handsome package—tall, brown hair, hazel eyes. He met Blake and Michael in middle school, and the three of them had been running together ever since. Sonny had eaten almost as many meals at my mamma's table as I had. Some folks initially wrote him off as a mild-mannered, somewhat slow Southern cop. Those people were fools.

I introduced Sonny to Calista, zipped over to order frappes for Calista and me, and hurried back to the table. I didn't want to leave her alone with Sonny any longer than absolutely necessary.

When I returned to the table, Sonny was still staring at Calista and sipping coffee. His eyes met mine, then darted back to Calista. He cleared his throat. "Ms. McQueen...ahhh...how did you know the deceased, Harmony, no last name?"

I wondered if she really didn't have a last name. Of course, she must have at one point. Harmony was clearly her professional name, but was it her real first name?

Calista gave Sonny an abbreviated version of the story, but covered all the salient points, like how Harmony was trying to save her from certain death, and this had no doubt led to her untimely passing.

Sonny chewed thoughtfully on a bite of pastry. "Liz, what's your connection to this case?"

"Calista is my client."

"And what is the nature of your inquiry for Ms. McQueen?"

Calista opened her mouth, and I put my hand on her knee and squeezed, giving her the signal not to speak—the same one Blake often uses on me.

"I'm assisting Ms. McQueen with security," I said.

"Security from what—who?" Sonny took a big sip of coffee, and eyed me over the rim of the cup.

"Hells bells, Sonny. You are familiar with the concept of private security."

"I am. I'm just curious why Ms. McQueen is in need of it. I'm not clear on where this imminent danger is coming from." He looked at Calista. "My apologies, ma'am. I'm a bona fide skeptic when it comes to the transcendental arts."

Calista pulled in her chin. "Well, my life coach was murdered just this morning. She was trying to warn me that someone was going to kill me. Until you've made an arrest, I'd say having my own security makes perfectly good sense. Have you? Made an arrest, I mean."

I noticed how Calista skipped over the part about how she'd hired me before Harmony turned up dead. She was a quick study in dealing with Sonny's dubiety.

Sonny avoided looking at Calista. "We're still in the early stages of the investigation. If I understand you correctly, you have no idea who Harmony was trying to warn you about?"

"That's right. My next reading was scheduled for this afternoon at three. I guess I'd be there now."

Sonny said, "You don't mind my asking, exactly what did a reading entail?"

Oh for crying out loud. Why did he have to go there?

"Well, we went into her therapy sanctuary. She would light candles while I relaxed with a cup of tea and quieted my mind. There was a fountain in the room, and she had soft music on. After the candles were lit, she'd come sit by me and chant. Then she took my hands and looked at them very closely and we would talk. Sometimes she used cards. She was trying to help me see and overcome obstacles in my life. It was part of her integrated approach as my life coach. She was very thorough."

Sonny had a poker face, but I knew exactly what he thought about Harmony's integrated approach to life coaching. "When did she first mention this man you were in danger from?"

Calista put her hand to her temple. "About two months ago."

"And you saw her every week?"

"That's right."

"So in roughly eight weeks, all she told you about this man was that he was from your past and he believed you owed him money?"

The bells at St. Matthew's announced three o'clock.

"Well, she did say he had dark hair."

Sonny nodded. "Any idea who this mysterious dark-haired man might be?"

"Yes. I'm certain it's my ex-husband, James Davis. He lives in Los Angeles."

"Any reason you believe it's him?"

"Well, who else could it be?"

"And, instead of asking you for this money he thought you owed him, he was just going to kill you?"

"That was her impression."

"Did she indicate how this would result in him getting his money?"

"No."

Sonny brushed the pastry crumbs from his hands. He reached into his jacket pocket. "Here's my card, Ms. McQueen. If you think of anything else that might help the investigation, please give me a call."

"All right," Calista said. "And would you do me a favor?"

Sonny stood. "I'll do anything I can."

"Try to keep an open mind. Just remember, 'Those who were seen dancing were thought to be insane by those who could not hear the music.' Your skepticism might cause you to miss the truth when you find it."

My blonde client was quoting Nietzsche now?

"Yes, ma'am." Sonny nodded. "Liz." He raised his eyebrows at me and took a step towards the door.

"Hey, Sonny," I said.

He turned and looked at me expectantly.

"Is there anything you can share about how the victim was killed, the crime scene?"

His look was all business. "The victim was shot twice in the back of the head, while seated at the desk in her private office. There were no signs of forced entry or struggle."

"Do you know approximately what time it happened?"

"According to the security company, the alarm was disabled at nine-thirty-three a.m., which, according to her assistant, was about the time Harmony typically arrived. The assistant had an appointment this morning and didn't arrive until twelve-fifteen. Harmony was deceased at that time."

"Was anything taken?"

"We don't know yet. A full inventory hasn't been taken, but according to her assistant, nothing appears to be missing."

"Did Harmony keep any files in her...spa?"

"Not the paper kind. Tech guys are going over her computer."

"Will you let me know if they find anything?"

"Open case, Liz."

"I am well aware of that. But if you run across anything that pertains to Ms. McQueen's safety, I would appreciate a heads-up."

Sonny gave me his signature, tilted single-nod-with-a-grin. "I'll give you anything I can."

SEVEN

That night I made tortellini for dinner. Pasta helps me think. Between Calista and all of her assorted issues and Harmony's murder, I had a lot to mull.

Gram had loved to cook for family and friends, and her kitchen—my kitchen—reflected that. Copper pots hung high over the black granite island and lined the shelves under the commercial-grade gas cooktop. Green painted cabinets and dark hardwood floors gave the room a homey feel. Fresh herbs grew in the greenhouse window above one of two farmhouse-style sinks. I reached for some basil, chopped it, and set it aside.

I was expecting Michael. We'd been having dinner together about once a week. This was my compromise. He wanted to marry me in a hurry. I knew I would never feel that way about him again, but we had a lot of history, and I couldn't cut him out of my life altogether.

And besides, no reason I should eat alone every night just because Nate Andrews was making a point by keeping himself in Greenville. That's what I was thinking when the phone rang.

I glanced at the screen and picked up my phone. "Nate." Could he hear the silly grin on my face?

"Slugger."

"Slugger? You haven't called me that in ages."

"Last time I saw you, you'd just given your cousin Marci a new beauty mark. Reminded me of the time you cold-cocked that guy who went across the table after his wife during their settlement conference. I'm seeing a pattern emerge."

"That was years ago, and if you'll recall, that jerk may well have strangled his wife in front of us if I hadn't intervened. And Marci had it coming."

"I had him covered," he said easily. "How're things?"

"Things are good. How're things with you?"

"They're okay. But I think they're about to get a lot better."

"Do tell?" Was he trying to sound mysterious?

"I wrapped up the Donnelly case this morning. Gave my testimony. I think it contributed to the sizable alimony check Mrs. Donnelly was awarded."

"That is good news. So, do you have a new case?"

"You could say that. How's Michael?"

Hells bells. "I suppose he's fine. Is there anyone else you'd like to inquire after?" I might have sounded a bit testy.

"No. It's him I worry about most."

"I'd say that was a pitiful waste of energy."

"I hope that's the case."

"Nate Andrews, did you call to bait me?"

"No. I called to see what you were doing for dinner."

I sighed. "I'm making pasta."

"Sounds good. I was thinking we could go out. But if you've already started cooking..."

My stomach flipped so high it bumped my heart and set it to pounding. "Where are you?"

"I'm just driving off the ferry. Should be there in less than ten minutes."

My mouth went dry. I couldn't form words.

"Liz?"

"Well, I guess I'd better finish getting dinner ready." I grabbed my hair with my free hand.

"See you in a few."

Oh boy. Oh boy oh boy oh boy.

Call Michael. I had to call Michael. Nate could not find him here.

I fumbled with the phone. My fingers weren't working right. I managed to tap Michael's name. Thank Heavens I didn't have to press all the numbers.

What did I look like? Okay. I had been out today. I had makeup on. I just needed to freshen up. The phone was ringing. Pick up. Pick up. *Pick up.*

"Hey," Michael answered. "I was just on my way over. You need me to bring anything?"

"No, thank you. No. Listen, Michael. I'm really sorry, but we're going to have to make it another night."

"Is everything okay?"

"Yes. Everything's fine. It's just—" What? What was I going to tell him? I would not lie. I sighed. "Michael, Nate's in town. He's just gotten in, and I haven't seen him in a while. There's just a lot we need to talk about."

"I see." Michael's voice was tight. "When would you like to reschedule for?"

"Ahh...can I get back to you on that?"

"How about Friday? Let's go out. Maybe someplace in Charleston. There's something I want to give you."

"Give me?" That sounded like trouble.

"Yes. It's yours, actually. I need to return it."

"What is it?"

"I'd rather show you. How about Friday?"

"Listen, Michael, let me call you back on that. I'll call you tomorrow, okay?"

"Liz, I really want to see you." He sighed, not happy. "Tomorrow then."

I employed my sunniest voice. "Talk to you soon. Bye now."

I pressed end, took three deep breaths and dashed up the stairs to change. I freshened, fluffed, and slipped into a mid-calf length, pink-and-white-checked sundress. My toes were polished in a complimentary color. I smiled slowly. I felt like being barefoot. I dabbed a little Chanel No. 19 behind my ears and on my wrists.

As I walked down the stairs, I heard Rhett barking from the yard. I walked out onto the front porch and watched Nate's grey Explorer roll down the gravel-and-oyster-shell driveway. I drifted to the top of the steps and waited. Oh my sweet Lord, I had dreamt of this moment—seeing him again, working up the courage to say all the things I wanted to say but hadn't since Nate walked down these same steps in April. He pulled to a stop and climbed out. Rhett greeted him with wagging tail and a sloppy grin.

"There's a good boy." Nate gave Rhett a two-handed head-rub, then reached back into the car and pulled out a bright green Hurley chew toy. He showed Rhett the toy, then threw it towards the forest at the edge of the yard. "Go get it!"

Rhett raced off.

For a moment, Nate just looked at me over the hood of the car. Then he closed the door and strolled towards me.

"What kind of pasta were you making?"

"Tortellini."

He started up the wide steps. I'd never seen a man look that good in jeans and a chambray shirt. "Have you put it on to boil yet?"

"No. I was just starting the sauce."

He stopped one step below me. We were eye-level. He reached out and tucked my hair behind my left ear. "I've missed you."

"I've missed you, too." I inhaled and savored the scent of evening jasmine mixed with Nate.

"All of a sudden I've lost my appetite...for dinner."

I felt my eyes widen, shocked to hear him say what I was thinking. "Nate..." I struggled for words. This was uncharted territory for us.

"You see, I've had ninety days since that afternoon I watched Michael Devlin propose to you on the beach, to think about how I should never have left you here with him."

"But—"

"I just threw the game. Walked off the field. What kind of idiot does that?"

I smiled. "I'm sure I couldn't say. At the very least you could have given me a clue you wanted in the game to begin with before you quit."

"Oh, you had a clue, all right."

"You should've said something." Maybe I did have a clue. But a woman needs to hear these things. What if I'd been wrong?

"You think that's what I shoulda done? Just laid my heart right out there and invited you to trample all over it when Michael—"

"Is an old friend and nothing more."

Nate's eyes searched mine for a long moment, assessing me. "I guess if he's chased you around this island, his home turf, for ninety days and hasn't caught you yet, he isn't going to."

"I told you that ninety days ago. Nothing has changed."

His lips curved oh-so-slowly. "Now see, that's where you're wrong."

"Am I, now?" My eyes searched his for confirmation. I came unmoored, drifting away on bright blue currents that held promise.

"Everything has changed." His voice was like a caress.

"How's that?"

"Now I know that *you* know you don't want him." He slipped his right hand behind my head and pulled it forward to his. Our lips touched, the first taste so gentle. We breathed in and out together. I grabbed the front porch post for support, half afraid I might fall otherwise.

He pulled his head back and searched my eyes with his. "Once we go down this road, there's no going back."

"I know."

"Are you sure this is where you want to go?"

"Quite sure."

His look went from question to hunger. I could read that look. It matched the yearning in the pit of my stomach.

In one fluid motion, he climbed the last step, picked me up, and strode inside. He kicked the door closed behind him. Without a word, he carried me up the stairs.

"I've moved into Gram's old room." When he'd left, I'd still been sleeping in one of the guest rooms that had been mine since childhood.

Nate chuckled. "How many beds are in this house?"

"Five. Well, six. One of the guest rooms has two twins."

"Good to know. Because right now, I'm not feeling picky." With purpose, he covered the length of the hall and navigated the doorway at the far end. He laid me gently on the bed, propped against my pile of pillows, then stepped back and gazed at me with wonder.

"Nate?" I said softly.

"What is it, Slugger?" How could he make Slugger sound so sexy?

"You were playing with Rhett..."

He threw back his head and laughed. "Be right back." He stepped into the bathroom.

I arranged myself in my most alluring pose to make him forget all about me being a little germaphobic.

Nate was still laughing when he returned, holding up his hands like a surgeon. "Sanitized for your protection."

I sent him my come-hither look.

His laughter settled into a sexy grin as he approached the bed. He sat beside me and caressed my ankle. His hand brushed up my leg to the hem of my dress. As if I were a precious gift, Nate unwrapped me slowly. When the dress reached my chest, I raised my arms and he lifted it over my head. He stretched out beside me and his lips claimed mine, his kiss no longer gentle. I wrapped my arms around him and slid my hands down his back, savoring the solid feel of muscle through the fabric of his shirt.

His left hand held my head to his, while his right explored every inch of me. He caressed my breasts through the lace of my bra until I whimpered. Then he reached around and deftly unclasped my bra, removed it, and tossed it across the room.

He pulled away from me and stood. He slipped my panties off and threw them over his shoulder.

I smiled. "I think you're over-dressed for the occasion."

"We can't have that, now." His eyes never left mine as he undressed. Then, Nate was on top of me. His mouth found mine again, and I lost all ability to think.

I touched his face. Overwhelmed by the surge of emotion, a tear slid down mine.

He pulled back and looked at me, a question in his eyes. I smiled through the tears and pulled his head back to mine.

Without a word, we possessed each other. We touched and felt, tasted and devoured, held and rocked. Something deep inside me moved, recalibrated. And then we took each breath together. Time slowed, and becoming one, our bodies synchronized.

I yelled something in a language I'm sure only Nate understood, and he cried out in answer.

Much later, we held each other, breathing together. The lines where I stopped and he started were blurred. That sense of fading into one person was intoxicating. He brushed the hair from my face and tilted my chin up, to hold me with his eyes again. "Are we okay?"

"Never better."

Nate rolled onto his back, pulling me with him. I rested my head on his chest and curled a leg across his. He stared at the ceiling.

"What are you thinking?" I asked.

"I'm trying to remember how long I've wanted to hold you like this."

"How long?"

"I distinctly remember having highly inappropriate thoughts about you when you were my brother's wife."

"Really? You hid that well. But that's been quite a while. How is it you've taken so long to mention these urges?"

"I think you know the answer to that."

"I suppose I do." Nate had been my best friend for years. He knew better than anyone how I'd pined for Michael, right up until he wanted me back. I hated how many years I'd wasted obsessing over someone I didn't really want. Odd how the mind games you play with yourself are the most seriously screwed up.

He tightened his long arms, wrapping me tight. "Let's look forward, not back."

I smiled. "I don't want you getting any ideas."

He pulled back and regarded me from under knitted brow. "What manner of idea should I not entertain?"

"Well, I can't have you thinking I'm a woman of easy virtue. Waltz in here and drag me up to bed like I'm a common... I expect to be properly courted."

Nate burst out laughing. "Slugger, I'm well aware that nothing about you is, or ever will be easy. And you are far from common."

"I'm serious. It occurs to me that we've never even been on a proper date."

"I will rectify that at the first opportunity. Are you free tomorrow evening? No, wait. A *proper* date should be on the weekend. I'll make reservations and order flowers. Will you have dinner with me Friday evening?"

"I'll have to check my calendar." Actually, I needed to relieve Michael of the notion he and I were going out. Oh boy.

"Please do that and get back to me. Now, as for tonight, I'm not eager to move, but I have worked up an appetite."

"How about I finish that pasta now?"

"I can help."

I kissed him slowly. "Meet you in the kitchen."

EIGHT

The next morning I was up at five for my run on the beach. Nate was sleeping soundly. I took a few minutes to watch him just for the pure pleasure of it, but didn't disturb him. I slipped into a pair of running shorts and a tank, pulled on my running shoes, and headed down the stairs with Rhett beside me. He loved our morning runs as much as I did.

The air was fresh, full of possibilities. The breeze blowing off the Atlantic was steady but not stiff. The only sounds were the soft rumble of the surf and the *thud, thud* of my shoes on the decking, across the walkway over the dunes, and down the steps. The darkness was beginning to pale. At five in the morning, I had the beach to myself, and that's the way I preferred it. Calista and all her issues invaded my head and I pushed her away. I needed my morning run to give her my best work.

I turned left at the bottom of the steps and jogged down the beach, around the north point of the island. They say that if you live at the beach you don't appreciate it. They're wrong. Every morning when my feet hit the sand I think how blessed I am to live in this magical place.

My family has lived on this island for generations. Between college, my unfortunate marriage to Scott, and avoiding home because Michael was married to Marci, I'd spent the last thirteen years in the Upstate, the South Carolina foothills. It had taken Gram's death and the need to solve that crime to get me home. I'd moved into the sprawling, yellow-and-teak, tin-roofed beach house she left me and took over her seat on the town council. Someone had to fill the void she'd left and protect our island home from developers. In some ways it felt like I'd slipped out of my life and into Gram's. Fortunately, my career in solutions consulting is portable.

Rhett and I turned around at Heron Creek and retraced our route past the marina and back around North Point. As I pulled the salt air deeply into my lungs and pushed it out again, it felt as though I was one with the island coming into sharper focus in the rising sunlight. I passed the house and ran south towards town. After I passed The Pirates' Den, the top of the white dome of Calista's house came into view.

From the beach, you could see only the top half of the house over the dunes. I decided to take a detour and see if Calista had exterior security installed. Rhett and I climbed her steps and headed down the walkway towards the house. Unlike mine, Calista's wooden path led to a wide pool deck. The amoeba-shaped pool had a waterfall at one end and a hot tub at the other. An outdoor bar with high stools stood at the right edge, next to the waterfall. A pool house with guest quarters sat adjacent to the bar. I rounded the pool house and took the steps down to the sand. I was looking for motion detectors and cameras. Either they were well-hidden, or Calista hadn't had them installed.

I walked around the house and down the length of the driveway, checking trees and bushes. When I was almost to Ocean Boulevard, I noticed a tan Toyota Camry across the street. I could see the top of a brown head in the driver's seat. Rhett sounded a warning bark.

"Shhh. Be still, boy."

He muffed out an indignant noise in response.

The driver started the engine and the car rolled forward. Whoever it was could not have seen where he was going over the dash as low as he, or she, was slouched. Clearly, the driver did not want to be seen.

Since he or she had obviously seen me, I dashed out into the street to get a tag number. When the car was a few hundred feet away, the driver sat up and the car shot away.

The Camry had California plates.

I skipped my usual morning skinny dip in the ocean and ran straight back to the house. The aroma of fresh-brewed coffee welcomed me as I opened the back door and stepped into the sunroom. "Nate?"

"In here," he called from the kitchen.

I followed his voice. Oh. My. Stars. There he stood, six-foot-three of prime Southern male, barefoot and bare-chested, in just a faded pair of blue jeans. I had trouble focusing on what I'd had on my mind when I came in the back door.

He grinned. "Coffee?"

"Yes, please—thank you." Did he know the impact he had on me?

He put three Splendas in a big mug, filled it with coffee, and added just the right amount of cream. Nate and I had been bringing each other coffee for years. Of course he knew how I liked it. But that morning it felt very intimate, significant.

"Thanks." I smiled.

"You should've woken me up. I'd've run with you."

"I didn't want to disturb you."

"The sight of you in those running shorts disturbs me."

"Does it now?"

"It disturbs me to think how gazing upon that much of your long, lovely legs might disturb any red-blooded male you pass."

I smothered a grin. "I didn't see a soul." I remembered why I'd come in early, shook my head to clear it. "Well, except I've got to check out a license plate." I headed out of the kitchen, down the hall towards my office.

"Before breakfast? What's up?" Nate followed.

I filled him in on Calista McQueen, the particulars of her case, and the man who'd been watching her house.

"Any chance he was doing anything besides surveillance on her?"

"Possible, but doubtful. Hers is the only house within half a mile along that stretch of road. And he went to comical lengths to keep me from seeing his face. If he'd just parked there to check a map or some such innocent thing, there'd've been no need for him to light out of there in such a hurry."

"True. Do you think this Harmony's death is connected to Calista?"

"Hard to say. Think about it. Harmony was killed in what appears to be an execution, by someone she knew, at approximately the same time Calista hired me because she's afraid someone will kill her. On the surface of it, it seems it would be an odd coincidence if her death wasn't connected to Calista somehow."

"That it would be. Breakfast?"

"I've got yogurt, blueberries, and granola. That's what I'm having. I'm afraid I don't have eggs and bacon on hand."

"I can make do with girl food this morning. I'll throw some yogurt together while you check out that tag."

"Thanks." I took a deep breath and willed my brain to work. Nate was all kinds of distracting. Being involved with my partner and still getting work done was going to be an adjustment.

I logged into one of my subscription databases. After a few clicks, I stopped and stared at the screen in disbelief.

James Edward Davis owned the Camry with California plates that had been parked outside Calista's house. The same James Edward Davis who had married Norma Jeane Mortensen on June 19, 1992 in Los Angeles, exactly fifty years after James Edward Dougherty had married another Norma Jeane Mortensen.

How had he found her after all these years?

Calista had interrupted me the day before when I'd been working on profiles, and I'd left in a hurry to go to Charleston with her. I hadn't had the chance to dig into Jim Davis yet. Had he been in cahoots with Gladys and Grace? Or, like Calista, had he been a victim of their schemes to turn her into Marilyn reborn and make her their meal ticket? I was busy creating his timeline when Nate set a bowl of yogurt on the desk.

"Find him?" he asked.

"Yep. Calista's first husband. This may be the strangest case we've worked since that guy hid his stripper-girlfriend's Indian python in his ex-girlfriend's mobile home."

Nate shuddered. "I hate snakes. Wonder what this guy wants with his ex-wife after all this time."

"I was wondering the same thing. I'd like to ask him."

"Well, why don't I start trolling hotel parking lots looking for the car while you finish finding out what you can about him online?"

"Sounds like a plan. Thank you."

He grinned. "I'm an easy dog to hunt with, Slugger."

I laughed. "I'd start with Isle of Palms, then work my way outward from there to Mt. Pleasant, then the greater Charleston and North Charleston areas. My hunch is he's close."

"Great minds."

We ate breakfast, both lost in our own thoughts. I struggled to keep my mind on Calista's problems and off what a dramatic turn my own life had just taken. It was strange how Nate was at once so familiar and suddenly so foreign to me. I needed to focus on Nate my partner and best friend, and think about Nate my lover after I knew Calista was safe.

NINE

I tracked Michael down at a construction site in Mt. Pleasant. He was restoring a home near the waterfront in the Old Village.

I'm reasonably certain Nate would not have approved of my excursion, but it hadn't taken me long to find out all there was to know about Jim Davis. He'd worked at Lockheed since he was nineteen and had never remarried. He had no criminal record and no children. If I wanted more answers about him, I was going to have to think up some new questions.

Michael was one of a handful of people on Stella Maris who had met Calista. I needed to interview him as a part of the investigation. That's what I would tell Nate and it was the truth. But I also needed to tell Michael he and I wouldn't be going out Friday night, or any other night. I needed to do that in person. Michael and I had a lot of history. I owed him that much.

"Liz!" Michael called across the yard when he saw me. He looked so happy to see me.

I felt just awful. "Hey, Michael."

"I'm so glad you stopped by I was thinking we'd go to Anson tomorrow night if it's okay with you. It's short notice, so we'll have to eat a little early. They're booked from seven on."

"Michael, I can't go tomorrow night."

"Would Saturday night be better?"

A little piece of my heart broke. I struggled to make the words I needed to say to Michael come out of my mouth. I stalled. "Can we talk about that in a minute?" I stepped into the shade of an enormous oak. It was late morning already and the heat was brutal. "I need to ask you something."

Michael followed me. "Shoot."

"You know Calista McQueen, right?"

"Sure, you remember. I took you through her house. We just got the occupancy permit a month or so back. She's had decorators in there ever since. I think she's moved in."

"She has. I just met her yesterday. What do you think about her?"

"What do I think about her?"

"Yeah, I mean...is she pretty?"

"What? You said you met her."

"Just please answer me. What does she look like?"

Michael shrugged. "She's not ugly or anything. Kinda plain. A little on the shy side. Liz, what's this about?"

Calista had dressed for Michael like she did when she went into the diner. "I'm just curious about her. She's my new neighbor, after all. I've got to get her a casserole made." Talking to Michael about Calista beyond asking the questions I needed answered violated client confidentiality. I didn't want to lie to him. But there were simply things I couldn't discuss with him. I offered him my sunniest smile.

Michael wasn't buying it. "You didn't come over to Mt. Pleasant to ask me what your neighbor, who you've met yourself, looks like."

"Was she always alone when you met with her?" I looked at him with a silent plea.

"This is about some case, isn't it?" He gave me a look that let me know he was biting back most of what he thought.

I gave him a part wince, part smile look, which was open to interpretation. "Was she alone?"

He relented. I felt sick on account of that was likely because he cared about me. "Most of the time. Robert Pearson was with her once. And we met with the Glendawns a couple of times about the property. There at the last some guy came with her for walk-throughs. She said he was her yoga instructor. Whatever. It wasn't any of my business."

"Did you know Elenore Harper was working for her as a housekeeper?"

"No, that's news to me."

"Did you install a security system?"

"Yeah. I sub-contracted that. I usually go with ADT, but she insisted on this outfit from Los Angeles. They were involved from the get-go. That place is a fortress."

"What about outside? Does she have perimeter security?"

"Sure. Cameras, motion detectors." His irritation level was rising.

"They're well hidden."

"That's a fact."

"Is all of that stuff monitored?"

"Now that I don't know. She would arrange for that service just like any other utility. But who would have all that stuff installed and not have someone monitor it? Will you please tell me what's going on?"

"It's related to a case. I'm sorry, I really can't."

Michael's brow creased. "See, every time you talk to me about a *case*, I start playing that scene in my head where you're on Blake's Jet Ski getting shot at. Have you thought at all about what I mentioned, about training to be a paralegal?"

Not this again. I put my hand on his arm. "Michael, I appreciate your concerns for my safety. It's sweet of you. But I like my job. I'm not looking to change careers."

He retrieved his arm, put his hands on his hips, and stared at the ground. "I want a family, Liz. Your job is not one that compliments motherhood well."

I took a deep breath. Michael had clearly read far more into our weekly dinners than I'd intended. Okay, I'd been on the fence at first, and maybe I hadn't clarified things for him when I climbed down. And even if Nate wasn't in the picture, even if I still felt the same way about Michael, the never-ending argument over my career would make a future with him impossible.

There would never be a good time for this conversation. "Michael." My eyes watered. "Michael, a little part of me will always love you. But you and I, we've had our time. We're just not the same people we were in college."

"I thought we were getting to know each other again."

I closed my eyes and nodded. "We have been. And what we've learned is that we want different things now."

"How can you say that? We both want a life with family and friends—a life on Stella Maris. We're island people, you and me."

"That's true. But you want a traditional family life. Nothing about my life is traditional anymore."

"Look, if your job means that much to you, forget I said anything. We'll work it out. I do want a family. With you. I can't see anyone else being the mother of my children. But we can wait until you're ready."

The more I let this drag on, the more I was going to say things that hurt us both. Better to make it quick and clean. I steeled myself and looked him in the eye. "I'm not going to be the mother of your children, Michael. We're not going to be getting married."

He looked like I'd slapped him. "I thought we were going to give this time."

"We have. Please, Michael. I never meant to hurt you, and it's killing me that I have. But I'm never going to be the kind of wife you want."

"Don't say that, now. Look, let's talk about this over dinner Saturday."

"I'm afraid not," I said gently.

"What do you mean?"

I needed to make him accept this, for both our sakes. "I mean we won't be going to dinner Saturday night. We've gotten reacquainted, like we talked about. And it's clear to me now that I'm never going to feel the way about you that I once did—the way you want me to. The way you deserve, Michael."

"This has something to do with Nate, doesn't it?" His tone turned ugly.

"I need to go."

"You've already married one Andrews. How did that work out?"

"That was just mean. I'm leaving now." Marrying Scott Andrews may well have been the single worst decision of my entire life. But Nate was nothing like his cheating scoundrel of a brother. I started walking towards my car.

"Liz, wait. Please."

"There's nothing more to say."

"You might be finished talking for now, but that won't stop me from trying to change your mind. I *will* change your mind. Dammit, Liz. We walked away one time. Please, let's don't do this again."

"We're done." I climbed in the car, started the engine, and stirred up the dust in the driveway as I left. I wasn't in love with Michael anymore. But I did care about him. And he sure could piss me off.

TEN

It had been less than twenty-four hours since Calista and I had met with Sonny about Harmony's murder. I hadn't heard from him since. That didn't particularly surprise me—he was conducting a murder investigation. This was his case. A Charleston PD case, not a Stella Maris case, so I had far less leeway to meddle. But Sonny didn't seem to be pursuing the angles that pertained to Calista. Naturally, those were my priority.

Jim Davis had been stewing in my brain like a pot about to boil over. I wondered if Jim Dougherty had ever remarried. Hells bells, I'd been listening to Calista too much. Nevertheless, on the way back home, I swung by Barnes and Noble in Mt. Pleasant. My natural curiosity was piqued by this biography of Marilyn Calista had mentioned. I loved the Book and Grind in Stella Maris, but a quick phone call verified they didn't have it in stock. I didn't have time to wait for them to order it.

It's not that I believed Calista was in imminent danger because she was Marilyn's doppelganger. But if Colleen had taught me anything, it was that there's much more to this life than what we could perceive with our five standard senses. I was open minded enough to be wary of the Marilyn angle.

I snagged a copy of the seven-hundred-page Spoto biography, another title called *The Marilyn Monroe Treasures* by Jenna Glatzer, and Marilyn's autobiography, published more than a decade after her death.

Then I headed for the Isle of Palms connector and voice-dialed Nate.

"How's the research coming?" he asked by way of greeting.

"Okay. Let's just say Jim Davis appears too boring on paper to have nefarious intent, but that in itself could be a red flag. I just picked up a Marilyn Monroe biography. You wouldn't believe how many books there are on her. I picked up a couple of others."

"What for?"

"I'm curious. How goes the search for Mr. Davis?"

"I've checked every hotel and vacation rental on Isle of Palms. I haven't spotted the Camry, and he's not registered anywhere under his name."

"That was quick. What did you do, hack the reservation systems?"

"Does that sound like me?"

"Why, yes, as a matter of fact."

"You make a fair point, Slugger. Just accept my word that Mr. Davis is not residing on the Isle of Palms at present unless he is using a false name, in which case I would posit the theory that he does have nefarious intent. I should add that the plate number of his car does not appear on the registration records anywhere."

"So, are you headed into Mt. Pleasant now?"

"I am."

"I probably passed you. Keep me posted."

"Will do. By the way, I have reserved a table for our date tomorrow evening at Anson. Seven-thirty."

Of course he had. Well, they both had good taste in restaurants. "Sounds good. What do you want for dinner tonight?"

"As long as you're at my table, I couldn't care less."

"You are a sweet-talker. Mamma always told me to be wary of sweet-talking boys." I hated how his sweet-talking ways reminded me of his brother, Scott. You couldn't believe a solitary thing that came out of Scott Andrews' mouth. Nate was not Scott. I had let Michael get into my head. I shoved him out.

"Your mamma is a wise woman. You should be very wary of me." There were a great many suggestions in his tone.

"I'll remember that. I've got to get back to work. I declare you are a distraction."

Nate laughed.

I loved his laugh. I smiled. This was Nate I was talking to. "Bye now."

When the call ended, I turned up the music. "Hemmingway's Whiskey" was playing. The brooding melody and lyrics sent me into a reflective mood. Thinking about Scott was enough to drive me to drinking whiskey.

I stopped by the house to grab something to eat and call Calista. My reading material would have to wait. I made a pimento cheese sandwich, poured a glass of diet Cheerwine, and took my lunch to my desk. My mamma makes the best pimento cheese in the world. I'd scored a take-home bowl when I'd dropped by Monday afternoon. Between bites, I called Calista and made an appointment to see her at two.

Then I had an idea. I pulled up Jim Davis's online profile. He'd never remarried, but he had family. His father had passed away a few years back, but it looked like his mother lived with his sister and her family. Maybe someone in the household knew where Jim was and what his intentions were. I could have used spoofing software to disguise where I was calling from, but decided to let that work in my favor. The truth or its third cousin might be my best hope.

I tapped in the number. On the fourth ring, a woman answered.

"Mrs. Davis?"

"Yes?"

The mother. How to play this? Maybe not the truth. I quickly donned my sweet-but-slightly-ditzy persona. "Ma'am, my name is Suzanne Thompson. I'm calling from South Carolina?"

"Is Jimmy all right?" The woman sounded alarmed.

I calculated her approximate age. Mid-sixties? I didn't want to go around scaring anybody's meemaw. "Oh, yes ma'am. I saw him just this morning."

"That's a relief. He hasn't called but once since he got there. I worry, you know."

"Yes, ma'am. I understand. It's a long way from California."

"What can I help you with?" she asked.

"Well, ma'am, Jimmy came into the diner this morning for breakfast. I waited on him myself. He's a good tipper."

"Jimmy?"

"Yes ma'am. But he left his wallet in the booth. Ma'am, would you happen to know where he's staying? He didn't mention it, and I'm sure he'd like to have his wallet back."

"Oh. Yes. He said he was at the Hampton Inn. I don't know if there's more than one of those in Mt. Pleasant or not."

Score. "Yes ma'am, there are two of them. But it won't take but a skinny minute for me to call and find out which one he's staying at. Then I can leave his wallet at the desk for him, or he can come back by and get it, either way."

"I know he'll appreciate that."

"Yes, ma'am. You have a nice day."

I hung up and called Nate. Hells bells, if Jim Davis was at the Hampton Inn just off the Isle of Palms connector, I'd likely driven right by him.

I took a bite of my sandwich and savored the rich marriage of five kinds of cheese, mayonnaise, and seven secret ingredients. Colleen faded in, stretched out on the back of the sofa in a way that would have been impossible for any mortal being. She looked at me with undisguised hunger.

"You miss food, don't you?" I asked.

"Boy howdy. When I learn to solidify, I can eat. I think. The first thing I want is some of your mamma's pimento cheese."

"I'll see to it," I said. "What do you know about doppelgangers?"

"Well, in the paranormal sense, like glimpsing yourself in your peripheral vision, omens, portents, and such, I haven't seen anything to credit the theories. But, in terms of folks having a double...think about the math. There are more than seven billion people alive on earth right now. Every day, more than twice as many people are born than die. In recorded history, nearly a hundred and ten billion people have lived. There are only so many combinations of features. I wonder why we aren't stumbling over ourselves coming and going."

I sipped my Cheerwine. "Do you think Calista is some distant relation of Marilyn's?"

Colleen shrugged. "Could be. There are known loose ends in Marilyn's family history. Read your research materials. Her mother's brother disappeared when he was twenty-four. He had a wife and three children. Went out for a newspaper and never came back. That's just one example. Anything's possible, isn't that what you always say?"

I nodded. "Anything is possible. Most things are even likely, given the level of crazy in the human race. Almost nothing is impossible."

"You say that now more than you used to."

"My best friend is a guardian spirit."

She shrugged apologetically. "Hey, Liz?"

"Yeah?"

"Don't take this as criticism, okay?"

"Okay."

"You know how sometimes you can be a little mulish?"

I stared at her by way of response.

"This is important. If Nate tells you to jump, just do it and ask questions later."

"*What*?"

"You heard me. Don't forget. Just jump." She faded out.

I finished my lunch and headed out to talk to Calista.

ELEVEN

When I walked inside the courtyard at the entrance to Calista's house, I considered studying up on feng shui. That feeling of serenity I'd experienced on my first visit wrapped around me again. It eroded when Elenore opened the door. Something about that woman got under my skin. No wonder Warren had traded her in.

"Ms. McQueen will receive you by the pool," she said.

I offered her a sunny smile. "Why, thank you so much."

"This way." She started through the house.

"Oh, don't bother. I can find her myself."

"Please follow me." She ignored me, escorted me to the pool deck, and announced me again. Then she disappeared.

Today Calista and Niles were in yoga outfits. They had mats on a shady spot of grass at the edge of the pool deck. It seemed awfully hot outside for yoga, but maybe the breeze made it bearable.

As I approached, they bowed at each other. Waves broke on the sand and sluiced back out to sea, creating the perfect soundtrack.

"I'm sorry to interrupt," I said.

"Liz." Calista walked towards a row of recliners shaded by a curved swath of concrete and white billowy drapes. "Let's talk over here." She arranged herself on a modern-looking chaise.

I took the one beside her. They were way more comfortable than they looked. Niles had followed her and stood nearby with a towel around his neck.

Calista looked up at him. "Why don't you get something to drink? And would you ask Mrs. Harper to bring some water with lemon for Liz and me?"

"Certainly. Can I get you anything else?"

"No, thanks. That was a great workout."

Niles nodded and exited stage left. He moved with hesitant steps, as if he weren't committed to the journey. I had the feeling he didn't like leaving. I watched him go.

"What did you want to talk about?" Calista asked.

"I don't want to worry you, but I need to let you know that Jim Davis is in the area. I caught him watching your house this morning around five-thirty."

Calista's hand fluttered up to her face. "You see, Harmony was right. Do you think he killed her?"

"Honestly, I don't know. I've done a good bit of research on him. He doesn't have a criminal background. There's nothing to suggest he's the violent type. But...people who aren't violent types turn violent when something sets them off. It's hard to figure what might have set him off after all this time. But, we can't rule him out as a suspect."

"I think he's only violent where I'm concerned."

"Was he abusive during your marriage?"

Calista stared out at the Atlantic. "He's not aggressive by nature. I think they made him a little crazy—Mother and Grace, I mean."

"Are you aware that Grace's real name was Donna Clark? And your mother, her name was Gwen Monroe. They both changed their names the week after you were born."

"But Mother's name is listed as Gladys Monroe on my birth certificate. I have a copy."

"I suspect Donna put her up to entering her name that way. Hospitals weren't barcoding patients back then. It would have been easy enough, I think, to give a variation on a first name. The initial was the same."

"I suppose you're right."

"I think they manipulated as much of your life as they could to create the illusion of a parallel."

"Well, they didn't manipulate the way I look."

"There is that. My theory is they took the coincidence nature offered them with your birth date and time and tried to capitalize on it. It seems they got wildly lucky with your looks." That double coincidence nagged at me. As coincidences go, either one of them would be a doozy. But combined they were nearly impossible to swallow. But, there she sat.

"That sounds right. I just didn't know they'd changed their names. That makes everything else a little suspect, doesn't it?"

"It explains some things. It's possible they paid someone off to alter the time you were born, especially if it was close." I pondered whether there was any margin in chasing that rabbit and decided against it. "So, you think their schemes made Jim violent?"

"He wanted me to get into modeling and acting. But that could easily have come from them. They were always around, always pushing me—pushing him. He never hurt me, but when I refused to go on auditions he would get really mad and throw things and storm out. He scared me."

Elenore appeared with a tray. She set it on a nearby table, served us each a glass of iced water with lemon, and slid away.

"Thank you, Mrs. Harper," Calista said.

"Calista, how did Elenore Harper come to work for you?"

"Niles introduced us. I think her daughter is one of his students. Something like that. She's odd, but very efficient."

I tucked that away to think about later. "Why do you think Jim has tracked you down eighteen years later?"

"Money? Revenge?"

"But how did he find you?"

"I'm hoping you'll find that out."

I sighed. "Me, too. Tell me about your security system. I understand from Michael Devlin that you hired someone from Los

Angeles to put it in. Is it possible someone at the security company knows your ex? The LA connection concerns me."

"First of all, the company's headquarters is based in Los Angeles, but I dealt with their office in Charleston. Their business is private security. They secure royalty and heads of corporations—billionaires. It's hard to imagine anyone there has loose lips. No one there knows anything about my background."

"Yeah, they wouldn't hold onto that clientele if they weren't keeping people safe. Still. Security companies have all kinds of resources for checking into people. Surely they could have uncovered your background if they looked hard enough. I was able to verify it. Of course, I knew where to look because you told me. Still. Money can be a powerful motivator."

"That's true." We listened to the waves for a few moments. "You know," she said, "everyone thinks they want to win the lottery. They don't. If you have great wealth, you have to spend your whole life guarding it from all the people who want to take it away from you. That's no way to live. You can never fully trust anyone. Almost anyone can be bought for the right price."

I felt bad for her. She was so beautiful, and rich enough to do anything she wanted. But she was so alone. "I can see how that much money would isolate you. When you were married to Jim, was he focused on money?"

"Very much so. He thought I could make us rich."

"Ironic how you came into more money than she ever made."

"Isn't it, though? I don't know how he found out where I am, but I think it must be like Harmony said. He thinks I owe him money, and he's come to collect."

"But, logically, if he kills you, he wouldn't inherit a dime." This was the biggest reason I didn't think he would kill Calista. But it didn't clear him regarding Harmony.

"He must have an angle."

"I think Grace and your mother were the ones with all the angles."

"They may be behind this. I'd sure hate to think my own mother would have me killed."

"Is she currently in an institution?"

"Last I heard, no. My attorney handles the trust that takes care of her. He might know."

"I'll need his contact information."

"It's Robert Pearson. He's local. You know him, right?"

"I've known him all my life. I heard he handled your land purchase, but he handles your other business as well?"

"Yes. He does now. Switching attorneys periodically makes me feel safer."

"I'll check in with him. But, I'll need you to sign a release so that he can speak to me."

"Sure thing."

"Back to the security system. Walk me through it."

"They consulted with Michael on construction. All the windows are bulletproof. Of course, the walls are as well. I have a safe room. The air is filtered. I have cameras inside and out. The exterior ones are motion activated."

"Who monitors the system?"

"Security Solutions in Charleston. That's the company that designed it."

We'd both been watching waves. I turned to look at her. "So you got a call when I walked through your yard this morning?"

Calista looked at me, alarmed. "No, actually."

"And you had armed the perimeter system?"

"Yes. I always do when I'm in for the night. To be honest, I only activate the interior cameras and motion detectors when I'm away. I can't bear the idea of someone watching me in my own home."

"Understandable. But the system failed rather spectacularly this morning. That could have put you at great risk. I'm going to need you to call and ask them to talk to me. You may need to sign a release for them as well. Who is your contact there?"

"Mack Ryan."

"Do you have the list of contacts we talked about, and the shopping list that was altered?"

"Yes. I put them both on the credenza in the foyer for you."

Elenore came out of the house, crossed the far end of the pool deck, and entered the guesthouse.

"She has a lot to clean between the house and the guesthouse," I said.

"Oh, she doesn't normally clean in there every day. She's staying in the guest house while the hardwood floors in her house are being refinished."

"That's very nice of you to let her stay here."

"It's more convenient for me, really. And after all, I have the guesthouse just sitting there. Why should she stay in a hotel? Plus, I feel safer having someone else here."

Somehow I couldn't reckon with Elenore as protection. "Do you have the same security features in the guesthouse?"

"Yes, but the guest house is a separate zone. The house has several zones."

"Is the master suite a zone?"

"Yes. Can I ask you a question?"

"Of course."

"Did you always want to be a private investigator?"

"No." I gave her a wan smile. "I wanted to be an actress. Mamma insisted I pick a college major that would give me something to fall back on if that didn't pan out. I decided on English. I thought maybe I could teach at the high school and manage the drama program. Everything changed when I took a course in criminal behavior as an elective. For a while I thought I might go into police work, maybe even the FBI. But all that bureaucracy seemed stifling—and don't get me started on the wardrobe. Private investigation was a better fit for me. Why do you ask?"

"Everyone else had dreams for me, but I never had any for myself until I left California. I just wondered."

I stood to leave. "Okay, I'm going to check in with my partner and see if he has eyes on Jim Davis. Call the security company as soon as I leave and let them know you had an undetected breach this morning. They should jump right on that. They have a reputation to protect. Then, for the next few days, I'd recommend you be vigilant about arming the security system inside and out. You can turn off the camera and motion detectors in the guesthouse and your bedroom and bath, but still have them on in the rest of the house. That will protect your privacy but alert the security company if someone enters the house while you're asleep."

"I'll forget to disarm it, and walk into the kitchen for water in the middle of the night."

"So, you may be billed for a few false alarms. That's the least of your worries."

"I guess you're right. If Niles stays over, I can disarm the guestroom as well, but leave the system on in the common areas."

I felt my face squinch. "Niles sleeps over?"

"Sometimes. If he's had a quarrel with his boyfriend, or if I'm feeling especially blue."

I took a deep breath and patted her on the shoulder. I wondered what it would feel like to have no family to rely on, no close friends to turn to. I had the urge to befriend her, but needed to maintain my professional objectivity. "I'll see you tomorrow afternoon. We'll talk more then."

"All right."

"Hey, I meant to ask you about your license plate. I'm just curious. What does it mean?"

"Fifty-cent soul."

"What's the significance?"

"It's something Marilyn said once. It stuck with me. She was so much deeper than people gave her credit for. She said, 'Hollywood is a place where they'll pay you a thousand dollars for a kiss and fifty cents for your soul. I know, because I turned down the first offer often enough and held out for the fifty cents.' I owe her quite a lot, when you think about it. If I hadn't known how her story ended, I might have let them turn me into a movie star. Instead, I kept my fifty-cent soul and left town."

TWELVE

Mamma called as I pulled out of Calista's driveway. "Liz, honey, your daddy has gotten himself another computer virus. Can you run by the barn? I'm positively mortified. I've heard from three members of the church, and Father Henry to boot. Your daddy's computer has been broadcasting pornography over email."

I resisted the urge to bang my head on the steering wheel. "I'll head over there now."

"Liz?"

"Yes, Mamma."

"See if you can get him to go to the doctor and have his blood pressure checked."

"I'll do my best." Daddy wasn't fond of seeing doctors, even Warren Harper. And he liked him, generally speaking.

"Thank you sweetheart. Come by and take some more of this pimento cheese if you can use it."

"Thanks, Mamma, but that's not in my best interests. That stuff is like crack cocaine to me."

"Well, I guess if I don't see you before, I'll see you at dinner Sunday."

"Okay. Wait, Mamma. Nate's in town."

"Well, bring him along."

My stomach clenched. "All right. See you then." I ended the call wondering how Nate was going to feel about having dinner with my family, and how they would receive the news that Nate and I were partners in more than one sense of the word. They purely hated Scott, with good reason. This might be weird.

Before she would let Daddy retire, Mamma insisted he find something to occupy his time besides sandpapering her nerves all day. Since his two favorite pastimes consisted of haunting flea markets and cussin' at the stock reports on cable news channels, we all put our heads together and came up with the idea for Talbot's Treasures.

It was in an old red barn on the other side of the island from their house on Marsh Point Drive just south of forty acres of woods. It was out of Mamma's hair, is what I meant. We pitched in to help renovate the barn, and air-conditioned it to the point you could've hung meat in there. Daddy didn't like to sweat. To help pay the outrageous electricity bills, he rented booths to a few of his cronies and the occasional bored housewife. Near the front door, he sat vigil over the stock ticker with his sad-sack basset hound, Chumley, surfed the World Wide Web, and occasionally sold junk.

And that's exactly where I found him when I stepped out of the sweltering heat and a swarm of no-see-ums and into his massive, frigid man cave.

"Top of the afternoon, Ms. Tutie," he called out, not taking his eyes off the television.

Apparently, he had trouble recalling the name they'd put on my birth certificate, because he seldom used it unless something was wrong. Tutie was the latest in a long succession of nicknames that came from the vast, unknown frontiers of my daddy's brain. It wasn't just me. When all was right in his world, he rarely called anyone by their actual name.

I hugged his neck, careful not to muss his hair. He looked much younger than his fifty-two years and was quite vain. There wasn't a single gray hair in his sandy blond head, which was the exact same color as mine before Phoebe got ahold of me.

"Hey, Daddy. How're you feeling? Mamma's afraid your blood pressure's up."

"The whistle pigs got into your mamma's bulbs again last night," he said, eyes still glued to the stock ticker.

Stella Maris had a thriving herd of wild hogs. In the aftermath of a hurricane back in the 1800s, most of the livestock wandered the island until fences and barns were repaired or rebuilt. This particular gang of hogs was never apprehended. Daddy called them whistle pigs. Don't ask me why. I was pretty sure that whistle pig was technically another name for a woodchuck, but Daddy never was much troubled by technicalities. Anyway, as far as I knew, no one had ever heard one of the hogs whistle.

They were mostly harmless, but they liked to snack on in flowerbeds and vegetable gardens, which made them unpopular. It wasn't clear to me from his response whether the hogs had Daddy's blood pressure up, or if it was something on the stock ticker.

"Those things are a menace." The idea of hogs running loose always bothered me. I harbored the suspicion one of them might attack somebody, although I'd never heard such a thing happening.

The town council had discussed at length what to do about them, but no consensus was reached. The island's matriarchs were too tenderhearted to hear tell of the hogs being exterminated, and the swine were wily enough to evade efforts at rounding them up.

"Computer's acting up again," Daddy said.

"That's what Mamma said. Let me take a look." I sat down at his desk and moved the mouse to kill the screen saver. I opened a web page. "Do you want all these toolbars on here?"

"Toolbars?"

"All these things at the top."

"I don't know how those things got on there. Get rid of 'em, why don't you?"

I updated his virus protection, scanned the computer, and removed the excess toolbars. "I'm going to change the password on your email account."

"Write the new one down for me."

"I'm taping it right where the old one was, inside your top drawer. I've underlined the letters you need to capitalize."

He stared at me for a minute. I could see his eyes dancing with mischief, though he didn't throw the game by grinning. He looked away. "Stocks are in the toilet."

"Daddy, when's the last time you had a physical?"

"A physical?" He looked at me like he'd taken a bite of something spoiled.

I sighed. "Listen. If you want to keep on tormenting Mamma with such nonsense as pornography blasts to the church, dragging me over here to fix self-inflicted computer problems, and selling junk, to a ripe old age, we've got to keep you healthy."

"That was no such thing as pornography. Is that what your mamma said?"

Chumley woofed in Daddy's defense.

"Well, Mamma's definition of pornography might be different from yours. Whatever it was, I'm sure it was hilarious. That's not my point."

"Well, state your business, Ms. Tutie."

"I'm going to make you an appointment for a physical."

"I am not going to sit and listen while Warren Harper jaws at me about exercise and fried foods."

"No, I don't think you should see Warren Harper."

"Why not? What's wrong with Warren Harper?"

Warren Harper treated many of the island residents, of all ages. That was the problem. He was a generalist. Daddy would see that as a criticism.

I sighed, closed my eyes for a second, then popped them open and gave Daddy a big smile. "There's nothing wrong with Warren Harper, Daddy. But, you've been friends a long time. I just thought it might be easier to talk about personal matters with someone who isn't one of your poker buddies."

"Hunh."

"I'm going to make you an appointment with an internist in Charleston. You can get all your tests run while you're there."

"Tests? What tests?"

"You know, lab work, EKG, colonoscopy."

"Are you *trying* to run my blood pressure up?"

"Of course not. Why on earth would you say such a thing?"

"'Swhat it sounds like. Here you are trying to give me a heart attack. Talking about letting some stranger stick a—"

"Don't be ridiculous. Everyone past a certain age has those tests done. Everyone who wants to keep on living. I'll let you know when your appointment is."

"Make yourself a doctor's appointment if you want to."

"I see a doctor, regularly."

"I guess that's your business." He turned back to watch the television.

A stray thought crossed my mind. "How long have you known Warren Harper?"

"All his life. Why?"

"How well do you know Elenore?"

Daddy snorted. "I can't imagine what he was thinking when he married *her*. Strange woman. She's from Summerville, if I remember right. She was running around with some man from there while she was married to Warren. Left 'im and those poor little children." He shook his head in disgust.

Those poor little children were a couple years behind me in school, and they'd made out just fine. Warren had remarried, and Lauren Beauthorpe Harper was a natural mother. "Elenore still lives here, though."

"She moved back a couple times. Never stayed long as far as I know. Kids won't have much to do with her. Who could blame 'em?"

"She was around enough for me to know who she was when I saw her."

"Where did you see her?"

"She's working for a client."

"Hunh."

I hugged him bye. "I've got to go, Daddy. Try to stay out of trouble. I'll see you Sunday."

"I'm not going to see any damn doctor."

Oh, yes, indeed he would. "Love you, Daddy."

THIRTEEN

Nate padded in from the hall as I was adding the white wine to the chicken. He sniffed the air. "Mmm...olive oil and garlic."

"How was your day?" I smiled up at him.

He came up behind me, wrapped two muscled arms around me, and kissed my neck. "Good," he said. "Getting better."

"Did you locate Jim Davis?"

He nuzzled the spot just below my ear. "Yes, I located our friend, Mr. Davis. But he can wait a bit."

I leaned into him. He felt solid, substantial. He smelled like soap and hot-blooded man. "I could keep this warm," I said.

"We can reheat it." He let go of me with his right hand long enough to flip the gas off.

"Just let me put it away..."

He nibbled my left ear.

Something melted and flowed inside me, while a shiver danced up my spine. I rested the wooden spoon next to the saucepan, then reached behind me and combed my fingers into his hair.

With the palms of his hands, he stroked my breasts in feather-light circles. I closed my eyes and arched my back, straining to press my chest against his hands.

Teasing, he pulled his palms away just enough to keep his caress just a whisper against my shirt.

Hungry for him, I let go of his hair, dropped my arms, and twisted towards him. He took my hands in his and stopped me, held me facing away from him. Then he lifted me and moved us in one quick motion away from the stove to the island. He placed my hands on the countertop and held them there, leaning over me to run his lower lip down one side of my neck and up the other. Every cell of me tingled.

He lifted his right hand and mine followed, reaching for any part of him. But he grasped my fingers and guided my hand back to the island. "Play nice, now," he whispered.

Oh, dear heaven, how nice I wanted to be to him.

He removed both his hands. With great effort, I kept mine on the counter.

He ran his fingertips from the tops of my thighs, slowly, up my sides, and to my breasts. He lingered there for a moment, making me gasp. Then, he slipped his hands underneath my tank and unhooked my bra. He pulled the shirt over my head, then released one arm at a time, replacing each hand in turn to the table. Finally, he slid down my capris, guided my legs free, and placed the ball of each foot on the floor with a squeeze indicating the foot should stay where he'd planted it.

I was standing in the kitchen in black silk-and-lace boy-shorts, bent slightly over the black granite island, on tiptoes. He was still fully clothed in jeans and a T-shirt. I was completely vulnerable and all-powerful.

I felt his lips on my ankle and gripped the table. He took his time, kissing his way up my left leg, then down my right. He lifted my right foot and stepped it out, spreading my knees apart. My hips gyrated in slow circles.

He reached around me and splayed his hands over my stomach. Gently, he pulled my bottom back against his jeans. I could feel the heat rising through the denim and lace. He kissed the spot between my shoulder blades. I rubbed against him and made a noise that was part moan, part whine.

"Are you getting impatient?" he asked.

"Yes," I hissed.

"No need to hurry, now," he said. "I want to savor you."

In answer, I ground against him more insistently.

He moved his hands slowly across my hips and cupped my bottom. I slowed the rhythm my hips danced to, pressing my bottom against his hands longer each rotation. He stoked me ever-so-lightly through the silk.

"I want to feel your touch," I whimpered. "Let's lose the lace."

"Soon," he whispered in my ear.

"*Nate.*"

"Yes, Slugger," he murmured in my ear.

"*Make love to me,*" I demanded.

"But I am."

An hour and a shower later we lingered at the kitchen table over Tuscan chicken and a bottle of Merry Edwards pinot noir. I rolled the stem of my glass through my fingers and watched the candlelight filtered through the wine. Waves broke on sand and sang softly outside the window.

"So how was your day?" Nate asked.

"Aside from Daddy's pornography-related emergency earlier, it was productive." I laughed as I told him about my visit to the barn.

Nate looked vexed. "I don't understand your daddy, or why your mamma puts up with him. He has to be a smart guy—he had a successful career selling industrial what, valves and such?"

"That's right."

"So why does he play this dumb, good-ole-boy routine?"

"Because it gets him what he wants. I went running over there, didn't I?"

"Why can't he just call, like normal fathers, and ask you to come by when you get a chance?"

I shrugged, thinking Nate really didn't want to talk about normal fathers. His was no poster boy. "It's who Daddy is. At his age, he's not likely to change. The rest of my day was interesting." I told Nate about Calista's security system, and how it failed to engage that morning.

He set his fork down. "It's a cinch this high-end security system comes with a staff of ex-Marine body guards for their high-end clientele. Why would she need to hire *you* for protection?"

"Maybe she's afraid of mercenaries. I don't know. What she needs right now is someone to figure out who wants to hurt her, and why. She hired me for my brains, not my brawn."

Nate shook his head. "I'd be tempted to think what she needs is a good therapist if it weren't for her ex-husband showing up here out of the blue."

"That, and the fake sleeping pills someone left by her bed."

"Didn't you say Blake suspected she did that herself, for attention?"

"That's what *he* suspects, not what I think."

"What do you think?"

"Based on the information I have right now, I'd say her ex-husband is possibly in cahoots with her mamma and that fake aunt. They probably found out about the money somehow and now they're up to their old tricks, trying to convince Calista that her life is a parallel of Marilyn's."

"Assuming you're right, how does that get them what they want—the money?"

"I haven't figured that out yet. I need to talk to Robert Pearson. He's her attorney now."

"That's odd. Looks like she'd stick with someone who specializes in lottery winners. It's a niche market."

"She said she feels safer changing attorneys periodically. Maybe she swaps everyone out. That could explain why she hired me—us—instead of taking her concerns to the security company."

Nate took a slow sip of wine and lowered his glass. "Well, that fits. And seeing how her fancy system failed to perform properly this morning, maybe that makes her smart."

"My thoughts exactly. About Jim Davis—I'm assuming if you'd seen him you'd have told me that by now."

"I called both hotels and asked them to ring his room. He's registered at the Hampton on the Isle of Palms Connector. Whoever checked him in didn't enter the make and model of his car or tag number on the registration. And they'd made a typo on the name, which is why I didn't find him when I scanned their system. He was registered as Kim Davis, who I took to be a woman. The lady at the desk caught it when I called.

"Anyhow, I parked where I could see two of the five doors guests use to enter and waited all afternoon. This Hampton Inn isn't configured like any I've ever seen. I called and asked for his room again right before I came back here. Still no answer. But, I called when I got out of the shower—the first time—and he picked up. I did a 'sorry, wrong room' and hung up."

"I have an appointment with Calista in the morning. If there is a real threat, and we have to assume there is, the only way I can ensure her safety is to stay with her twenty-four seven until we've eliminated the threat. But that will seriously impair my ability to investigate. I can take her with me for some things..."

"I can handle the rest. But we need to get into Jim Davis's room before you go to Calista's for the duration. That's a two-person job if we don't want to get caught."

"Then we'd better do that tonight."

"Tommy and Suzanne?"

I grinned. "Okay, but I'm not playing the hysterical female this time. You lose the earring. I'll check out Davis's room."

"Fine by me. I'm secure in my masculinity." His lips curved, and he sent me a sizzling look from beneath hooded lids.

"Let's do it." I returned his gaze with one that made all kinds of promises for later.

FOURTEEN

The parking lot at the Hampton Inn was quiet when we arrived. It was scattered with cars, but their drivers were either inside the hotel or had parked and left the lot. We parked a few spots down from the Camry, and I stood on lookout while Nate attached a GPS tracker under the back driver's side wheel well. Now we wouldn't have to wonder where Jim Davis was at any given moment.

We hopped back into the Explorer and parked just around the front corner of the hotel, out of view from the lobby. I put a Charleston-area tourist map and a few brochures with coupons in an envelope, sealed it, and wrote Jim Davis's name on the outside. When he received this packet, he likely wouldn't think anything about it—just that local businesses were advertising.

Dressed in jeans, t-shirt, ball cap, and aviator sunglasses, Nate headed inside to drop off the envelope at the front desk and ask the clerk to see that Jim Davis got it.

I waited in the Explorer. As soon as Nate was on his way, I called the hotel and chatted with the front desk clerk about possibly holding my wedding by their pool. It was after nine on a Thursday and there would be only one person on duty. My job was to keep her busy so she didn't look at Nate closely and didn't have time to complete the transaction of looking up Jim Davis's room number on her computer and calling him. I focused on enunciating my r's and g's and keeping my vowels to one syllable so she wouldn't place my voice later.

Nate climbed into the back seat and flew into a wardrobe change. Moments later, he emerged transformed.

I was prattling on about how I wanted swans in the pool for my wedding, and whether or not chlorine would hurt swans. While the desk clerk was explaining how they'd never had swans in their pool before, and I'd need to speak with the manager in charge of all such as that, I put my hand over the phone and whispered to Nate, "Damn, you clean up good." I usually only saw Nate in a business suit and tie on court days.

He grinned. "Give me thirty seconds, no longer."

I waited, then rolled my pink overnight bag across the parking lot while discussing fireworks with the clerk. I'd taken a curling iron to my hair, fluffed it out, and slipped in a headband. In a flowing sundress and sandals, I was hoping for an air of innocence. I told the clerk on the other end of the phone that I'd set up an appointment for me, my mamma, and my soon-to-be mother-in-law to meet with the sales manager and ended the call just before I walked into the lobby.

Nate stood at the far end of the reception desk with his suitcase. His phone was to his ear, his pretext that he'd been about to check in when he got a call, and had politely stepped out of the way of other guests.

The desk clerk was a brunette, early thirties. She gave off an efficient vibe. Her nametag claimed she was Barbara. Barbara was on the phone when I walked up. "Good evening, Mr. Davis. We have an envelope for you at the front desk."

The second Barbara hung up, I smiled widely. "Hey." I stretched the word out, employing my thickest drawl. "I'm Suzanne Thompson? I called earlier?"

Barbara smiled at me and stepped away from her computer to the front counter. She was oblivious to Nate. I was the customer in front of her. "Do you have a reservation?"

"I didn't make a reservation because the man I talked to said y'all had plenty of rooms available. Should I have made one? Oh, please tell me y'all have a room. I declare, I just can't sleep in that hot house. The air conditioning repairman can't get to me until tomorrow."

This was Nate's opportunity to look at Barbara's computer screen and get Jim Davis's room number. With any luck, it would still be displayed. She hadn't had a chance to start another transaction.

Nate said, "What's that address?" into the phone. He pulled out a notepad and pen and jotted something down.

Barbara said, "I'm sorry to hear your air conditioning is out, but we're happy to have you here this evening."

"Thank you so much." I smiled and tilted my head at her. Then I leaned in, widened my eyes, and whispered, "I'm not feeling well. Would it be all right if I powdered my nose before I check in?"

"Certainly. Can I get you anything?"

"I'll be fine. Thank you so much." I made a left turn at the end of the counter.

Phone still to his ear, Nate looked out the front, away from me. He slipped me the piece of paper with the room number. The counter was high, our hands out of Barbara's view.

"Miss?" Barbara said.

"Yes?" I stopped.

"The ladies lounge is down that way." She pointed the opposite way down the hall, towards the ladies room and one of three elevators.

"Oh, my. Thank you so much." I shook my head in dismay, as if I hadn't known full well where the ladies room was located and made for the other end of the hall.

Behind me, I heard Barbara greeting "Tommy," who had finished his phone call. Before she could check him in, he said, "Ma'am, could I ask your opinion on something?"

"Why, certainly," said Barbara.

I glanced at the room number—354. I pressed the elevator button.

Tommy spoke loudly and his voice carried. "I just bought these for my girlfriend. We've been dating almost two months. Do you think they are too much? I don't want to scare her away, but I don't want to disappoint her, either. She has very discriminating tastes."

My elevator arrived.

A man of medium height and build, with brown hair, got out and turned towards the front desk. Odds were it was Jim Davis, coming for his package.

I slipped inside the elevator and pressed three.

Sadly, before Tommy could open the jewelry box to show Barbara what was inside, he would drop the box containing one very large, very good fake diamond stud. He would spend the next fifteen minutes looking for the matching earring, which would seem to have bounced right out of the box, but was actually in Nate's pocket. He would surreptitiously hide it very well while hunting. Before it was over with, he'd have Barbara and, hopefully, Jim Davis, helping him look. If Jim failed to join the search, Nate would text me.

I reached into my purse and pulled out a gadget that looked like a dry-erase marker. I'd bought it six months ago at our favorite online toy store, but we'd only used it a handful of times. The elevator opened and I made my way to room 354. Nate was right about one thing. This Hampton Inn had an odd layout, with four hallways surrounding a courtyard.

I propped my purse against my suitcase, glanced up and down the hall, pulled the top off the dry-erase marker tool and inserted the tip into the power jack on the bottom of the key card-reader. In seconds, the electronic gadget hidden in the shell of the marker had hacked the code to open the door and the light on the card-reader turned green. I opened the door, picked up my purse, and slipped in, pulling my suitcase behind me.

I set the timer on my phone for ten minutes and put the door opener back in my purse. Then I started with the nightstand. Nothing there but a prescription bottle of Nexium. The name on the bottle was James Davis. I was in the right room. The other nightstand held nothing but the hotel's clock radio, phone, and Bible in the drawer.

I checked the closet next. Nothing there but two changes of khaki pants and three golf shirts. Nothing in the pants pockets.

I turned my attention to the dresser drawers under the TV stand. Jim Davis's socks and underwear held no secrets.

I glanced at the timer on my phone. I had four and a half minutes.

I rummaged through the suitcase. Empty.

I moved to the desk. The surface was clear except for the hotel information. I opened the single drawer. Calista stared back at me. At least it looked like Calista from eighteen years ago. There were three photos. One of them was of Calista and Jim together at what must have been a simple home wedding. The other two were candid shots of Calista.

Underneath the photos was a postcard with a beach scene. Stella Maris, SC, was printed across the top. What the hell?

I turned it over.

On the back, someone had printed, "Your wife is here," in block letters. The postmark was two weeks old. There was no signature. I grabbed my phone and took a photo of the postcard front and back, and the pictures.

Then, I put everything back in the drawer exactly as it had been and tore my clothes off.

I opened my suitcase and pulled out a black dress with a slit up to there, stilettos, and a wide brimmed hat. I crammed the clothes I'd had on inside the suitcase and slid into the black dress just as the alarm on my phone sounded.

I stuffed my shoes in my purse, grabbed my suitcase and purse, took one last look around the room. I eased the door open a crack. No one was in the hall. I rolled my suitcase behind me, and headed for the elevators at the other end of the hall. In the elevator, I fished a hairband out of my purse, pulled my hair into a knot on top of my head, and settled my hat top at an angle that partially hid my face.

When the elevator doors opened, I was on the ground floor, but on the backside of the hotel, away from the lobby. I exited through the door closest to where we'd parked and ran as fast as I could across the asphalt in bare feet, dragging the suitcase and holding my hat on.

I threw my suitcase into the Explorer, grabbed my pumps from my purse, and slipped them on. I grabbed my phone and the black handbag from the car. I took the red lipstick from the purse and slathered on a coat. Then I darted towards the hotel lobby in five-inch heels.

Just before I rounded the corner, I stopped. I glanced at the phone. No texts.

I smoothed my dress adjusted my hat, and slid on my largest pair of sunglasses. Then I sauntered into the lobby employing my best imitation of a femme fatale. Nate, Barbara and Jim, I presumed, were doing a grid search of the lobby floor, pine board by pine board.

Barbara stood and adjusted her suit. She smiled a welcome. "Good evening."

"Got it!" Jim said. He was holding the earring in his palm.

"You found it?" Nate stood, a perfect, awestruck look on his face.

"Is this it?" Jim stepped towards Nate, red-faced and grinning.

Nate said, "Thank you, sir. I can't thank you enough. Where was it?"

"Right by that basket of games." Jim pointed.

"Well, I'll be. I just looked over there myself, and I missed it."

"It was almost underneath it. It's no wonder you didn't see it."

"See?" Barbara had returned to her customary position behind the counter. "I knew we'd find it. Shall we get you checked in now?"

"Tommy," I said in as haughty a voice as I could manage. "What is the meaning of this display?"

"Sweetheart," Nate said. "Nothing. Everything's fine. We were just looking for something. But we found it."

Barbara said, "Will you need one room or two this evening?"

I looked at my watch. "We'll have to check in later. There's no time now. Tommy, father is waiting."

"I'm sorry, Sweetheart. That's fine. We'll check in after we meet your father for drinks." He smiled graciously at Barbara and Jim. "Thank you both again."

Nate took my arm to escort me out the door.

"Why are you thanking these people?" I asked loudly.

"They were just very nice while I was waiting for you," he said. "Bye, now," he called over his shoulder.

"Bye," called Jim and Barbara in unison. I thought I detected a hint of confusion.

We stepped into the thick night air and held hands as we walked towards the car.

"You do high-maintenance bitch very well," Nate said. "But I confess I prefer your portrayal of the hysterical Southern belle. Both are positively award-worthy."

"Why, thank you. You know I was in the drama club in high school."

"You have any problems upstairs?"

"None. This routine is so much easier with this new tool than back when we had to swipe a housekeeping key."

"Find anything?" he asked.

I grinned. "As a matter of fact, I did." I told him about the pictures and the postcard.

"Someone sent him a postcard telling him where Calista is? You've gotta be kidding me."

"I kid you not. How did things go in the lobby?"

"It was a damn disaster. I had to beg Davis like a little girl to help look for that earring, and Barbara kept wanting to go check on Suzanne Thompson in the ladies room. It was hard work keeping them both in that lobby."

Nate opened the door to the Explorer for me. This was new. I offered him my brightest smile. "Thank you, sir."

He walked around and climbed in the driver's side. "I just can't gain sympathy from folks as easy as you can."

I looked at him sideways. Something in his tone aroused my suspicions.

He grinned like a kid caught sneaking a cookie before dinner. "Everything went according to script."

I punched him in the arm. "Then why didn't you tell me that straight off?"

He laughed. "Just to see you get riled."

I threw him a look. I was aiming for aggravated, but he was so damn handsome I gave up and laughed. "You just prefer searching hotel rooms to crawling around the lobby."

"Who wouldn't?" he asked. "Davis seems like a nice enough guy. I tried to get acquainted while we were crawling around on our knees. It'd sure be handy if we had the software to use Bluetooth or Wi-Fi to force pair cell phones. He probably had his in his pocket. We could tell pretty quick what his intentions are if we could monitor his calls and texts."

"That technology is not available from any of our toy stores. I'll keep looking. Being able to force a proximity pair would be slick."

I mulled Jim Davis and the postcard. The postcard seemed to suggest Jim Davis had been lured to South Carolina by someone. But Mr. Davis could still be involved in a conspiracy with this unknown party. "What do you say let's call Sonny Ravenel and tip him off as to Jim Davis's current location? I'm thinking he might want to question him regarding Harmony's murder."

Nate tipped his head from side to side, appearing to weigh the options. "Or...maybe we should talk to Davis first. Just in case he's feeling more chatty before law enforcement is involved."

"Might be he's more forthcoming after the threat of the long arm of the law has reached out and touched him. We could play good cop."

"Could go either way."

"I'm going to want information from Sonny. He's more likely to give it to me if I give him something first. He'll owe me."

Nate started the car. "Well, then. By all means, let's do our civic duty."

FIFTEEN

Friday morning arrived before I was prepared to offer it a proper welcome. I'd stayed up too late reading Donald Spoto's biography of Marilyn Monroe. Dragging myself out of bed took every bit of self-discipline I could muster. It helped that Nate jostled me awake while Rhett barked encouragement. I almost barked at them both. I'm not at my sunniest when I haven't had enough sleep, my run, or my coffee.

A run, a swim, and a shower later, I slathered on sunscreen and consulted my closet. I had several appointments that day and it was going to be hotter than the gates of hell. I needed cool and comfortable, but cute. I slipped into an Anthropologie white-on-white embroidered skirt and a blue sleeveless chambray popover. I added a wide brown belt, my brown Kate Spade flat sandals, and my silver hoop earrings. A little mascara, a little lip gloss, and I was down the stairs.

Nate and I took our coffee and yogurt parfaits into my office and got to work. He had research to do for a case in Greenville, and I had Calista's lists to process. It felt warm and familiar, working with Nate, even with the hum of electricity that flowed between us.

"Hey, can you do a bug sweep for me?" I asked.

"Sure. Calista's house?"

"Yeah. Whoever's gaslighting her has access to the house. They may well have bugged it. I'm going to move our ten o'clock to noon at The Pirates' Den. Once she's out of the house, I'll call and ask her to send Elenore on an errand and clear Niles out if he's hanging around. If you'll meet us at The Pirates' Den, you can pick up a key and the security code." I tapped Calista's name on my iPhone.

"Roger that."

After I spoke to Calista, I donned latex gloves. I examined the shopping list I'd picked up with a tissue the day before from her credenza. Blake might not have the resources to test the contents of capsules absent compelling reason, but he could surely have this piece of paper checked for fingerprints.

I pulled out a magnifying glass and studied the lined page. Calista had told me their normal procedure was for Elenore to keep a running list of grocery and household needs, and Calista would add personal items. Monday was shopping day. It was easy to tell Elenore's tight script from Calista's loopy handwriting. The last item on the list was the enema kit. At first glance, it did resemble the entries for sunscreen, toothpaste, and shampoo. But under the magnifying glass, I detected subtle differences. The "m" in particular was off. I compared the entry to the list of names Calista had given me and noted that the "m's" were similar everywhere except the last entry in the shopping list. It was a good forgery. I slipped the page into a plastic evidence bag and labeled it.

Calista's list of connections was poignantly short. Every person on it was either on her payroll or someone who'd exploited her in the past. From what I'd read, here was one more parallel to Marilyn Monroe. Even when Calista tried to break away from the pattern her crazy family established, she seemed to stumble into similar situations. Like moving to the East Coast and changing her name. Although the studios had been behind Marilyn's name change. Still, both women were vulnerable to people they should've been able to trust. I took a moment to give thanks for every member of my family and all my friends and neighbors.

Jim Davis headlined Calista's list. If I had my guess, he currently occupied Sonny's interrogation room. Nothing in his background seemed suspicious except his efforts to cash in on the coincidence of Calista's birth and her appearance by forcing her into a career she didn't want. In fact, the only incriminating things about him were that he was the ex-husband and he was present in the area. He was a piece of the puzzle, but I wasn't convinced he was Calista's biggest problem. I set him aside.

Grace and Gladys were next. These women made my skin crawl. Just to see what I could stir up, I tried calling the latest home phone number I could find. Apparently, when Gladys wasn't institutionalized, she still lived with Grace. No one answered. I didn't leave a message.

I turned back to the list. After a space, Calista had recorded the people currently populating her world. Harmony was at the top. Her being dead and all, I didn't think she posed a danger, but her death was likely connected. I searched my usual databases. Harmony's profile produced a shocker: Under the name her mother had put on her birth certificate, Helena Patrice Calhoun had an MBA from the Darla Moore School of Business at the University of South Carolina. She'd married a Rigney and lived on Tradd Street, South of Broad.

Hells bells, poor Sonny was deep into a hot mess. Dealing with old money, society types whose people had occupied the tip of the peninsula since well before the Revolutionary War, complicated any investigation.

Phoebe DiTomei was next on the list. The owner of Phoebe's day spa, she colored every female's hair on the island over age fifteen. I could vouch for Phoebe.

But the next name gave me pause. Charles Gadsden was Calista's therapist. After what I had read about Ralph Greenson, Marilyn Monroe's therapist, I shared Calista's suspicions of him. According to Donald Spoto's well-documented biography of Marilyn, Greenson appeared to control every aspect of Marilyn's life. He gave her high dosages of various barbiturates and arranged for other doctors to do so, isolated her from her friends, and even maneuvered himself onto the Twentieth Century Fox payroll as some sort of consultant. Then there was a chilling incident in June—just two months before Marilyn's death—where Greenson went to elaborate measures to conceal bruises of suspicious origin on Marilyn's face. There was something very sinister about his relationship with his most famous patient.

I wanted to know everything there was to know about Calista's Dr. Gadsden. I spent an hour profiling him. He was a life-long Charleston resident, had no criminal background, and as far as I could tell he was financially secure. He was married and owned two separate residences, one in Charleston and one in New York City. No children. He'd never been sued by a patient. Dr. Gadsden set great store by his own abilities, judging by the articles he'd published. Calista had marked him as having access to her home. This was a big red flag. I needed to interview Dr. Gadsden.

Elenore and Warren Harper were next on the list. Calista had started seeing Warren as her personal physician when she moved to Isle of Palms. But why would he have access to her home? Warren Harper had treated me until I left for college, and still treated most of the island residents. I had to believe he was above reproach. Nevertheless, I profiled him and Elenore, finding nothing I didn't already know.

Robert Pearson had recently taken over Calista's legal needs, but was not marked as having access to her home. I had an appointment with him at eleven. I'd known Robert my whole life— he married one of my best friends from high school. I'd profiled him in April when I'd been working on solving Gram's murder. He was a member of the Stella Maris town council, and I'd suspected someone was blackmailing him, but hadn't been able to prove it. I pulled a copy of his profile and added it to Calista's case file.

A Google search told me that Bruce Williams, Calista's wealth management advisor, had a plastic smile that warranted scrutiny. I spent half an hour vetting him, but turned up nothing suspicious. At least he didn't have a key to Calista's house. Still, I put him on my "pay him a visit" list.

Which brought me to Niles Ignacio. The rest of the list was alphabetical, but Calista had listed Niles last, which told me she found him the least suspicious. My gut screamed something else entirely. Niles had more access to Calista than anyone except Elenore. And the way he hovered over Calista made me queasy. I wanted Niles to be the culprit. That would have been easy. I turned his life inside out.

Unfortunately, Niles Ignacio was the squeakiest-clean name on the list. He'd been born in Vermont, and except for his stint in the Peace Corps in Mozambique, he'd lived there until March of 2011, when he moved to Mt. Pleasant. He'd worked in a series of yoga studios in the Burlington area, the most recent a wellness center that offered yoga, massage, and the like, for five years. A few of his client testimonials were still posted on the website: "Niles changed my life... Niles helped me achieve peace and strength for the first time in twenty years... Niles is an old soul... Working with him has taught me so much."

"Oh, good grief."

"What's wrong, Slugger?" Nate looked up from his laptop.

"I just hate it when my instincts are off."

I called Serenity, the yoga studio in Mt. Pleasant. The owner there thought Niles walked on water, too. Her only complaint was that he'd cut back on his group classes since he started giving Calista private lessons at home and volunteering as a Big Brother.

Just to be sure, I checked his financials. He lived simply, it appeared, and within his means. He'd rented a studio apartment in Mt. Pleasant. No criminal record. Clean credit. He was everything Calista believed him to be. *Damnation.*

I needed to get moving. I made a quick call and scheduled an appointment with Mack Ryan at Security Solutions in Charleston. Then I tried Dr. Gadsden, but his receptionist informed me that due to patient confidentiality, regardless of whatever release Ms. McQueen might sign, Dr. Gadsden would not meet with me. We'd see about that.

I grabbed my tote, kissed Nate goodbye, and headed to see Robert Pearson.

Robert came around the mammoth desk when I walked into his office. "Liz, good to see you. Have a seat."

I made myself comfortable in a supple leather chair, asked after Olivia and the kids. We spent the next ten minutes on pleasantries. Robert was handsome—good bones, brown hair, blue eyes, and an easy smile. I'd always thought of him as a Boy Scout, honorable and all. The idea that he might've been a blackmail victim still troubled me. But, as all the parties involved in the underlying scheme were either in jail, in the ground, or in another country, I'd decided to leave it alone. Finally, he sat back in his chair and asked me what I had on my mind.

"I need to know who would get the money if anything happened to Calista McQueen," I said.

Relief flashed across his face. He quickly hid it with a half-chuckle. My instincts told me he was relieved I wasn't asking him questions of a personal nature. "Interesting question. That one keeps things close to the vest. Uncanny, isn't it? The resemblance?"

"Yes, it is." So, Calista had dressed normally when she met with Robert. I'd wondered about that.

"I handle oversight of her charitable foundation and manage the trust that cares for her mother, along with several other charitable trusts. The foundation raises and donates money to children's charities—orphanages, children's hospitals, et cetera. It has its own staff. It's well funded. Along with the trusts, it will survive Calista and keep right on giving where they currently give. All the trusts are revocable until she passes, at which point they convert to irrevocable trusts. Every beneficiary gets exactly the same thing whether Calista's alive or dead."

"No motives there."

"Has someone tried to harm her?"

"Not yet."

Robert squinted at me.

"It's complicated. Let's just say she hired me to make sure no one does."

"And you're following the money."

"That's where these things usually lead. What happens to the foundation and the trusts when the money runs out?"

Robert shook his head. "Everything is funded through earnings on the money and fund-raising campaigns. The principal is never touched. That kind of money, properly managed, doesn't run out."

"Wow." I pondered that for a moment.

Robert tapped the desk with a pencil. "The money in those trusts represents—and I'm guessing here, you understand—maybe half of her wealth. The rest she manages herself. She has a background in banking and finance. Oh, she pays a wealth management advisor good money, but I don't think she pays him much mind. He doesn't have power of attorney. Neither do I. I doubt anyone does. She took the lump sum payout option on the jackpot. From what I gather, her investment strategy has been quite lucrative. Conservatively, she's made more money investing the lump sum than she would've if she'd taken the annuity. You'd never guess it—she seems a little ditzy—but apparently she has a head for money."

"Is it unusual for someone with her assets not to have someone hold power of attorney?"

"Yes. Calista has trust issues. That's why she hired me, and why she'll only keep me for a year or so."

"So, what happens to the rest of the money if something happens to her?"

"She's cagey. But to the best of my knowledge, everything is owned by a trust she's established, similar to the ones I manage. She is the grantor, the trustee, and the beneficiary. When she passes, the trust department at First Federal becomes the trustee.

The remainder beneficiary list is a long one, but they're all charities."

"Are they real charities? Or are some of them scams to take her money that resemble charities?"

"I asked that very question, more delicately, perhaps. She invited me to research them if I was of a mind. Not only are they all legitimate, every one of them spends seventy-five percent or more of their donations on programs that directly benefit their causes. They all have transparent reporting and low operating costs."

"So how would anyone benefit from her death?"

Robert shrugged. "You're the detective. I haven't any idea."

"The mother, Gladys Monroe. Is she currently in an institution?"

"She's living with her friend, Grace. That's where I send money, anyway, and she's cashing the checks."

"She just comes and goes at the nervous hospital whenever she feels like it?"

"For all intents and purposes. I mean, of course, the doctors give their opinions, but she's never been a danger to anyone. Involuntary commitment is almost unheard of anymore. If she wanted to leave and her doctors had a serious problem, they'd call me. My two cents? She's not as crazy as she thinks she is."

"It's all part of the game." Marilyn's mother had been crazy— or maybe not, according to Marilyn's biographer. Oddly, Calista's mother could be more like Marilyn's mother than either she or Grace McKee realized, in that she wasn't really crazy at all. I took a deep breath and let it out slowly. "Does she know the money she receives is from Calista?"

"Yes, but she doesn't know where Calista is, or even her current legal name. The checks are drawn on my account, and a series of other attorney's accounts before mine."

"Back to the money. If Calista's the trustee of a trust she established, she can do anything she wants with the money while she's alive, right?"

"Absolutely."

"So she has an investment portfolio, owned by these trusts, and she makes the investments herself?"

"That's right."

"Seems like there'd be a lot of accounting involved, if only for tax purposes."

"Dixon Hughes Goodman handles all of that. But trust me, no one has access to her money. They just file the paperwork."

"Robert, I declare, you're not giving me much to work with here."

"If she's in some sort of trouble, hard as it may be to believe, I doubt it's about the money."

I dug both hands into my hair thinking about Calista's crazy family and their bizarre preoccupation with molding her life after Marilyn Monroe's. "Things would be so much simpler if it was about the money."

SIXTEEN

Steel-drum music and cool air greeted me as I stepped from the midday heat into The Pirates' Den. John Glendawn called out a greeting from behind the mahogany bar and told me to sit wherever I liked.

I chose a corner table between the wall of aquariums and the glass wall overlooking the Atlantic. A medley of savory aromas laced with island spices made my mouth water.

I was hoping Calista wouldn't be long when she walked through the door. I waved her over.

"I see you've given up disguises," I said as she lifted her polka dot skirt and slid into the chair across from me.

"If this is going to be home, people here will have to get used to me, won't they?"

"Folks here are friendly and accustomed to the unusual. Trust me. You'll get a few stares for a couple weeks and then you'll just be one of us."

She gave me a skeptical look and picked up a menu. "So far I'm still getting a lot of stares. We'll see. What's good here?"

"Maybe people are just staring at a beautiful woman. You could have worse problems. I like the cheeseburgers, but I'll probably have a salad. The jerk chicken is good, but spicy. And you can't beat the shrimp and grits."

Calista regarded me gravely. "Any news about Harmony's death?"

"Not specifically. Nate and I are eliminating suspects with ties to you one by one. I haven't heard anything new from Sonny. Are you using the alarm system?"

"Yes, and they came to check the system out. They were there for hours."

John came from behind the bar to take our order. Lunch wasn't as busy as dinner at The Pirates' Den. "Eh law. That sun's like to cook us all. What can I get for you ladies? Something cool today?" To his credit, he didn't stare at Calista.

We both ordered salads with grilled chicken and iced tea. John brought our tea, then ambled towards the kitchen just as Nate appeared to pick up Calista's keys and security code.

Calista grinned as we both watched Nate walk towards the door. "He's cute."

I returned her grin. "Yes, he is."

"You're very lucky."

"I'm aware. But how did you know he's more than my partner?"

She smiled slyly. "The way you two look at each other screams, 'we're having sex.'"

"Really?"

"Why do you look so alarmed? Neither of you are married are you?"

"No, but we're having dinner with my parents on Sunday."

"That sounds fun." She looked wistful.

"It will be. When things settle down—after we're sure you're safe, and all guilty parties have been dispatched—I'll invite you over for Sunday dinner. Meeting my family might help you see how everyone has nutty relatives."

She shifted her eyes and raised her eyebrows in a look that flashed doubt like a neon sign. "I'd love to come to dinner," she said. "But my family will always take the blue ribbon for dysfunction."

I couldn't argue that point. I took a sip of my tea.

"So," she said and smoothed her napkin. "You think someone bugged my house?"

"It's possible. Checking is a reasonable precaution."

"Why did you want Niles and Elenore to leave? You don't suspect them, do you?"

"Until we know who is trying to make you and everyone else think you're crazy with those gaslight stunts, I suspect everyone who has access to your house. Which brings me to my first question. I've been reading the biography of Marilyn you suggested—call it curiosity. Given her history with her therapist, the fact that *you* suspect he had a hand in her death, and your...*situation*, why are you seeing a therapist, and why on God's green earth does he have access to your house?"

Calista paled. "Dr. Gadsden has been treating me off and on since Joey died. He helped me through all the deep, dark blues. Helped me cope. He'd never hurt me. And I told you, I don't take pills. He's a therapist. He doesn't give me drugs. He has a key to my house in case of emergency. He's one of the few people I trust."

I absorbed that information. "Exactly how much do you trust him?"

"I don't understand."

"I'm not sure if *I* know your whole story yet. Does anyone? Know everything, I mean. About the money, your family issues..." I rolled my palms toward her.

"Dr. Gadsden knows everything. He'd have to, wouldn't he? You can't hold back with your therapist and expect to make progress."

"You don't take pills?"

"None. Well, just my vitamins, but Elenore gets those at GNC."

"You told me you'd been treated for mental illness."

Calista grimaced and waved a palm at me. "That was a joke. I thought you knew that. I mean, yes, I'm in therapy. I get blue sometimes. What of it?"

"How often do you see Dr. Gadsden now?"

She looked out the window at the surf. "Three, sometimes four times a week."

I stared at her, waiting for her to tell me that was a joke, too. She didn't. After a moment she said, "He helps me keep things in perspective."

"We've got to get you some girlfriends."

She gave me another wistful look. "I never have had girlfriends. I've always thought that would be the most wonderful thing, to chat about normal things. Giggle. Have a girls' night out..."

My heart hurt for her. Screw professional boundaries. "Let's do that. Let's have a girls' night out. I'll bring my sister, Merry. You'll like her. Maybe we'll ask Moon Unit. You know Moon Unit? From the diner?"

"That sounds like fun. What would we do?"

"Probably come here. They have karaoke on Friday nights, and my brother's band plays."

"I thought your brother was the police chief."

"He is. He also plays in a band—The Back Porch Prophets. He plays pedal steel guitar. Keyboards. He writes some of their music."

"Your brother sounds like an interesting man."

I shrugged. "He lives on a houseboat, just so you know," I said by way of warning.

From the glint in her eyes, I couldn't tell if Calista was warned off or more intrigued.

"So are we on?" I asked. "Next Friday? I have a date tonight."

"Sure." She pressed her lips together and smiled.

John delivered our salads and topped off our iced tea. "Can I get you ladies anything else?"

"We're good, John. Thanks."

I put together a bite of salad. "I think, for your safety, it would be a good idea for me to stay with you until we've figured out who is behind the barking dog, the pills, et cetera."

"I think you'll have better luck getting to the bottom of all of that if you're not trying to babysit me."

"You hired me to keep you alive. At first, I wasn't convinced there was a real threat. But your life coach has been murdered. And not by a relative or a burglar either. She was executed. We both believe there's a connection. Why take a chance?"

"I'm perfectly safe until the evening of August fourth. If you haven't figured this out by then, you can stay over that night."

"Calista, it makes no sense that someone would try to kill you only on that night. If they want you dead, that's going to be the priority, not when you get that way."

"I know how it sounds, but please. Just focus on proving who is behind all of this. Stop them before they get to me."

I sighed a long-suffering sigh that called Mamma to mind. Resigned, I reached inside my handbag. "I was afraid you'd mule up. If you won't let me stick close, put this on and don't take it off—not even to shower." I handed her a silver pendant.

"It's not very attractive, is it?" She wrinkled her nose.

"It's not that bad. A little clunky maybe. But it's not supposed to be a fashion statement. Take it. Put it on. You can wear it inside your blouse. It has a GPS inside, and if you press the center swirl, it sends an alert to my cell phone. I can tell where you are and I'll know you're in trouble."

She took the necklace from my hand. "It's like those things they give senior citizens in case they fall?"

"Sort of. But you can't talk into it. May I have your cell phone?"

"Why?"

"Because I'm going to install some software on it that will allow me to spy on your phone calls, texts, emails—pretty much anything you do on your phone. I can also track the phone's location this way. The pendant is in case you get separated from your phone or can't call for help."

Very slowly, she pulled her phone from her purse. She placed it on the table and slid it to me. Her eyes stayed locked on mine. "I'm a very private person."

I searched for the website I needed from Calista's phone, logged into my account, and downloaded the app. "This is a very temporary arrangement. As soon as the threat is neutralized, you can watch me remove the software."

"If I survive August fourth—when she actually died—and August fifth, which is when she was officially declared dead, then that's the end of it. There's nothing left for them to try to pattern."

"You're assuming that your Aunt Grace, your mamma, and your ex-husband are behind this. I think that's a dangerous assumption."

A commotion broke out near the doorway. Two women of a certain age with big sunglasses and teased hair headed our way with open arms, making all kinds of racket.

Calista said, "It makes perfectly good sense to me."

"No."

"I'm afraid so."

The brunette pulled the fake blonde towards the table. "I can't believe it, Gladys, here's our girl!"

"Oh, honey, I can't believe it's you. It's just so good to see you," said the blonde, who didn't look a bit like Calista in my opinion.

Calista was unnaturally calm. "Mother, Grace, this is Liz Talbot. Liz, Gladys Monroe and Grace McKee. Or do you prefer Gwen and Donna?"

That shut the women up. They both stepped backward. Grace, or whoever she was, gave Calista an appraising look. Gladys looked at Grace for her cue. After a moment, Grace regained her composure and continued her act. "Sweetheart, we've missed you so much. Why, you're just as beautiful as always. Look at her, Gladys, isn't she gorgeous?"

"Gorgeous," Gladys echoed.

I couldn't think of a thing to contribute to the conversation.

"Why are you here?" Calista asked.

"We came to see you, of course," Grace said.

"We came as soon as we got the postcard," added Gladys.

"We've been looking for you ever since you left California. We kept thinking you'd come back to us..."

"Excuse me, ladies," I said. "But did you say you received a postcard?"

"Why yes," said Grace. "Postmarked right here in Stella Maris. It said, 'Norma Jeane is here.' It was so pretty. Had a picture of a beach."

"Who sent it to you?" I asked.

"We don't have any idea. It wasn't signed," said Grace. "I hoped maybe you'd sent it, Norma Jeane."

"I certainly did not send it. And my name is Calista. Don't either of you dare call me by that other name. I won't stand for it, do you hear me?" She had steel in her voice, her eyes, and her spine.

"Ladies, pardon me, but I'm curious how you came to be right here, at The Pirates' Den right now," I said.

They looked at each other. "We asked the woman at the bed and breakfast for a recommendation. We wanted a restaurant overlooking the ocean. Neither of us have ever seen the Atlantic Ocean before this trip. She recommended this place. When we walked in the door, the first thing we saw was our girl."

"That's quite a coincidence," I said, wondering if it was a coincidence at all. Another Grace – my godmother, Grace Sullivan – owned the only bed and breakfast. She was a psychic. I needed to talk to her.

"Isn't it, though?" Grace smiled, oozing satisfaction. "Here, Gladys, you shouldn't stand so long, let me pull us up some chairs."

Calista stood. "We were just leaving."

"What?" Gladys looked confused. "Baby girl, we just found you, after all these years. Why would you leave now?"

"Because, Mother, I simply don't care to stay any longer. Liz?"

I did a quick calculation, and decided neither Grace nor Gladys would deviate from the script while they were together. I needed to speak to Gladys alone. I opted for solidarity with my client.

"Coming. How long do you ladies plan to stay on at the bed and breakfast?"

"As long as necessary," Grace said. "Please talk to her, won't you?" She grabbed my hand.

I stood and pulled my hand along with me. "I surely will."

"Norma Jeane?" Gladys cried out. "Where are you going, Norma Jeane?"

"We'll wait to hear from you," Grace called.

"That's an excellent idea," Calista said.

Gladys started wailing as the door closed behind us.

SEVENTEEN

The afternoon heat in Charleston didn't nearly bother me as much as usual after the scene with Calista's family at lunch. Half my salad had been left in the bowl, but I didn't mind. My appetite had gotten lost in all the crazy.

Security Solutions, Incorporated occupied a squat, nondescript, concrete office building on the section of East Bay between Chapel and Charlotte Street. It wasn't the kind of place you could wander into by accident—the front door was steel, and it was locked. I pressed the call button and identified myself to a curt gentleman.

"Step inside, Ms. Talbot," he said after making me stand in the afternoon heat for longer than should have been necessary. "Last office on the left."

The door was so heavy it would likely survive a bomb blast. I proceeded down a hall lined with closed doors to the office at the end, which stood slightly ajar. I tapped two short knocks and pushed the door open.

The office was unexpected. It screamed testosterone, but tastefully. I'd bet a high-dollar decorator was responsible for the wide-plank paneling, local artwork, and tailored window treatments. Of course, the window was opaque, so you couldn't see the bars on the outside.

The man behind the heavy desk stood. "Ms. Talbot, I'm Mack Ryan. Have a seat."

"So nice to meet you." I shook his hand, then settled into a leather wingback. He was definitely ex-military. The man was one big muscle with a brown crew cut. The crease in his khakis would slice bread. His black golf shirt bore the SSI logo.

The release form Calista had signed was the lone piece of paper on an uncluttered desk. He glanced at it, then regarded me with piercing gray eyes. "How can I help, Ms. Talbot?"

"I'm concerned that Ms. McQueen's system did not activate yesterday morning. I would imagine that would be rare for a company with your reputation."

"Not rare. Never happened. I pulled the electronic records. The system was activated with her code at twenty-three forty-seven Wednesday night. Someone turned on perimeter security and the outdoor cameras. At one fourteen, the system was deactivated using the same code.

"Nevertheless, out of an abundance of caution and concern for our client's welfare, I dispatched my technicians. They were onsite within an hour of her call yesterday afternoon. Every component of her system has been tested—twice, by different techs. Everything checks out."

"Does anyone have the system code besides Ms. McQueen?"

"Only SSI personnel and anyone Ms. McQueen has shared the code with. I assure you there was no technical failure with our system or monitoring. The motion detectors didn't activate the cameras because someone turned them off. Someone inside the house."

I squinted at him. "How many keypads are there?"

"Three. One by the front door, one in her bedroom, and one in the pool house."

I mulled that. "And because she doesn't turn on the inside cameras, there's no way to know who turned it off."

"Affirmative."

"Can you tell which keypad was used to turn it on and off?"

"It was activated and deactivated from her bedroom."

"So you're thinking she disarmed it herself."

"Ms. McQueen says that she armed the system but did not disarm it. She is my client. Not my business to speculate otherwise."

I liked Mack. He struck me as a straight arrow. "Is this a pattern? Has the system been deactivated other nights, or was this an isolated incident?"

"It's happened every night for the last four nights. Before that, never."

"Would you have known this if she hadn't reported that the system failed to activate?"

"The information is part of the electronic log, but we'd have had no reason to check it or frankly question it absent her call. Clients turn their systems on and off all the time for various reasons."

"It happened again last night?" Who had been in the house besides Calista?

"Affirmative."

"And was it activated and deactivated from her bedroom every time?"

"Yes."

"When the system has been working normally—before the last four nights—have the cameras ever picked up anyone outside her house?"

"Since the system was installed, no one has approached the house while the system was armed except Ms. McQueen and Mrs. Harper."

"Mrs. Harper has gone in alone?"

"Affirmative."

"Then she must have the code, right?"

He nodded. "That's right. Typically domestic employees have alarm codes. The cameras were also activated by swine in the flower beds three times the first week they were installed."

"You have got to be kidding."

"I wish I were. The techs had to raise the angle on the cameras so the crew in the screening room didn't have to monitor hogs all night."

"Damnation. I hate those hogs. How many were there?" As soon as the words were out of my mouth, I wanted them back. How many were there? I sounded like a wild hog hunter.

Mack gave me a look that telegraphed how he thought the question odd. "I couldn't say. We didn't keep that footage."

I coughed gently into my hand, searching for a natural segue anywhere. "The interior cameras are motion activated as well?"

"Yes."

"So, hypothetically speaking, if Ms. McQueen turned on all the interior cameras when she went to bed, she would activate the cameras if she got up for a drink?"

"The cameras are aimed at doorways and windows with access. There's incidental coverage of every room except the bathrooms. The cameras in her bedroom cover the sliding glass doors and windows that access the porch. There's access to her private bath and the kitchen without activating a camera. We set it up that way for privacy reasons. If she gets up in the middle of the night and goes to the bathroom or kitchen, she won't trip a motion detector."

"And she's aware of this?"

"Affirmative."

"Why would she go to the expense of having equipment installed and not use it?"

"I couldn't speculate on that."

"The keypad in her bedroom. Does a camera cover that?"

"No. It's on the wall near her bed."

"Is there a delay on the motion detectors?"

"Negative. If there's an intrusion, seconds count."

"There's always someone monitoring the cameras?"

"We have three people in the surveillance room at all times. Of course, they're monitoring multiple cameras for multiple clients. But remember, all the cameras are motion activated. Most of the screens stay dark most of the time. An alarm sounds and a red light comes on any monitor that's activated. If someone takes a bio break, we still have two sets of eyes on the screens."

"And if someone other than Calista shows up on her screen?"

"Unless she sent us a photograph and asked that the subject be added to her cleared list, we would dispatch a team and call the Stella Maris PD. Your brother is closer. It takes us forty minutes to get there."

I raised my left eyebrow. "You know Blake?"

"We're familiar with law enforcement in every jurisdiction where we have a client. I also check out private investigators who make appointments to discuss clients."

"Naturally," I said. "I've asked Calista to use the interior system. I'll reiterate that she can access the kitchen and bath without being on camera."

Mack nodded. "That would be optimal."

I offered him a sunny smile. "I was unfamiliar with your company prior to this case. There's not much goes on in Charleston County I miss."

"We keep a low profile."

"How do your clients find you?"

"Word of mouth. Our clients tend to have some connection, not necessarily social, though I'd guess some do. Many have the same attorneys. In Ms. McQueen's case, the referral came through her accountant at Dixon Hughes Goodman."

"Are all of your staff members ex-military?"

"Ninety percent. We have a few former police officers and a spy or two. Are you exploring a career move?"

"No. Just curious."

He stood. "Let me know if you change your mind."

I turned right on East Bay, headed to meet Sonny at Kudu. I needed caffeine and an update. Sonny probably had the same two things on his mind. The driver of a black Mustang with dark tinted windows turned right onto Calhoun behind me. The car followed me way too close—almost on my bumper. What the hell? When I lucked out and found a spot halfway down the block from Kudu on Vanderhorst, the Mustang pulled past me, paused at the stop sign, and turned right onto St. Phillip Street with a short squeal of rubber on asphalt. Jerk.

On the sidewalk, I stepped over a tangle of laundry, no doubt dropped by a College of Charleston student on the way to the laundry mat. This area of town, adjacent to campus, was their domain. Laundry on the sidewalk was not uncommon.

Hot as it was outside, I still craved a mocha latte. The air conditioning inside Kudu was in high gear, so I ordered my coffee, then checked the back left corner of the shop. Sonny was there, and on the phone.

He waved, and I pointed at the giant red cappuccino machine. I'd wait for my double soy mocha latte while he finished his call. I smiled and thanked the barista as he handed me my cup. I loved the signature twin swirls on top. It's the little things.

Sonny was off the phone and munching on a danish. I took the seat across from him. "Hey, Sonny."

"Hey, yourself. Thanks for the tip about Jim Davis."

"Any time. Did you get anything useful from him?"

Sonny eyed me over his coffee cup. "It didn't get past me that I just did your job for you."

I widened my eyes and gave an innocent look my best shot.

"You can save all that," he said. "It's a good thing I'm an easy going guy."

"Why, that's what I love best about you, Sonny."

"Uh-huh. So, Mr. Davis received an anonymous postcard alerting him to his ex-wife's presence in the area. I saw the postcard. Looks legit. His story is that he still loves her, and he has been searching for her for since she left California in nineteen ninety-four. His motives are pure, and so forth, and he has no knowledge of Ms. McQueen's association with Harmony, aka Helena Calhoun Rigney."

"Do you believe him?"

"Frankly, he seems like a simple guy—what you see is what you get. He's never remarried." Sonny shrugged. "I can't say how he fits into your case, but I don't like him for Mrs. Rigney's murder."

"You think that's South of Broad drama?" Behind the wrought iron gates to brick-walled gardens, stately, moss-laden oaks guarded historic homes where George Washington had slept. Inside those regal residences, the pedigreed and the nouveau riche inhabitants of South of Broad had problems just like everyone else. Wealth created its own theatrics. But unpleasantry among the upper crust had the added layer of keeping up appearances, avoiding scandal.

Sonny winced. "Unfortunately not. That would be too easy. I'm only telling you this because it's got the hair on my neck up. You need to steer very clear of this case. Something happens to me, you go straight to the Post and Courier. Hell, screw that. Call Nancy Grace. Mrs. Rigney was a pretty little thing—Nancy Grace loves those. Comes to it, I might call Nancy myself."

"What on earth?"

He spoke so softly I had to strain to hear him. "Mrs. Rigney was killed with a Glock used in a murder outside a King Street nightclub four years ago. The gun was found in a nearby dumpster. The murder is an open case, so the gun should be in evidence. But it's not there."

I inhaled sharply.

Sonny nodded. "Someone removed the gun from evidence. Only two reasons anyone would do that. To protect the murderer—but it was an unregistered gun, so that doesn't fly—or if someone needed an untraceable gun for another purpose."

"Could it be misplaced?"

"Case has never gone to trial. No reason anyone would move it. Only thing makes sense is someone took it."

"Would someone take it to sell it?"

"Nah—it wouldn't be worth the risk except for the express purpose of committing a crime."

"And the only folks with access are police officers?"

"Of various roles, but yeah."

"Hells bells."

"You got that right. Needless to say, I'm watching where I step here, and you should, too. You hear me, Liz?"

"Yeah. I hear you." I pondered what he'd told me for a few moments. "That makes it unlikely Harmony's death is connected to Calista."

"That's what I thought, too. Mrs. Rigney—that was a hit. And the hitter, at a minimum, has connections inside the department. Your client's issues, entertaining though they may be, are of a different variety." Sonny stood. "Anything comes up makes you think otherwise, call me. But do not do anything other than pick up the phone to call me."

"Mmm-kay. Sonny?"

"Yeah?"

"Watch your back."

He nodded and left me alone to finish my mocha and try to figure any way Calista might be connected to a hit connected to a police officer. A feeling of gratitude for her screwball family washed over me. Just then I was hoping they were the root of Calista's troubles. They were far less scary than a rogue police officer. But I was worried about Sonny.

EIGHTEEN

On my way home, a black Mustang pulled beside me on Johnny Dodds Boulevard. It had the same dark windows as the one that had been behind me in downtown Charleston, making it impossible to see the driver. Was this the same car? Surely my conversation with Sonny had made me paranoid. Nevertheless, I tried to slow down and let it pass so I could get the plate. The driver kept his speed consistent with mine. Then, he slowed down and pulled in behind me. He followed too close. I took my foot off the accelerator. Abruptly, I tuned right at Anna Knapp Boulevard, planning to circle around and maneuver behind the car. The driver switched lanes, made a U-turn, and sped off. What the hell?

By the time I negotiated my way back to the intersection, the Mustang had disappeared into traffic. I slid into the left lane. The light was red, traffic steady. I willed the light to change so I could chase down the Mustang and inquire after the driver's intentions. Was he just a jerk, or was he following me because I'd rattled his cage in connection to Calista's case? Fourscore and twenty years later, the light finally turned green. I hung a left and changed lanes. I drove as fast as traffic would allow, weaving back and forth, flirting with reckless driving. Was the Mustang still on Johnny Dodds, or had the driver turned somewhere? There was no sign of him. I slammed my palm against the steering wheel. *Damnation.* No sense going back over the bridge when I couldn't be sure my quarry had headed back to Charleston. I turned around at Houston

Northcutt Boulevard and made for home. I took a cleansing breath. The jerk in the Mustang was probably just a jerk.

I brooded about Sonny, the Mustang, and all things Calista until I was on the ferry. As it always did, the water soothed me. I stared out to sea and focused on the evening ahead. I had a date to dress for. Nate had made reservations at Anson for seven o'clock. My mouth watered thinking about Anson. Their she crab soup was to die for.

Nate's car wasn't in the driveway when I turned in, so I called to check in with him.

"Where are you?" I asked.

"I had some shopping to do. In my haste to get to Stella Maris, I neglected to pack proper attire to escort a lady to dinner."

"Oh, Nate. You didn't have to do that. We could have gone someplace more casual. Honestly, I've seen people dressed very casually in Anson."

"Cretins. A gentleman wears a jacket for fine dining. I'm looking forward to this evening."

"Me, too. Hey, what did you find at Calista's?" I pressed the button to close the garage door behind me.

"She's bug free. I did an RF sweep, an IR sweep, checked the wiring—I checked the house from top to bottom. The only people monitoring her are the folks at SSI."

"They only monitor her when she actually turns the system on."

"Fair point. But, no one else is listening in."

"Thank you for checking. Ohmygosh. I have to tell you what Sonny told me."

"Tell me when I get there. See you in ten."

"I may be in the shower."

"In that case, I'll hurry along. Take your time."

I felt a huge, silly smile take over my face and floated up the stairs. I'd barely made it from the garage to the mudroom when Rhett went to barking. It couldn't be Nate yet. I scooted through the kitchen, down the hall, and peeked out the door. Michael's Jeep Cherokee was in front of the house. What on earth did he want?

Hoping to make whatever it was quick, I opened the door before he could knock. "Michael."

"Liz...can I come in?"

"I'm getting ready to go out. What's up?"

"I just need a minute."

"Michael, we've said all there is to say."

"Liz, please."

I closed my eyes, inhaled deeply, and opened the door. I waved him into the living room, and he made himself at home on the sofa.

He looked up at me with such vulnerability my heart softened. I sat down in the chair to his right. "What did you want to talk about?" I asked.

"I have something that belongs to you." He reached into his jeans pocket and brought out a ring box.

I raised both hands to my face and drew back. "Michael—"

"It's not what you think."

I squinched my face at him.

He opened the ring box.

"Gram's engagement ring," I gasped. "Marci took this—well, technically, Gram's will specified Marci could choose a piece of jewelry—how did you get it back?"

"She needed more money. I bought it back from her. I had planned—never mind. Here." He held out the open box to me. I was transfixed by Gram's two-carat, emerald-shaped diamond ring. I reached for it.

"This is unexpected." Nate stood in the living room doorway, confusion and hurt battling on his face.

"Nate." I jumped up and Michael followed.

"Liz, talk to me," Nate said, his voice calm and even.

"This isn't what it looks like at all," I said, moving towards him as I spoke.

"Please tell me what it is, then."

Michael took a step in our direction, seeming reluctant to cede ground. "I was just returning Liz's grandmother's ring."

"Marci had it," I said.

"I see," Nate said.

"Liz..." Michael said.

"Thank you so much for returning Gram's ring," I said. Heaven help me, I didn't want to hurt Michael, but my first priority was to make sure Nate did not get the first wrong idea. "Was there anything else?"

Michael looked defeated. "No, that's all. Nate." He nodded and passed us on the way to the door.

"Thank you again," I said. "I can never thank you enough. This piece is very precious to me."

"I know." Michael nodded, with his hand on the door.

I was almost home free.

Michael hesitated. "You know, this island is your home, Liz. You and me, we share that. This place means something to us. We have roots here. Roots are important."

"Michael—" I needed to make him stop talking, but I had no idea what to say or do.

Nate did. He placed his hand lightly at the small of my back. "Thank you for returning Liz's ring. If you'll excuse us, we have a dinner reservation in Charleston."

Michael nodded twice and left.

I started babbling the second the door closed behind him. "He showed up here without calling or anything. I was just about to hop in the shower. I don't want to keep my handsome date waiting." I kissed Nate lightly and scurried up the stairs without looking back.

NINETEEN

Charleston is a foodie's paradise. From oyster shacks down a dirt road where they serve salty bites of heaven with a shovel, to white-table-cloth restaurants that make the toughest food critic drool, we have it all. I was pleased that Nate had chosen Anson—it was one of my favorites.

Anson is right off Market, in the heart of historic Charleston. We parked in the lot beside the restaurant, and I waited with a little smile on my face for Nate to come around and open my door. He reached in and took my hand to help me out. The current that passed between us made me lightheaded. I studied his eyes as I stood and was relieved to find no hint of tension from the earlier scene with Michael. It seemed neither of us was inclined to let Michael spoil our first date.

Nate pulled me a little closer. "Nice dress." His voice was a caress, ripe with promise.

"Thank you." My smile promised him things, too, like how maybe later he could help me out of my favorite red V-neck Ann Taylor sheath.

Hand in hand, we strolled towards the restaurant. A horse and carriage clopped by. The guide, dressed in confederate uniform, waxed poetic about Charleston's history.

We stepped beneath the overhang covered in little white lights and through the door. Several couples perched by Anson's massive cypress bar, each in their own private worlds. The décor was dark woods, muted green walls, plantation shutters, and warm candlelight. The hostess led us to a velvet-backed booth with a leather seat. Murmured conversations and sensual jazz comprised the soundtrack. I inhaled a medley of savory aromas and sighed a happy sigh.

"Good evening, my name is Jonathan, and I'll be the one taking care of you this evening." Our waiter had a tie clip made of a bent fork.

"I love your tie clip," I said. "Do all the waiters wear those now?" I'd never noticed them before.

"No, I made this myself." He smiled, then was off to bring water. He took our cocktail order and returned momentarily with my Grey Goose pomegranate martini and Nate's Woodford Reserve.

Nate raised his glass. "To my lovely dinner companion."

I smiled, suddenly shy. "Why, thank you, kind sir."

I couldn't say why Nate unsettled me after all these years. We'd sat across the table from each other hundreds of times. But this was our first date. My best friend and partner Nate had all sorts of new, unexplored dimensions now that he was my fellow Nate. Off balance, I searched for familiar territory. "I never told you about Sonny."

"Can it wait? I'd rather talk about you tonight."

"Well..." There was nothing either of us could do about Sonny's case, which now seemed not to intersect with our case, so I let it drop. "Of course."

"It was nice of Michael to bring your grandmother's ring back."

"It was, wasn't it?" Here was a topic I'd like to avoid.

"I'm not sure I'd be such a congenial loser if you were dining with him this evening."

"No sense even entertaining such an idea. Have I ever mentioned what sexy eyes you have?"

"Not that I recall."

I flirted shamelessly with him until Jonathan came by to discuss specials. After he mentioned the fried green tomatoes and pimento cheese appetizer, I didn't hear another word he said until he started talking about grits. "I'm from up north," he said. "I hope that won't affect my tip."

We all laughed. Jonathan continued his routine. "I never liked grits until I tasted these. We grind them ourselves, and if you've heard of Anson Mills grits, that's us." Of course I'd heard this before, but his pitch was part of the experience. He slid away to give us a few minutes with the menu.

After we'd picked out way more food than we needed, we set the menus aside and I pulled my hand sanitizer from my clutch. I slathered some on and set it on the table for Nate.

"No, thanks." He almost swallowed a grin before I caught it.

"There's nothing funny about getting sick. You don't know how many people have handled those menus, not to mention the door handle." I nodded at the sanitizer.

"I prefer to keep my immune system well-practiced at defending all comers."

I tilted my head at him, giving him a look I borrowed from Mamma. He relented and picked up the sanitizer.

Jonathan appeared.

Nate said, "We'll start with a couple of oysters each, the lady would like hers fried. I'll have mine on the half-shell. Then we'd each like a cup of she crab soup. I'll have the pork belly appetizer, and the lady will have the fried green tomatoes. And I'll have the pork chop main course, and the lady will have the fried flounder. And we'd like a bottle of J pinot noir."

"Very good." Jonathan topped off our water and stepped away.

"I didn't realize I'd ordered so much fried food until you said it out loud," I said. "I'll have to run ten miles in the morning."

"We'll work it off somehow."

"We'll need to. You know Mamma's not serving health food come Sunday."

Something flickered across Nate's face. "You haven't had to intervene between your daddy and his computer anymore have you?"

"Thankfully not. Not this week, anyway."

"Have you been doing that a lot since you've been back?"

I shrugged. "Some. He's just trying to get attention. I've been gone a long time. When he's used to me being home all that nonsense will settle down. I hope."

Nate took a sip of his drink. "We haven't thought very far ahead, I'm afraid."

I felt as if I'd been turned into a salt pillar. How had I not thought this through. Nate still lived in Greenville. He hadn't mentioned how long he planned on staying in Stella Maris. I picked up my drink and downed the last sip.

"We'll work it out," he said. "It's not like Greenville's on another planet."

"I guess I was hoping you'd move here." Hoping, hell. I'd assumed he'd move. Stupid, stupid, *stupid.*

"Well, I like spending time here. But I have a condo in Greenville. Yours hasn't sold yet. We have established relationships with several attorneys who send us a nice stream of business there." He shrugged. "Greenville's home for me—it's my place in the world."

"Your parents still have a home there." All of the things I hadn't thought of piled up in my head.

"Hunh. They spend most of their time in Florida. Who knows where Scott is—somewhere with no extradition agreement. Besides, he's so damaged our best hope is to die in something other than a gunfight. I know you're close to your family...." His face creased.

"I am, and I stayed away so long for stupid reasons."

"Because of Michael. And Scott."

I pondered the truth of that. Scott's career and Michael's marriage to my cousin, Marci the Schemer, had held me in Greenville.

"And now, you want to stay here because of your family and because you have roots."

Michael's words echoed in my head and I knew that's precisely what was running through Nate's. "And the house," I said. "I have a house here. On the beach. I've committed to the town council."

"What if we divide our time between here at the beach house and Greenville."

I did love Greenville. And he made a great point about the attorneys we worked with. But, I couldn't entertain the thought of leaving Stella Maris again. And it hadn't escaped my notice we'd skipped right over talking about such things as love and gone straight to where we'd live. That didn't sit right with me, but I didn't want to spoil our evening with a quarrel. "We have time to figure all this out, right?"

"All the time we need." He smiled, and the edge had left his voice.

Jonathan arrived with the wine. As soon as it was tasted and poured, our oysters appeared in front of us and we began the feast. We lingered, sharing bites of each other's food, and talking about nothing more complicated than creating the perfect bite of pork belly, corn and cheddar waffle, hot pepper jelly, sunnyside-up egg, and succotash. After entrees neither of us finished, we topped off the meal with three bites apiece of mile high apple pie.

Nate was quiet on the ride home. We took the long way, bearing right onto Coleman Boulevard coming off the Cooper River Bridge. We crossed Shem Creek, lined with fishing boats and shrimp trawlers. Lights from the restaurants that lined the shore reflected in the water and lit the scene like Christmas.

Coleman Boulevard turned into Ben Sawyer. We crossed the Ben Sawyer Bridge, turned left, and drove the length of Sullivan's Island. When we crossed the bridge over Breach Inlet onto Isle of Palms, I thought of Colleen, as I always did. How like her, to take her life somewhere other than Stella Maris, sparing her family a constant reminder.

132 Susan M. Boyer

It was nearly ten-thirty when we pulled into the Isle of Palms marina parking lot. We'd have a short wait for the next ferry.

Nate lowered the windows and turned the car off. Music from the band playing at Morgan Creek Grill drifted across the lot.

"The night smells good." I filled my lungs with salt air. "This time of year, the only time you can enjoy fresh air is at night. I'm sick to death of air conditioning, but grateful for it just the same."

"Something tells me your disposition would suffer if you spent summertime in the Lowcountry without air conditioning."

"Most likely." I glanced right. At the far end of the parking lot, I spotted a black Mustang. "Seriously?"

"What?"

"I thought maybe I was being followed this afternoon. Some idiot in a black Mustang. And bless Pat if there's not one parked right over there. I'm going to check it out."

"Probably a lot of black Mustangs."

"Still...I want to get the plate." I opened the door.

Nate opened his door and climbed out. "You stay in the car, I'll get it."

"Nate, it's just a license plate—" We were apparently going to have a period of adjustment where work was concerned now that our relationship had turned romantic. He'd dialed his protective streak way up. I shrugged and closed my door.

He came back a few moments later. "Dark tinted windows?"

"Yes—I bet you anything that's the same car."

Nate scribbled the plate in a notebook he pulled out of the console. "Maybe so, but he wouldn't leave his car here and take the ferry. The Marina Market is closed. Maybe he's visiting someone on a boat—or over at Morgan Creek. They've got a crowd tonight."

"No one would park that far away."

Nate shrugged. "He didn't follow us here. And there's no one in the car. We'll run the tag when we get back to the house just to be on the safe side."

I scoured every corner of the parking lot I could see.

"Relax. There's no one here but you and me." He twined his fingers through mine and we watched the ferry approach.

The Amelia Ruth was named in honor of my third great-grandmother, a Beauthorpe who'd married a Talbot. The Beauthorpe's had donated the land for the dock on Stella Maris and contributed generously to the original ferry. Amelia Ruth docked and the side of the boat, which lowered to form a ramp, opened. Nate pulled the car onto the ferry. We were the first ones on. "Do you want to get out?" he asked.

"Sure. The breeze will feel nice up top." We got out of the car and climbed the steps to the top observation deck. The middle deck was nice when you wanted air conditioning. But tonight I wanted to see the stars and feel the wind.

We walked to the front of the ferry. No one else was on the deck, so we had our pick of spots. I stood next to the rail, and Nate snuggled close behind me, wrapping me in both arms.

"What are you thinking?" I asked.

He brushed my hair back and kissed me on the side of my neck. "This."

I leaned into him for a moment, then turned in his arms. He placed a hand behind my head and pulled me close. With his bottom lip, he caressed mine. Then he kissed me soundly and rested his forehead to mine.

The engine noise picked up, and the Amelia Ruth pulled away from the dock. Time was passing too quickly. It felt as if we'd barely been on the ferry five minutes. I smiled playfully and turned to watch the trip. I loved being on the water, especially at night. Once we were away from the marina, the sky was jet black and the stars twinkled and the moon glowed just for us.

The warm breeze felt soft on my skin, and its rush dampened the sound of everything outside the two of us. I was cocooned in the arms of the man I loved, and all was right with the world. It was magical. We cuddled and soaked in the night, totally lost in each other.

Halfway into the twenty-minute trip, after we'd cleared the northern point of Isle of Palms and were starting across Pearson's Inlet, the ferry jerked, and swayed a bit. I snuggled closer to Nate. The tide was on its way out and inlet currents were often swift.

The groan of metal under stress and a splash loud enough to penetrate the wind announced trouble.

Nate stepped away from me.

I turned around. "What in this world?"

Nate was on high alert. "That splash was too loud to be a person."

We scrambled towards the back of the boat and made our way down the stairs. The second level deck was as deserted as the top had been.

My alarm level climbed. This was very unusual for a Friday night. As we started down the flight of stairs to the car deck, I gasped. The back side of the boat, which served as a ramp when lowered, had been opened and was closing.

"*Holy shit.*" Nate muttered. "Looks like the ferry has some equipment issues."

I followed Nate the rest of the way down the steps. The car deck was empty.

The Explorer was gone.

We were the only passengers on the ferry—how?

"Oh my God." Terror rose in my throat.

"Not a malfunction," Nate said.

I searched the deck. For a moment I thought we were alone on the ferry. Where was the captain? A lone crew member stepped out of the wheel house. He wore the standard uniform, cap and all. Only the ski mask and two pistols were out of order. He walked towards us deliberately, keeping one gun trained on each of us.

"Nate, are you armed?" I spoke softly.

"Regrettably not. Didn't think I'd need a gun tonight."

"I had a Taser in my purse, but it's in the car."

"Where are the life vests?" he asked.

"In the chests under the seats."

"When I say go, you jump over the side. Don't hesitate. I'll try to get two vests and follow you."

"Nate—"

The armed crewman closed the distance between us by half.

"No time to argue, Slugger. Do it. *Now.*"

I vaulted over the rail.

Two silenced gunshots followed me over the edge.

I hit dark swirling water and went down. Damnation. The water was deep. Deep enough to hide an SUV until it was sucked out to sea. I kicked towards the surface. It seemed miles above me.

My heart and lungs exploded as I broke the surface.

The tide was running out. I struggled against it, treaded water, and watched the ferry slide away.

Bullets pinged off metal.

Nate flew over the side. Was he hit? He plunged into the water and I swam towards the spot I'd seen him go in. With every stroke, I fought the water intent on tugging me towards the Atlantic.

"*Nate?*"

He popped out of the water maybe a hundred feet away. Praise God he had two life vests.

"Were you hit?"

He coughed and sputtered. "No. Swim towards me."

"I'm trying."

He wiggled out of his sport coat, then kicked and floated in my direction. After what seemed like an eternity, I reached out and grabbed a life vest. We struggled into them. I was exhausted already from fighting the current. Without the floatation jackets we would surely have drowned.

"Are you okay?" Nate asked.

"For now. We've got to get to land."

The ferry continued towards Stella Maris. Nate said, "At least we're out of gunshot range and no doubt invisible now in the water. Who the hell was that guy?"

"My best guess is the driver of that Mustang. And it has to do with the thing I didn't tell you about Sonny. Later. We've got to get to land."

We floated in a circle, looking at all the options.

"We're too far from Stella Maris," Nate said. "That small islet might be in range, but it would mean swimming against the current. No way that'll work."

"We've got to make the water work for us," I said. "If we swim with the current, but angle towards Isle of Palms, we might be able to reach the northeast shore there."

"Sounds like a plan."

"I need to rest a minute. Let's just drift."

"For a minute."

I laid back in the life vest and floated. Nate followed suit. Five minutes later, I'd caught my breath. The lights on the north end of Isle of Palms seemed impossibly far away. "We'd better get moving. Swimming in these vests is going to be awkward and slow. But I think we have to leave them on in this current."

"Agreed."

We kicked slow and steady and moved our arms in semi-circles in front of us. Resting periodically, we made our way towards shore. Behind us, the ferry glided back from Stella Maris to Isle of Palms on schedule, then returned. What felt like days later, we crawled onto the sand. I flopped over on my back and sent up a silent prayer of thanks.

Nate sprawled beside me and reached for my hand.

I gripped his hard, and tamped down the hysteria threatening to overwhelm me.

Nate said, "That's the closest we've ever come to being killed on this job. Something tells me that what we're into is a lot deeper than we think. I'd've sworn we hadn't kicked near enough hornets' nests yet to warrant this kind of trouble."

"Sonny found out the gun used to kill Calista's life coach came from the evidence room at Charleston PD."

"Not good."

"I thought that meant Harmony's—Helena's—death wasn't connected to Calista. But since Helena isn't our case, and Calista is..."

"No one would try to kill us over a case we're not investigating."

"Precisely," I said. "The two cases must be connected. And we must be a hellava lot closer to whoever is behind it all than we imagined."

"We'd better stay on Isle of Palms tonight. We need to make sure the house hasn't been compromised, and we're in no shape to deal with that tonight."

"I fed Rhett this morning. His water bowl automatically refills. He'll be fine until tomorrow. Unless someone has been to the house."

My panic level rose again. Surely whoever our assailant was, he'd have no reason to harm a friendly dog. Only Rhett didn't sound all that friendly to intruders. There was nothing we could do. "We don't have a choice but to stay here. The last ferry has come and gone, and I don't know about you, but I don't think I want to get back on anyway."

"Excellent point." Nate staggered upright and removed his life vest. He reached down and gave me a hand up.

My legs buckled. I felt dizzy.

Nate steadied me. "Are you okay to walk?"

I took a few deep breaths. "I'm good." I slipped off my vest.

Nate pulled me close and we clung to each other for a few minutes.

Finally, I said, "Whoever that was, they left the dock before anyone else could get on the ferry. Nate, what about the regular crew?" I pulled back and looked up at him.

He looked grim, but didn't respond. He didn't have to.

I started to tear up. "We better find someplace for me to crash, cause I'm close."

"Here we go, Slugger." Nate tugged gently and we started moving towards the nearest walkway. "Look at the bright side. I think we just worked off all that fried food."

I giggled. "This dead ends into a golf cart path. Our best bet is to turn left and stick to the cart path until we can cross over to Back Bay Drive. We're inside Wild Dunes, of course, which means we'll have to walk all the way to the Boardwalk Inn to check in this time of night. Any idea what time it is?"

Nate glanced at his watch. "What do you know? This thing really is waterproof. It's almost midnight."

"I would have sworn it was three a.m. We must have gone into the water at about twenty 'til eleven. I think your watch is broke. We were out there longer than any hour and twenty minutes."

"Far be it from me to argue with a lady under such circumstances as these."

We made it to the golf path. "If it really is close to midnight, we might get lucky and catch a shuttle. They have service within the resort to carry guests around to restaurants, bars, and such."

Nate patted his pants pockets. "Remarkable. I still have my wallet. You figure out how to talk us on to a shuttle. I've got cash. It's soaked, but it should still work. I'll figure out a way to talk us through check-in without giving a credit card. Until we know more about what's going on and who's involved, I don't want to do anything that can be traced."

"Deal."

TWENTY

I woke Saturday morning to Nate waving coffee under my nose.

"Let's get some of this in you before I open the blinds," he said.

I pulled a pillow over my face and burrowed deeper under the covers.

"Come on now. We need to get moving. I called Blake. A buddy of his has a house with a dock at the end of Seahorse Court. We thought that would be better than the marina right now. He's borrowed a boat and is on his way to get us."

I groaned, sat up, and reached for the coffee. "What did you tell him?"

"Everything I know specifically about last night. I didn't go into any of the whys or wherefores. I'm not sure if this case belongs to him, to the Coast Guard, or to the sheriff's office, but Blake can sort all that out. If anyone else wants to talk to us, then they'll be around. Meanwhile, we've reported the incident to local law enforcement."

I gulped coffee. "I bet he's fit to be tied."

"Rightly so," Nate said. "Our clothes aren't nearly dry. I picked up some shorts and t-shirts while I was out."

"How long have you been up?"

"About an hour. I brought breakfast." He dangled a bag.

Suddenly I was ravenous. I grabbed the bag and tore into it.

Nate opened the blinds, and sunlight exploded into the room. I blinked and stuffed a bite of croissant into my mouth.

"Nice hotel," Nate said. "Accommodating staff." He picked up his own coffee cup.

"Well, most people are when tipped that well. Why on earth do you carry so much cash around?"

"In case I need to rescue a mermaid, of course. I'm not nearly as creative with improvisation as you are. That shuttle driver enjoyed your little, 'We fell into the pool shagging at a party,' story."

"Oh, please. That probably happens once a week here in the summer. He didn't even blink."

Nate chuckled.

I stared at him. I was still flirting with coming unhinged. "I'm glad you can joke about this. We almost died last night." I stuffed another bite of croissant into my mouth to soothe myself.

"I'm aware."

"We need to call Sonny."

"Maybe. Pass me that bag."

I handed it to him and he pulled out a muffin.

"Why maybe?" I asked.

"I want to think all of this through with a clear head before we talk to anyone other than Blake."

"Surely you don't think Sonny is involved?"

"I've never met Sonny Ravenel. I've heard you mention him a time or two. I know you trust him. That's good enough for me. But anyone who would go to the lengths that jackass last night went to is capable of anything. Sonny could be under surveillance. Someone could be listening to his calls. As far as our would-be killer knows, we're dead. Best play dead a while."

"You're right. But if he thinks we might be alive, won't he look at my house first? Wouldn't he be watching to see if we show up?"

"Very likely." Nate looked somber. "Let's just take things one step at a time."

I stood, wrapping the sheet around me. Nate wore khaki shorts, an Isle of Palms T-shirt, and an Isle of Palms baseball cap. "You look like a tourist," I said.

He handed me another bag. "You will too, as soon as you put some clothes on. I'm sorry, but the store didn't carry undergarments."

I blushed. "I'll manage." I waddled into the bathroom. I'd rinsed my bra and panties last night while closing in on a dissociative state. I hadn't wrung them out well, and they were still pretty damp. My dress was ruined. I wiggled into my underwear, tore the tags off my shorts, T-shirt and cap, and dressed. Thankfully, Nate had thought of flip-flops. My red Kate Spade wedges were at the bottom of Pearson's Inlet.

I recognized my brother at the wheel of the Boston Whaler before he came clearly into view by the way he stood, and the fact that he was rubbing the back of his neck and periodically adjusting his ball cap.

He tossed out a couple of bumpers and tied off the boat at the dock. Nate and I climbed aboard.

"Are you all right?" Blake's face was creased, his eyes wide with alarm. He scanned the area. Blake rarely looked scared.

I nodded. "I'm fine."

He hugged me, which was also rare for Blake. I hugged him tight and teared up. I was still overdue for a good cry.

Blake released me and reached for Nate's hand, then pulled him in for a back slap. "Nate. My God, what the hell?"

Nate shook his head. "We're still sorting that out. Has to do with the Calista McQueen case."

Blake's face contorted in disbelief. "That whacko? You've gotta be kidding me."

"We're not saying she had anything to do with it," I said. "But the people who want to harm her are apparently the same people who killed the new age guru in Charleston."

"Harmony what's-her-name?"

"Right," I said.

"Sonny caught that case," Blake said.

"We know," I said. "And I'm afraid Sonny's in danger, too." I brought Blake up to speed.

He stared at me for a long moment, processing. "Let's get you two home. I'll text Sonny on his burner and ask him to meet me. We have under-the-radar communications established. Never thought we'd need it. Anyway, I'll fill him in. I'm coordinating with the sheriff's office and Isle of Palms PD to investigate."

"Did someone check the marina parking lot for the black Mustang?" I asked.

"I asked Isle of Palms PD to check it out last night when Nate first called. It's gone," Blake said.

I squinched my face at Nate. "You called Blake last night?"

"While you were freshening up. You passed out so fast, I figured I could tell you this morning."

Blake said, "What IOP PD did find, however, was the scheduled ferry captain and a crew member, each in the trunk of his car. Good thing they got to them quick as hot as it is."

"Are they okay?" I asked.

"They've taken them to Medical University of South Carolina as a precaution, but yeah. Looks like they'll be fine. Just shook up. Neither of them remembers much after relieving the crew from the previous shift at seven p.m. Captain says someone grabbed him from behind. Thinks something was sprayed into his face. Neither of them saw a thing."

I mulled that. "If the Mustang is gone, that likely means our guy is long gone. For now. Did you run that plate Nate gave you?" We hadn't had the equipment to run the plate since we hadn't made it home. While the notebook Nate wrote the tag number in was long gone, he had a good memory.

"Stolen. Both the car and the plate. Probably in a chop shop by now."

"Whoever he is, he sure is brazen. Calling attention to himself in a stolen car?" I took a seat under the canopy. I hadn't had sunscreen to put on that morning, and I could feel my arms starting to burn.

Blake said, "Unfortunately, while brazen, he also appears to be very resourceful. I don't guess I can convince you two to go back to Greenville for a while?"

"Don't start," I said.

Nate said, "Sorry, Blake. I can understand your position, but we have a client who's depending on us."

Blake pressed his lips together and shook his head. "This guy didn't just want to kill the two of you. He wanted to make you disappear. You get that, right?"

"Of course we get that," I said. "And that fits. Whoever killed Harmony wouldn't want two more bodies connected to Calista turning up. He needed us to disappear. For folks to think maybe we'd gone off for a long weekend or something."

Blake's look issued a warning. "What is it about that woman? What have you not told me?"

I sighed, looked at Nate.

He nodded.

"Calista inherited that Powerball jackpot from a couple years back. Seven hundred million dollars," I said.

Blake closed his eyes and rubbed the back of his neck. "That kind of money can buy all kinds of misery." He started the boat and headed towards home.

TWENTY-ONE

In case someone was watching the house, Blake parked at The Pirates' Den and the three of us walked up the beach. Rhett was happy to see us. I poured him a heaping helping of kibble and promised him extra attention later. Blake and Nate searched the house for any sign someone had been inside. I pulled up the DVR recordings from my security feeds. If our ferry driver had been in my house or yard, he was invisible.

After completing their manual sweep, Nate and Blake joined me in my office.

"Nice setup." Blake studied the split screen. I'd never shown him my security system, which rivaled what Calista had with SSI. The difference was that when my cameras activated, an alert went to my phone and everything was recorded to a DVR. No outside service watched the feeds from my system. I needed to replace my iPhone, which had been in my purse, to make sure I was notified of future intrusions.

"I think we're safe for now," I said.

Nate said, "All the same, I'm going by the store to pick up heftier door and window deadbolts. Someone wants in badly enough, we won't be able to stop him, but we can slow him down."

"Good idea." Blake looked grim. "Nate...you gonna be in town a while?"

I could tell exactly what was on my brother's mind. He'd haul me over to Mamma and Daddy's in a skinny minute if he thought I was going to be by myself—or worse, send Daddy over to sit vigil on the porch with a shotgun.

A look passed between the menfolk.

"I'm not going anywhere," Nate said.

"Blake, you have got to promise me you *will not* mention any of this to Mamma and Daddy. The absolute last thing I need is Daddy and his shotgun-toting cronies over here."

"I'm not convinced of that," Blake said. "Seems to me the more people around, the safer you'll be."

I said, "We've got a case to work on, and also client confidentiality to consider. Not to mention Mamma's sanity and Daddy's safety."

Blake blew out a long sigh. "Have it your way. For now. Nate, if you'll come by the station, Nell will get you a copy of the police report. The insurance company's gonna want that."

"Will someone try to recover the car?" Nate asked. "I know it's ruined, but the insurance company will ask about that for salvage value, anyway."

Blake winced. "Honestly, nothing like this has ever happened around here before. My understanding, the sheriff's department will send divers in later today. If they can locate it, they'll strap it in a harness and lift it out onto a barge. But, yeah. It's been in salt water overnight. It's totaled."

Nate nodded. "I need to pick up a rental and replace my phone and some of the equipment I had in the Explorer."

"Let me get changed." I opened my desk drawer and pulled out my Sig Sauer. No way was I going anywhere without Sig until the guy on the ferry was behind bars.

I stepped out of the shower, wrapped myself in my favorite fluffy robe, and hurried into the bedroom.

Colleen waited in a chair by the French doors leading out to the balcony. "Scary night."

I glanced at the bedroom door, verifying it was closed. If Blake and Nate thought I'd gone to talking to myself they'd worry I was having a breakdown. "You were there?"

Colleen shrugged. Her face was painted with worry. "I had the night off."

"You helped us escape." I'd been too panicked to consider that possibility before. I sat down on the chair at my dressing table and stared at her.

She studied a spot on the wall. "That would have been outside the scope of my mission."

"Odd. That guy impressed me as someone well-practiced with handguns. And yet he missed us both multiple times." I hadn't had the chance to reflect much on this aspect of the evening.

The edges of her mouth curled a little, but her eyes were wide with innocence. "Maybe he's not that good. Could have been Divine Intervention."

"I suspect you were our Divine Intervention."

"Best keep those suspicions to yourself."

I rummaged in the closet for clothes. "Colleen, I appreciate your help—so much. Really. We nearly died last night. But, I'm not sure what happens to guardian spirits run amuck, so please don't go out on any more limbs for me, okay?"

"You just let me worry about my business. You have more pans on the stove than you can manage."

I slathered on sunscreen and slipped into yellow capris, a white tank, and a lightweight blouse. "I thought about you last night. I always do when I cross Breach Inlet. But, when we were in Pearson's inlet, and I thought we might drown...."

"I know," she whispered softly. "It was a bad moment for me, too."

"I miss you," I said. "I miss being able to do normal things with you."

Her eyes misted. "We can't change what's been done. No point in going there. I miss you, too."

Our eyes held for a long moment. I reached to stroke her arm and stopped myself. She was at once so real and so ethereal.

She grinned. "I'm working on materializing. It's an advanced skill. Once I master it, you'll be able to feel me. The downside is others can see me when I do that. But really, who would recognize me?"

Colleen had changed quite a bit since her death. She'd become a perfect version of herself. She was slim now and her skin was flawless. Her hair looked like she'd just stepped out of Phoebe's Day Spa. Anyone who saw her might think she reminded them of someone. But she was right. No one would recognize her.

"Nate's waiting for me," I said.

"Be careful. If you need me, holler I'll come if I can."

"What happens to you if you get caught going off the reservation?"

"As long as I'm not neglecting my primary duties or meddling in my family's lives, and as long as I'm on the side of the angels, I think I'll be okay. Like I said, let me worry about that." Her voice and form faded simultaneously. She disappeared in a poof with a single spark.

I wasn't comfortable with what Colleen thought about afterlife rules and consequences. But as often happened, when I had more to say, she'd gone elsewhere. I flew through an abbreviated fluff and makeup while pulling my head back into reality.

TWENTY-TWO

Blake called thirty minutes later. "There's no one parked anywhere near the house. No signs it's under surveillance."

"Thanks, Blake," I said. "For everything."

He cleared his throat. "Sis, maybe you and Nate should just stay in the house. Lay low a while. Let me pick up the new locks. I can bring you whatever you need."

"I promise we'll keep our heads down. But we can't just hole up here and wait for him to come and get us."

Silence.

Then he said, "Be careful. Stick together. And keep me posted."

"We will. I promise."

Nate and I had to go into Charleston to replace our phones and pick up a rental car for Nate. When we drove onto the ferry, I gripped Nate's hand and the door handle.

He put the car in park and cut the ignition. "Come on. Let's check out the guy who's driving this thing."

I took a deep breath, steadied myself, and nodded.

Before the ferry left the dock, Nate and I chatted up the captain and crew. I recognized them as regulars, and there was one extra man on duty. Their eyes moved constantly, checking out every vehicle and person.

For our part, Nate and I walked all three decks and greeted as many people as possible, looking into their eyes. Most of them were people I'd known my whole life. None of them had any known connection to Calista.

When we left the Apple store on King Street, I sent up thanks for iCloud backups. Our new phones were clones of our old ones.

"The guy from the boat last night was a pro," I said. "We need to look Jim Davis in the eye to be sure, but my gut says he's nothing more than a pawn, lured here to play the role of suspect."

"Agreed. Anyone who handles two handguns with silencers with that much confidence is probably ex-military."

"Ex-something," I said. "Nate?"

"Yeah?"

"Does it strike you as odd that he had two guns and clearly knew how to use them, but missed us both?" Of course I knew exactly why this happened. But I wanted to know what Nate had seen.

He didn't respond.

I stopped walking and looked at him. "What happened after I went over the side?"

"I was focused on two things. Grabbing life jackets and following you into the water without getting shot. It's a blur." He looked uneasy.

"What are you not telling me?"

He was ruffled, which was very un-Nate. He glanced skyward for a moment, then back at me. "I saw sparks. Bright, silver sparks. I keep telling myself it was bullets pinging off metal, but there were too many. Looked like someone lit a roman candle on the deck. Must've distracted the gunman. Whatever it was, I'm grateful."

"Me, too." I'd seen Colleen's pyrotechnics before. I took his hand and started walking again. "What say I call Calista and see if I can get her to agree to a sit down with her past. We can kill several birds with one stone if we can get her and Jim to meet with the rest of her loony family at the bed and breakfast. That way, we can interview them all at once and get Grace's take on their intentions."

"Sounds efficient."

"Do you want to interview Jim Davis separately first?"

"I don't see the point. Let's see if Calista will go along with a meeting."

I dropped Nate off at the Budget Rent-A-Car on Meeting Street, then called Grace Sullivan, my godmother the psychic, who owned the bed and breakfast. Grace had indulged me my whole life, and today was no exception. She commenced pulling together a late lunch.

"Everyone will be on their best behavior at the dinner table," she said. "I'll speak to Gladys and Grace. They seem a little...confused...misguided, perhaps. But I don't think they have violence in them."

"Good to know," I said. "Thanks so much, Grace."

"Darlin', I can't wait to see you."

I hung up and called Calista. Initially, she didn't think much of the plan. But when I told her what had happened to Nate and me, I think she would've done anything I asked. My last call was to Jim Davis. The GPS we'd put on his car placed him at his hotel.

He answered his room phone with hesitation in his voice. "Hello?"

"Mr. Davis, my name is Liz Talbot. I'm a private investigator employed by your former wife."

"Norma Jeane hired a PI? Why would she do that?"

"For security, Mr. Davis. She seems to believe you mean her harm."

"I'd never hurt Norma Jeane. She's the love of my life. I only wanted to talk to her. Now the police have questioned me. I'm not sure I'm supposed to leave town. This is all a big misunderstanding."

"I'd like to help you clear that up. Would you care to join us for lunch at Sullivan's Bed and Breakfast on Stella Maris at two o'clock?"

"You mean you and Norma Jeane?" The hope in his voice was pitiful.

"Yes." I decided not to debate the name issue just then. I also left out who all else would be in attendance.

"I'm on my way right now. I can't believe I'm finally going to see her." The joy in his voice sounded genuine, but I'd met good actors. I reserved judgment.

"See you at two."

"Ma'am, I can't thank you enough. Thank you. Thank you. I can't believe I'm finally going to get to see her. After all this time. I just can't tell you—"

"I'm so sorry to interrupt, but I need to go now and finalize the arrangements. I'll see you at two."

He was still thanking me when I hung up.

Sullivan's Bed and Breakfast was a huge Victorian affair with a wide, wrap-around porch dotted with rockers. Live oaks and palm trees punctuated elaborate landscaping that featured private seating areas, a fire pit, and a fountain. Grace Sullivan's family, like mine, had resided on Stella Maris as long as the sand. The house was over a hundred years old, but had been meticulously maintained and upgraded with all the modern conveniences.

Grace Sullivan was Mamma's best friend, and the two were the same model of female. By the time I'd dropped off my car, hopped into Nate's rental, and we'd driven around the north point of Stella Maris, Grace had a lunch spread that would've put a gaggle of Junior Leaguers to shame. My mouth watered when Nate and I walked in the room. She had the table set with china, crystal, silver, linen, and lace. Fresh cut hydrangeas spilled out of a Waterford vase. The food was still the prettiest thing on the table. Chicken salad croissants, cucumber sandwiches, deviled eggs, potato salad, pasta salad, marinated tomato salad, cheese straws, and on and on.

"Liz, darlin'. It's so good to see you." Grace advanced with outstretched arms and hugged my neck like she hadn't seen me in years. I had to tear my eyes away from that spread of food.

"Hey, Grace. You look gorgeous as always." Every blonde hair in her elegant, shoulder-length bob was in place, her pink St. John pantsuit accessorized with a scarf and simple gold earrings.

She hugged me tighter. "You're such a sweetheart to say so."

"Thank you again for doing all of this. When in heaven's name did you have time to make all this food?"

Grace dismissed my question with a wave. "Just a little something I threw together. Nothing special."

"Where are my manners? Grace, you remember Nate?"

Nate reached for Grace's hand. "Hey, Ms. Sullivan. So nice to see you."

"Why of *course* I remember him," Grace said. Her eyes gleamed at Nate. I could see the wheels turning in her head. "Aren't you just the handsomest thing? My goodness, you two must be starving. I'm so relieved you're all right. Of course, I knew you would be."

Nate said, "I forgot how fast news travels here."

Grace smiled. "Oh, no, darlin'. I haven't heard a thing."

He nodded, apparently connecting Grace's words to her psychic abilities. Nate wasn't a certified member of the paranormal believers, but he accepted that Grace had a gift because I did.

"Where is everyone?" I asked.

"Gladys and Grace are upstairs freshening up. My, those two are excited. No one else has arrived yet. Would you like to sit in the front parlor until everyone gets here?"

"That sounds great, thanks," I said. The bed and breakfast was in an isolated beachfront spot on the west side of North Point. We were as well hidden there as anywhere on the island. Folks didn't stroll through unless they were guests.

Nate and I followed Grace across the polished wood floors of the wide front hall.

"Maybe we should leave the chairs for those that might not ought sit by each other," I said.

"Good plan." Nate sat beside me on the sofa.

Grace glided out of the room on a puff of perfume to finish lunch. No sooner had she left the room than Calista opened the front door. She wore a navy fitted boat-neck dress that only served to make her look every inch the movie star she didn't want to be. Nate and I went to greet her.

"I wasn't sure if I should knock or just come on in," she said.

"You only need to knock if it's locked. Guests come and go all hours. We're waiting in here." I gestured to the parlor.

"I see." She sashayed into the room and perched on a Queen Anne chair. "I'm terribly worried about what happened last night. I never meant to put you in danger."

"We're fine," I said. "But for all our sakes, we need to drain this swamp PDQ. Nate and I would like to establish whether your family poses a threat to you in any way. Honestly, we don't believe they do. It appears someone lured them here by telling them where you were. That created a distraction from what's really going on."

"And what do you believe is really going on?" Calista asked.

At the same time Nate and I said, "Someone wants your money."

Calista sat back in her chair. "So few people know about the money, that's hard to believe. You can't imagine the lengths I've gone to."

"We'll talk about that later," I said. "Right now, we want *you* to get a comfort level that neither Jim, your mother, nor Grace McKee mean you harm. We're not suggesting what you should or shouldn't do in terms of your relationships with these folks. That's not our business. Let's just try to eliminate them as suspects, okay?"

"That's going to take quite a bit of convincing," she said.

"Let's have a nice lunch and see what they have to say for themselves," I said.

"Norma Jeane." A man's voice, filled with reverence, cracked.

We all turned towards the door. I hadn't heard Jim Davis come in.

"My God, honey. Can it really be you?"

"Hello, Jimmy." Calista's voice was neutral.

Jim rushed towards her chair and stopped short three feet away. "I've been looking for you for eighteen years." The adoration on his face was bare.

Still, people killed the objects of their adoration at an alarming rate. Best to make sure he wasn't a sociopath. "Mr. Davis, would you have a seat?"

Jim looked around, as if realizing for the first time Nate and I were also in the room. "Hello," he said. "Of course, I remember you."

I nodded. "Good to see you."

Urgent whispers and creaking stairs alerted us to Gladys and Grace's approach. Nate, Calista and I froze, bracing ourselves. Jim looked confused. Not nearly enough moments later, the women appeared at the French doors.

"Baby girl," Gladys squealed. "I *knew* you'd come."

"Norma Jeane, honey, we're so happy you're here," Grace gushed simultaneously.

They both rushed Calista's chair and stopped short when Jim wouldn't budge.

"Jimmy?" Grace looked quizzically from him to me, searching for an explanation.

"What the hell are those two doing here?" Jim demanded.

"I don't understand." Gladys clutched Grace's arm.

Nate stood. "Would everyone please take a seat?"

The three of them ignored Nate. The women's chirping, harping, and squealing got louder. Jim grumbled something, but I couldn't make out what. Then Gladys went to wailing. For her part, Calista sat perfectly still, chin up and ankles crossed. She didn't utter a word.

Nate looked at me. "Slugger, you are clearly more gifted at lunatic whispering than I."

"You're taller. You be the bad cop. Get them seated and quiet. I'll take over from there."

"That's enough," Nate yelled over the cacophony. "Everyone please take a seat. *Now*. And let's all listen to what Liz has to say."

They didn't look happy, but Jim, Grace, and Gladys found chairs.

"Thank you all for coming," I said.

The three of them regarded me with a mixture of curiosity and hostility.

My godmother, Grace, breezed into the room, arms wide open. "Welcome everyone. I'm so happy to have you all here. If y'all don't mind, I'll visit with you for a while, and then we'll have a nice lunch." She slid into a side chair near the door.

Of course I'd asked Grace to join us. I read people well, as did Nate. But Grace saw things no one else did. Her psychic abilities traced back to a near fatal drowning as a teenager, with white light and all the trimmings.

"Let's start by agreeing on some basics," I said. "My client changed her name years ago. She's Calista McQueen and would like to be addressed accordingly."

Muttering, averted gazes, and chair shifting ensued, but mutiny did not break out.

"If I understand correctly, y'all received anonymous postcards alerting you to Ms. McQueen's location approximately two weeks ago. Please nod if this is accurate."

Three heads bobbed.

"And Mr. Davis, you did not contact Ms. Monroe and Ms. McKee to let them know you'd received a postcard?"

"No way. Those buzzards ran my Norma—I'm sorry baby—Calista—off to begin with. All that star crap was their—"

I held up my hands. "Thank you, Mr. Davis. We'll get to all of that. Ladies, likewise, you did not contact Mr. Davis?"

Grace McKee spoke for them, "No. We wanted to see our girl. To try to make things right. We didn't think she'd want to see him."

By way of response, Calista directed a gaze at Grace that would have frozen napalm.

"You ladies drove across country, and you did as well, Mr. Davis?" I asked.

Nods and affirmative murmurs came from all three.

I said, "So—one at a time, please, beginning with Mr. Davis—exactly what did you hope to accomplish by traveling across country without so much as a phone call first?"

Jim said, "I've never loved anyone else. Never remarried. I wanted to try to win back my wife. It's as simple as that." If he was a sociopath, he was very good at it. But that was the trouble with sociopaths. Most were accomplished liars.

Grace—my godmother—stood and crossed the room. She placed her hands comfortingly on Jim's shoulders. "How very romantic. And gallant. A gentleman fighting for his love." She held onto him for a moment, then patted his shoulder and stepped away.

Jim nodded at Grace, the expression on his face telegraphing that he was unaccustomed to strangers laying hands on him. "Thank you."

"Ms. McKee?" I raised my left eyebrow.

Grace McKee clutched her chest and looked at Calista. "I've loved you like a daughter from the day you were born. I wanted to see you again before I died. Tell you how much we miss you and just want you to come home. I'd hoped for a more private reunion, of course."

Calista pressed her lips together and crossed her wrists on her lap.

Grace Sullivan stepped over and hugged Grace McKee. "It was very brave of you to come all this way. Two women alone. I bet the journey was quite an adventure."

Grace McKee submitted to Grace's embrace, but sat stiff, eyes wary. After a moment, my godmother rubbed the woman's arms and stepped back.

"Ms. Monroe?" I asked.

"Norma—Calista, honey, I'm so sorry. You're my only child. We never meant to hurt you. We just got caught up in it all.

Marilyn's mother's maiden name was Monroe. That wasn't a made-up name. That was her family name. I've dreamed since I was a little girl about whether we might be related somehow. It was my one connection to someone important—someone who people will remember."

Calista looked at her mother. Her expression softened a bit.

Encouraged, Gladys continued. "Grace and I watched her movies over and over. My favorite is *Gentlemen Prefer Blondes*. Grace always liked *How to Marry a Millionaire*. Grace has worked for years on our family tree. It's not out of the question. I mean we really could be re—" She seemed to catch herself. "There I go again. We never meant to hurt you. Please believe that."

Grace Sullivan slid over to Gladys and wrapped her in an embrace. "There now. Bless your heart. I know it's hard to be a parent. I never had children of my own, you understand, so I can only imagine how you must feel."

Unlike the others, Gladys hugged Grace back. She clung to her for a long moment, then pulled back and looked at her with gratitude. Gladys's chin trembled. I glanced at Calista. She raised one shoulder and lowered it.

Our hostess turned her attention to what she did best, getting us fed. "Everyone, why don't we finish chatting over lunch. Everything is sitting on the table." She gestured dramatically and led us into the dining room, where she waited by her chair at the head of the table.

"Calista, come sit by me." I smiled and guided her to a chair on the end between Grace and me.

Nate took the chair to my right. Jim Davis claimed the end of the table, and the two women I'd started thinking of as harmless flibbertigibbets hesitantly settled into chairs across from Calista and me, leaving an empty spot between them and Jim.

My godmother took her chair. "Isn't this nice? Did you all have a pleasant drive from California? I hope y'all didn't run into bad weather."

No one answered, and Grace continued with a stream of pleasant chatter, covering the flowers, the weather, and excursions our visitors might enjoy.

I put my linen napkin on my lap, served myself a chicken salad croissant and passed the platter left. The California crowd watched me, then followed suit with whatever happened to be in front of them.

Beside me, Nate scooped a large serving of potato salad onto his plate.

"Better save room," I said. "You'll love Grace's chicken salad."

For the next few minutes, the only sounds in the room were the soft ping of serving utensils on platters and bowls. There was a strained moment, after everyone's plate was piled high. No one began eating. We all just looked at each other.

Unflappable, Grace said, "Everyone dig in. Let me know if I can get anyone anything."

I picked up my fork. Whether anyone else ate or not, I needed sustenance. Near-death experiences took their toll on a person. Nate dug in, and Calista commenced pushing food around on her plate.

Gladys took a bite of her chicken salad croissant. "This is quite good. I'd love to have your recipe."

Grace McKee rolled her eyes and propped an elbow inelegantly on the table. "When have you ever cooked?"

"Ms. Sullivan," Calista said, "thank you ever so for doing all of this for us. This is a difficult situation, and you've been such a dear."

Grace beamed and patted Calista's hand. "You're quite welcome my dear." Her hand lingered on Calista's for a moment. Then, Grace looked at me, her eyes wide with alarm.

She'd picked up on something, no doubt about it. Figuring whatever it was would require sustenance, I focused on my food.

Jim ate with little enthusiasm. He stared at Calista with hound dog eyes.

Grace McKee sipped her tea, and finally put a bite of potato salad on her fork. "I'm still not clear what we're doing here." She slid the fork into her mouth.

I patted my mouth with my napkin. "Ms. McKee, we are reassuring Calista, whom you profess to care about, that she is safe with the three of you."

Grace McKee's face blazed.

Oh, boy. I'd been too blunt. "What I'm saying is, Calista has concerns, based on all of y'all's history. We want to put those to rest if we can."

Grace McKee shoved her fork into the potato salad. "Why is our private business any of yours, is what I'd like to know."

Calista leveled a look at her. "Liz represents my interests."

"Your *interests*?" Grace McKee scoffed. "All any of us ever did was tend to your interests. And what did we get for it?"

Calista drew back and raised a hand to her face.

Jim muttered something that sounded like, "Crackpot harpy."

My godmother tried to steer us toward a neutral topic. "Do you ladies know how to get your hydrangeas to come out blue?"

"Let's simmer down," Nate said.

Gladys looked bewildered. "This is such a nice lunch."

Grace McKee scowled at Gladys. "Is that all you care about? Lunch?"

"I just thought..." Gladys looked at me, then Calista. She seemed lost.

Jim said, "Heaven's sake, Grace, can you just act civilized for one meal?"

"Don't *you* dare start with me. If it hadn't been for you, Norma Jeane would never have left California. She'd be in her rightful place."

"And what is my rightful place?" Calista's voice was cool.

"Look at you." Grace drew back her shoulders. Her eyes widened and seemed to swirl, broadcasting that her remaining screws were coming loose. "All these years later, you look more like her than ever. You're fighting destiny, girl. You can't do that. You can't fight who you are. You were born to carry on Marilyn's legacy. You're a Monroe."

"Oh boy," Nate said.

Gladys said, "Grace, just eat your lunch and leave Calista alone." It was the most forceful thing she'd said so far.

Calista regarded her mother with a little smile.

Jim said, "That's what I'm saying. Good chicken salad." With apparent effort towards enthusiasm, he took a bite of a sandwich.

"You like the chicken salad so much, *have some more!*" Grace McKee flung her croissant down the table and beaned Jim in the head.

Nate, my godmother, and I inhaled sharply.

Jim stared at Grace McKee. "Didn't take long for you to drop your act, did it?"

"I don't have an act. You're the one playing all lovesick."

"I couldn't care less what you think, you crazy old witch. I love...Calista. My mistake was letting you call the shots way back when. If I hadn't listened to you, I might still be married to the woman I love."

Quietly, Gladys said, "It's all my fault."

"What is all your fault?" Calista asked.

"I should never have let her talk me into any of that fame nonsense," Gladys said. "It cost me my daughter."

Grace McKee was incensed. "Let *me* talk *you* into it? You're the one who thought you were related. You were every bit as excited as I was when she was born."

"Of course I was excited. I had a daughter."

"You couldn't stop talking about the date and time," Grace McKee said.

"Well, it was interesting, I thought," Gladys shrugged.

"Interesting?" Grace screeched. "*Interesting*? I'll *show* you *interesting.*" She grabbed a handful of potato salad and hurled it at Gladys.

For a few seconds, we watched it slide off Gladys's face.

Then everything happened at once.

Nate jumped up and headed around the table. "Okay, that's all—"

"Oh, my," said my godmother.

"What the—" I couldn't believe that nut had thrown food at Grace's beautiful table. I moved my chair back.

Grace said, "Sit still, darlin'. Let the menfolk handle this."

Jim said, "That does it." He pushed back his chair and rounded the table towards Grace McKee. But Gladys was closer than either of us. She put a hand behind Grace's head and smashed it into her plate.

Calista said, "Ms. Sullivan, I'm very sorry about this."

"Nonsense, dear," said Grace. "This is quite entertaining."

"That's the first time I ever remember Mother standing up to Grace," Calista said.

The two women smeared handfuls of food into each other's face, alternately caterwauling and cursing, until Nate and Jim separated them.

"Well," said my godmother, "she certainly did it in spectacular fashion."

Nate had ahold of Gladys. She drew close to him. Grace McKee struggled against Jim's none-too-gentle grasp.

Jim said, "I believe you've overstayed your welcome. In this nice lady's home, and certainly in our lives." He hauled her out onto the porch.

Gladys started to cry. Nate released her and she ran up the stairs.

I looked at my plate. Why hadn't they waited until I'd finished eating before they started the food fight?

My godmother sipped her tea. "I don't know about y'all, but I'm ready for dessert. I made a strawberry shortcake, and the berries are simply luscious."

Nate ran a hand through his hair. "That went well."

"One thing is clear," I said. "None of those three had a hand in trying to kill us last night. Their weapons of choice are on a whole nother level, and their violence of a more spontaneous nature. These folks aren't planners."

"Agreed," Nate said.

"None of them has the head for that sort of thing," Grace said.

"What else can you tell us?" I asked.

"I sense Mr. Davis and Ms. Monroe feel genuine remorse for the past, and would like to have Calista back in their lives in any way she'll go along with. That McKee woman is a fine piece of work. But she's mostly harmless."

"So who is playing all these tricks on me, if not them?" Calista asked. "Who killed poor Harmony and nearly killed the two of you last night?"

Grace's forehead creased. "Elizabeth and Nate will figure that out, I'm sure. But you are in danger. I'm certain of it. There's a dark-haired man in your past who thinks you owe him quite a lot of money."

TWENTY-THREE

After dessert—the strawberry shortcake was a divine combination of sweetened strawberries, freshly whipped cream, and buttery shortcake—Nate, Calista, and I helped Grace clean up the aftermath. Then Nate and I climbed into his rental.

I said, "The only people in this whole mess who appear anywhere near equipped to pull off a professional hit and commandeer a ferry are our friends at Security Solutions."

"You took the words right out of my mouth, Slugger. Shall we shake their tree and see what falls out?"

"Let's."

Nate and I stopped by the house to change and pick up stakeout essentials. I'd had Granddad's old landscaping van repaired and retrofitted in May. With its new tinted back windows, captain's chairs, and built-in desk, it made the perfect surveillance vehicle.

I packed the cooler with water, Diet Cheerwine, and sandwiches. For snacks, I grabbed nuts and trail mix bars. For stress, I snagged a bag of dark chocolate. Our swim the night before had me exercising an abundance of caution. I added an extra clip to the toys in my tote—my shiny new Taser, pepper spray, and telescopic steel baton. I checked Sig and snugged him into the holster on the waistband of my jeans. Everything else we'd conceivably need was stored in the van.

I flipped through my stack of magnetic door signs. "I'm thinking for the neighborhood we're headed to, caterers and pet groomers are out. Wanna be electricians, security system techs, or plumbers?"

"Security system techs," said Nate. "It's ironic."

It was almost five-thirty when I parked across the street from Security Solutions. I turned the engine off, and turned on the auxiliary camper air conditioner I'd had installed.

Nate said, "Now that's handy. We'd cook in here without it."

"It runs off a battery. We'll have to run the engine periodically to recharge it, or else plug in the extension cord somewhere."

"I've never done surveillance on a security company before. Feels strange."

"Yeah, it is a little weird. But I'm telling you, of all the people I've run across since I met Calista, the ones most equipped to pull off that stunt last night are inside that building."

"You don't have to convince me. They also know she's very wealthy, even if they don't know about the jackpot."

"That's the thing that bugs me. All their clients are ridiculously wealthy. And their reputation depends on keeping them safe."

"Only takes one guy who wakes up one morning and decides he wants to live that good life he's been guarding all this time. Figures he'll take the cash and disappear. He's not worried about the company's reputation anymore."

I raised my left eyebrow at him. "Isn't that the same thing I told you two hours ago?"

"Yeah, but arguing both sides must get exhausting. I figured it would help you out if I took one of 'em."

"It's a good thing you're easy on the eyes. I might be tempted to put you out on that sidewalk I could fry an egg on."

"Am I now?" He grinned.

"Don't be letting it go to your head. Conceit is most unattractive."

"I'll bear that in mind."

"Do you want the binoculars or would you rather run the tags?"

"Lady's choice."

"I'll run the tags. I can keep an eye on Calista at the same time. That's easier on my laptop than my iPhone. Camera is in the console." I slid out of the driver's seat and back to the desk. I initialized my hotspot and opened my laptop. According to both the cell phone tracking software and the pendant, Calista was at home.

For the next thirty minutes, Nate zoomed in on the license plates of every car in the Security Solutions parking lot and read them to me. One by one, I logged them and searched my subscription database for the car's owner. We could depend on the cars in SSI's lot being employee cars. Their clientele did not visit SSI's operational headquarters—SSI representatives went to them. And it was Saturday evening.

After we had a list of everyone in the building, I started on profiles. Mack Ryan wasn't on duty, but I profiled him as well. Everyone I checked was a former member of the military. Most were not married. None of them appeared to have ties to the community going back further than a few years. Unless some of them walked to work or carpooled, there was only one woman in the building.

At quarter 'til seven, Nate said, "Shift change. We just got the first arrival."

"Get a picture." I stopped typing and spun towards Nate.

Of course, he'd already framed the shot. He clicked away. "Every time we work a case together, I'm surprised anew that you let me wander around on my own. I'm concerned you don't hold my common sense in high regard."

I threw Nate a level two *oh puh-leeze* look, which was lost on him because he was snapping pictures. "You know that's not it."

"Really now? Because if that's not it, all we're left with is that you're a control freak."

I tried to look offended and failed. "I'm just dotting my i's."

"You have trust and control issues."

"It's possible I'm a bit of a type A personality. This isn't news to you, so quit acting all injured."

His voice was velvet. "We may have to work on your issues later. Perhaps I can help you, in the interest of your well-being, of course."

Something warm flowed through my core. I shook myself. "Nate. Would you stop distracting me? Did you get that guy's plate?"

"No," he said mildly. "I'm taking pictures of everyone who comes and goes. After all the cars are swapped out, I'll get the plates."

I was glad he was focused on folks across the street and couldn't see how flushed I must be given how hot my face felt. I downed half a can of Diet Cheerwine. "Good idea."

The corners of his mouth curled up. Had my voice quivered? Damnation, that man knew the effect he had on me. Stakeouts had developed a whole new dimension.

I turned back to the computer and tried to remember what I'd been doing. Right. Mack Ryan. He'd struck me as such a squared-away, Boy-Scout type. But his background was almost abnormally neat. I had the basics. Date of birth, social security number, home address, education—he'd graduated from The Citadel—and dates of military service.

He'd never been married. His credit was squeaky clean. He owned his house in West Ashley outright, no mortgage. He was only thirty-six. Private security must pay better than private detecting. Somehow, I'd've felt better if one thing about the man had been less than perfect.

Nate said, "Okay, Slugger. Ready for the next batch of plates?"

I flagged Mack for follow-up. His background smelled manufactured. "Ready when you are." I clicked back to the plate search window.

As I was running the third plate, my iPhone trumpeted the news that Calista had a text. Not surprisingly, her phone and text traffic had been light and unremarkable. I switched screens. "Hang on," I said to Nate.

The text was from Niles: *I know u had a trying day, dear one. R u all right?*

Calista replied: *I'm fine. Sweet of u 2 check.*

Niles: *Sorry I can't b there 2 pet u.*

Calista: *I understand. Hope all is well w/ u & Kyle.*

Niles: *Don't u worry abt me. I'll b fine. We just need 2 spend some time 2gether. C u 2morrow.*

"Oh, please," I said.

"What is it?" Nate asked.

"Just the yoga instructor. Fawning over Calista and making up with his boyfriend. It's nothing. Let me run that last plate."

As soon as I'd run all the plates from the second shift group, I put together basic profile data on them. I was running employment background checks when I found what I was looking for.

"Got you." I felt cold all over, as if someone had flash-frozen me.

"What did you find?" Nate slipped out the captain's chair and came to look over my shoulder.

"Ryder Keenan. He's ex-Charleston PD. That can't be a coincidence."

"Sounds like a porn star. Is that his real name?"

"I'm checking." I accessed four additional databases, piecing together Ryder Keenan's life. I had all the basics of his digital footprint, beginning with his birth certificate.

"Looks like," I said. "He was born in Summerville—his parents are still there, too. He's lived in the Charleston area his whole life. He worked for Charleston PD from two thousand two until two thousand eleven. Then he went to work for Security Solutions. He was on the job when the gun that killed Harmony was logged into the evidence room."

"That would be a remarkable coincidence."

"He has a wife and three kids. Damnation." I hated it when one person's greed and stupidity destroyed innocent family members' lives. I'd seen it all too often.

"Best have Blake contact Sonny."

"Let me run the rest of these names first."

"All right. But I think you have your man."

"So do I, dammit." What in the name of sweet reason made men who had everything throw it all away for money? I finished running the employment profiles. Marine. Army. Marine. Marine. "Hells bells."

"Well. What do you know about that?" Nate was still looking over my shoulder. The last name, Tim Poteat, was also an ex-Charleston police officer.

I finished outlining his background. "This guy grew up in Summerville, too. He went to high school there, anyway. I can't find his birth certificate. His military service records indicate he was born in Florida. That'll just take a little more digging. But, he also went to work for Charleston PD in two thousand two. Poteat left in two thousand ten, a year before Keenan. He was also still there when that gun went into the evidence room. At least he's not married."

"These guys have history together and with the Charleston PD. And they're working together now. Could be they're both involved."

"But how in hell are they connected to Calista?"

"I'd say by virtue of the fact they work for SSI."

I scrunched up my face. "When the life coach told Calista a dark-haired man from her past thought she owed him a lot of money, I didn't pay it any mind. I didn't know Harmony. I wrote her off as a scammer. But when Grace said the exact same thing..."

"You're thinking the connection preceded the security system contract?"

"Yeah. My instincts are screaming there's more to it. Also, I trust Grace."

"Let's have Calista take a look at the photos. See if she recognizes anyone."

I opened the pictures folder on my laptop. Photos taken with any of our cameras automatically uploaded via the cloud to our computers. "I want to look at these myself." I scanned the fourteen snapshots and cross-referenced the cars they were getting into or out of to pick Keenan and Poteat from the group. Ryder Keenan was walking away from a black Chevy Traverse. Tim Poteat's photo was by a silver Nissan 370Z.

"Sonavabitch." At seven o'clock on a July evening in the South Carolina lowcountry, it was still bright enough for sunglasses. "With those ball caps pulled low and the aviator sunglasses, they could be anyone. You can't even tell what color hair they have."

"Can't you pull their driver's license photos?"

"No, the system I use has data, but no photos. But Sonny can get us copies. There may be other photos of them online. I'll have to do some digging."

"If nothing else, we follow them until they take off the caps and sunglasses. Getting photos of them won't be hard. We know where they work, where they live, and what they drive."

"You're right. We need to talk to Sonny."

We were still operating under the assumption someone was watching and possibly listening to Sonny. Someone with access to better toys than us could have paired his phone. Nate and I kept the Bluetooth and Wi-Fi access turned off to prevent pairing. Out of an abundance of caution, I opened the Burner app on my iPhone, created a new phone number, and labeled it "Suzette."

With this app, I could create new numbers anytime and delete them when I was finished with them. Once deleted, it was as if the numbers never existed. This was more convenient than buying burner phones.

Sonny wasn't as enthusiastic about technology as I was. He'd bought a burner phone, and Blake had given me the number when I'd checked in earlier.

From my newly created number, I dialed Sonny's burner. He answered on the second ring and I immediately hung up. Ten minutes later I called back. By now, he should be someplace safe from eavesdropping. Just in case, we talked in code.

This time he answered on the first ring. "Yeah."

In the most seductive voice I could muster, I said, "Hey, Sonny. This is Suzette."

"Well, hello, hot stuff. How are you tonight?"

"It's Saturday night, and I'm all by myself. You want some company?"

"Sure doll face. You want to get a drink at The Blind Tiger?"

"That sounds divine. How about nine o'clock?"

"I'll be there. And Suzette?"

"Yeah, Sonny?"

"Don't wear any underpants."

I ended the call and burst out laughing.

Nate was not amused. "What was all that about?"

"I was just selling the pretext, Nate. So was he. If anyone was listening, they'll think he's meeting someone for a drink at The Blind Tiger, after which he's going to get lucky."

Nate gave me a level look. "Sonny's never been that lucky, has he?"

I laughed. "Oh, *puh-leeze*. Sonny's like a brother to me."

"See, I'm not so reassured by that since there was a time you might have said the same thing about me." His tone was teasing, but with a layer of something else.

I lowered my chin and sent him a smoldering look, full of promise. "Darlin' I have never, ever, considered you anything like a brother. Sonny's a friend. He's never been anything else."

"Uh-huh."

I slid into the driver's seat and started the engine. "Have you ever been to the Banana Cabana on Isle of Palms?"

"No. I thought we were meeting at The Blind Tiger over on Broad Street."

"So does anyone else who might have been listening. Blind Tiger is code for Banana Cabana." I turned onto East Bay.

"We're cutting it close to get to Isle of Palms by nine. It's quarter 'til."

"Nine means ten."

"When did y'all work all this out?"

"Blake and Sonny came up with it this afternoon. They figured we needed a way to call clandestine meetings. Came in handy."

"You gonna call Blake?"

"Would you? This van doesn't have Sync." I missed the voice-activated system in my Escape.

"As long as I don't have to seduce him."

TWENTY-FOUR

Blake, Sonny, Nate, and I huddled around a table on the far perimeter outside at the Banana Cabana. The guitar player was on break, so we could hear the surf.

The waitress brought a round of margaritas and we ordered shrimp and oysters to snack on. Then Nate and I told Sonny and Blake how two ex-Charleston police officers worked at SSI.

Sonny shook his head. "Why would a professional security guy be after this McQueen woman?"

I sipped my margarita. "She's worth a lot of money."

"This may be good news for me," he said. "I'd rather have ex-police officers after me than someone I depend on to watch my back. With missing evidence, you don't know who to trust. I hope you're right."

Blake said, "We don't have anywhere near enough to be sure. You still need to act as if anyone could be involved."

"Trust me," Sonny said. "I don't trust anyone except the people at this table right now."

"Are you staying someplace safe?" I asked.

"Yeah. I'm off the grid. Camping."

I asked, "So, do you know Ryder Keenan or Tim Poteat?"

Sonny nodded. "I know them both. Neither of them very well. Both had already been on the job a while when I started as a uniform. Couple years later, both of them were working undercover. Deep undercover. I never saw either of them after that. Couldn't tell you what kind of cases they worked. I don't remember Keenan leaving the force. But there was trouble with Poteat. Memory serves, he was fired over some kind of abuse of power complaint."

Nate asked, "Do you remember if they were friends?"

"Nah," Sonny said. "Like I said, I didn't know them that well."

"I don't guess you could access their files?" I asked.

"That would be a definite 'no,'" Sonny said. "It's not like on TV where I can chat up someone in HR and they'll slip me a file. That's a serious breach."

"Well, can you ask around?" I asked.

"Of course I'll ask around," he said. "Discreetly."

My phone alerted me that Calista was receiving a call. I picked up to listen. I didn't put the phone on speaker, but stepped away from the table so the guys could continue talking.

"Calista, I've just gotten in for the evening. I was concerned about you. You seemed overwrought this afternoon. Are you feeling better?" A man's voice. Not Niles. Not Jim.

"Dr. Gadsden," Calista said. "Thank you for checking on me. Yes, I thought a lot about what you said. I am feeling better."

Hells bells. A therapist that checked on patients after ten on Saturday night? I must have made a face.

"What's wrong?" Nate called.

I shook my head.

"It's best to allow only positive energy into your life. Don't let anyone disturb your peace of mind. Don't let them have that power over you," said Dr. Gadsden.

"I'll remember that," said Calista.

"Dear girl, I do wish you'd let Warren write you a prescription for something to help you sleep. It's important that you get proper rest," said Dr. Gadsden.

"I appreciate your concern. I'll have some herbal tea. It really does help. You know why I can't take pills," said Calista.

The doctor sighed. "Calista, we have got to work more on this obsession of yours. It is causing you to make inappropriate choices that can be harmful to you. Try to get some rest. I'll check on you tomorrow."

"Good night," Calista said.

"Oh," said Dr. Gadsden, "I need to move our Monday appointment to ten o'clock."

"That's fine. I'll let Elenore know to expect you."

"Good night, my dear." The doctor hung up.

Something about him made my skin itch. I'd never seen a therapist, but it was hard for me to imagine it was commonplace for them to call patients on the weekend absent some crisis.

Blake scowled at me. "Are you listening in on someone's phone conversation?"

I closed the app. "Not anymore."

"That's illegal, you know," Blake said.

"Not if she gives me her phone and I tell her what I'm installing. She's my client. I'm looking after her best interests." I wondered if that's what the good doctor was doing. "Did you get any fingerprints off that shopping list?"

Blake sighed loud and long. He shook his head. "None except Calista's and Elenore's. We printed them for elimination."

"Did you run Elenore's prints?" I asked.

"Why would I do that?" Blake asked.

"I don't know. She's just odd. She has a murky background. I didn't find anything incriminating—nothing I didn't already know—when I profiled her, but there are still some holes I can't fill," I said.

The waitress appeared with our shrimp and oysters.

I pulled out my hand sanitizer and slathered some on. I offered it around and got three sets of exasperated looks. "Fine. One of us has to stay healthy."

The waitress left and, while we served ourselves, Blake took the opportunity to lecture me. "If I ran the fingerprints of every odd person on Stella Maris, all I'd get done is running prints."

I tilted my head at him. "I know full well you don't do that yourself. You could have someone do it."

"Would you like me to get DNA samples as well?" Blake asked.

"That's a great idea. Why don't you swab Elenore, Niles, that therapist, Calista's crazy family—"

Nate said, "Slugger, your food's getting cold."

I gave him and Blake both a look of disapproval. Then I dipped an oyster in cocktail sauce and popped it in my mouth. I hadn't even finished chewing when my phone trumpeted again. I glanced at the screen. "Oh, for heaven's sake."

"What now?" Nate asked.

"It's just the yoga instructor checking in with her again."

"She still at home?" Nate asked.

I pulled up the GPS screen. "Yep."

"Since you're checking locations anyway—just dotting i's— where's Jim Davis?" Nate asked.

"Nate, he's harmless," I said.

Nate shrugged. "What's Harmless's current location?"

I tapped the screen a few times and pulled up the GPS tracker we had on Jim Davis's car. "Sonavabitch."

"What?" Nate and Blake spoke at once.

Sonny had a mouthful of shellfish. He gave me an inquiring look.

"He's at Calista's house," I said. "Probably parked out front just mooning over her."

"If he really is harmless, that may not be a bad thing. Another set of eyes," Blake said. "Do you want me to have Rodney run him off?"

I pondered that for a moment. Rodney was one of Blake's patrol officers. "No. Have Rodney drive by just to make sure he is parked across the street and not in her driveway. Nate and I will go by and speak to him on the way home."

Blake made the call. We polished off the food and said our goodnights.

At eleven forty-five, I pulled the van to a stop under a live oak in front of Jim's car. He was right where I thought he'd be. "Poor guy," I said. "He's pined after this woman a long time, and she's never going to want him again. You have to feel sorry for him, even if he is kinda stalking her."

Nate reached for the door handle.

I put my hand on his arm. "Let me talk to him. He needs a gentle touch right now."

Nate rolled the window down. "Holler if you need me."

I got out and walked towards the car. It was pitch black under that oak tree. Shadows danced around in the breeze. I approached the driver's side window. Jim was leaning against the door. Must have fallen asleep. I reached out to knock on the glass.

My hand stopped inches away. Blood covered the window and windshield. I stumbled backward.

Nate came out of the van. "What's wrong?"

"He's been shot."

A siren blasted from Calista's house. The alarm had been triggered.

I bolted towards the house. There was nothing we could do for Jim Davis. Nate's legs were longer. He got there first. He took the right side steps two at a time. I went round the left. Nate waited at the door. We drew our weapons. I tried the door. Locked.

"Calista!" I pounded on the door.

No response. I ran around the porch to her room. Nate followed. The blackout shades were drawn. I knocked on the glass. The siren continued to wail. By design, the house was impenetrable without codes and keys. There would be no picking locks and no knocking down these doors. Where the hell was Elenore? I ran around to the pool house calling to her over the shriek of the alarm. I pounded on the glass doors.

"Checking the other side of the porch," Nate said.

"Got it. Elenore!" I put my face to the glass. Movement inside.

Long seconds later, Elenore unlocked the door and slid it open. She was in pajamas and a robe, and appeared groggy. "What is the meaning of all this noise, Ms. Talbot?"

I gaped at her. Could she not hear the alarm? Was she holding me responsible for it? "The alarm's been set off. I can't get inside to check on Calista. Let me in—now."

She glared at me with open hostility. "One moment." She stepped away and came back a few seconds later with a set of keys. Unbelievably slowly, she weaved towards the house. Was she drunk?

I was hopping mad, and ready to snatch those keys away from her. It took her three excruciatingly clumsy tries to get the key in the lock. Finally, she opened the door to the great room and slid it open.

"Can you put in the code and kill that noise?" I shouted and didn't look back.

"Calista!" I ran towards her room.

In a pile of covers and pillows, she laid very still.

Thankfully, the siren stopped.

I ran to the bed. "Calista." I placed two fingers on her neck. Her pulse was strong. But she wasn't moving.

Nate came into the room. "I had to punch in the code for the housekeeper. She's snockered. What have we got?"

"She's alive, but not responsive. Call 911."

"Already done."

"Dammit, someone should have already been here in response to the alarm. Get me some water."

I sat on the bed and raised Calista's head. She was limp.

"I didn't hear a thing until you knocked on my door." Elenore appeared a few feet away.

"How is that possible?" I asked. "That screeching would've woke the dead."

She looked very unsteady on her feet. "I don't feel very well," she said. Then her knees buckled.

Nate set the water on the bedside table and caught Elenore just before she hit the floor. He eased her into a chair. "They've both been drugged. Whatever it was, Calista got more of it."

I patted Calista's face and wrists. I wet a corner of the sheet and dabbed at her face. Her eyes fluttered.

I shook her gently. "Calista, wake up."

She didn't rouse further.

"Did you see anyone—anything?" I asked Nate.

He shook his head grimly. "Nothing."

"Did you unlock the front door?"

"Yes. I'll see—"

Voices and the sound of fast moving feet announced the EMTs.

"In here," Nate called.

Two EMT's, Blake, and Rodney Murphy came spilling into the room.

I moved to let the EMTs take care of Calista. "She's been drugged. Mrs. Harper, too."

One of the EMTs went to check Elenore.

"Liz, brief me," Blake said.

I motioned towards the great room with my head. Blake, Nate, Rodney and I moved out of the bedroom.

"Jim Davis has been shot in his car out front," I said.

"Rodney, check it out," Blake said. He tapped a few buttons on his cellphone. "Coop. Wake up Sam and call Warren Harper. We've got a body in a late model Camry in front of the McQueen place."

"Did you get a call from the security company?" I asked Blake.

"No. Just the 911 call from Nate."

"I knew it," I said. "The audible alarm was going crazy. The monitoring service should've been alerted and called you immediately. In theory, one of their teams should show up here any minute. Someone inside that office is tampering with her system."

The EMTs rolled Calista out on a gurney. "We'll be right back for Mrs. Harper," one of them said.

"Where are you taking them?" I asked.

"East Cooper Medical Center."

I looked at Nate. "I'll go with Calista. You want to stay here in case Blake needs anything from us?"

Blake started to say something, then looked at Nate and shut up.

Love or something like it, fear, and frustration battled on Nate's face. Resigned, he nodded. "Watch your back."

"You do the same," I said. I wasn't any happier separating than he was. We were both safer together. I darted out of the room and headed for the van.

"Wait just a damn—" Blake hollered after me, then laid into Nate. "What the hell are you thinking? I depended on you to keep her here. She's got no business whatsoever running around by herself—"

Something else must have demanded Blake's attention. He had a crime scene to process.

TWENTY-FIVE

I hate hospitals. I'm afraid to breathe in them. People catch things in hospitals, sometimes worse things than what they came in with. I tried not to touch anything in the ER waiting room at East Cooper Medical. After what seemed like days, a nurse came out and told me Calista and Elenore were being admitted for observation. She gave me a room number for Calista and told me I could wait there—she'd be brought up shortly. I punched the elevator button with my elbow and held my breath for the ride.

I found the room and perched on the edge of a chair. Eventually, two nurse's aides rolled Calista in and moved her to the bed. She was so still.

"When can I speak to a doctor?" I asked, wondering when someone was going to ask me who exactly I was. I'd known going in that sooner or later I'd have to lie and say I was family. I had zero time to discuss HIPPA regulations.

One of the aides smiled. "Someone will be in shortly."

Shortly turned out to be forty-five minutes. An Asian woman, whose nametag read Dr. Sharma, came into the room. "Hello, you are with Ms. McQueen?"

"Yes. I found her, unresponsive, at home. Is she going to be all right?"

"Are you a member of her family?"

"Yes," I said. "I'm her sister."

"I see. Yes, Ms. McQueen should make a full recovery."

"Do you know what she ingested?"

"Yes. It was flunitrazepam. Rohypnol. You may have heard it referred to as the date-rape drug. It's unusual for us to get patients quickly enough to verify it was Rohypnol. It's only detectable in the blood for four hours. Longer in urine. But, most often in the patients we see, it's out of their systems."

"And Mrs. Harper...she had the same thing in her system? She's Calista's housekeeper. We're all the family she has." I gave her a look that added, *the poor thing.*

The doctor hesitated. "Yes, Mrs. Harper had the same drug in her system, though her symptoms were not as pronounced. It can affect people differently. Also, your sister had alcohol in her system. That dramatically increases Rohypnol's adverse effects."

"Thank you, doctor."

"You are very welcome. We'll just keep them both until they're fully alert and make sure there are no complications. The nurses will check on them periodically. If you need anything, press the button." She smiled and left the room.

I pulled out my iPhone and opened the app that monitored Calista's phone. She'd been fully alert when she spoke with the therapist. That had been at ten fifteen. When Niles texted her at ten forty-five, she never replied.

She'd told the therapist she was going to have tea. Had Elenore made tea for both of them? Had she spiked it, then drank a little herself to avoid suspicion? Possibly, but I didn't peg her as having shot Jim Davis. I had a bad feeling he was dead because of who he'd seen coming or going.

Calista stirred. "Liz?"

I jumped out of the chair and to the bedside. "Hey. How are you feeling?"

"Like I have a bad hangover. I only had one glass of wine."

"I thought you didn't drink."

"I told you I don't drink hard liquor. I do have wine occasionally, though not much of it. What happened? Where am I?"

"You're at East Cooper Medical Center. We had a hard time waking you up."

"I don't understand. Isn't it nighttime?"

I looked at my watch. "It's almost two-thirty in the morning."

"So why were you trying to wake me up to begin with?"

"What's the last thing you remember?"

"Ummph...." Calista screwed up her face. "I had a glass of wine to relax me. But I still felt wired. Mrs. Harper made us a pot of tea. We drank it together in the living room."

"Was anyone else there?"

"No. Just Mrs. Harper and me."

"Do you remember setting the alarm and going to bed?"

"No."

I'd tell her about Jim later. "Nate and I were driving by on our way home. We heard your alarm." I told her about waking Elenore to let us in. "I think Elenore must have had less tea than you did."

"No, we each had two cups."

"Did she have wine?"

"No. Mrs. Harper doesn't drink alcohol."

"Okay. Just rest. I'll be right here."

"Did someone poison our tea?"

"It looks that way."

"Is Mrs. Harper all right?"

"She'll be fine. Rest now."

Calista drifted back to sleep.

Did the wine account for Calista being that much more drugged than Elenore? Had someone else been there?

I needed to know Jim Davis's time of death. I couldn't think of a solitary reason why Elenore would go across the street and kill him. Unless maybe it was to keep him from mentioning that no one had come or gone. But how would she have known he was there to begin with?

And would she have been able to do such a thing after ingesting the Rohypnol? From what I knew about the drug, and the timeline of when Calista stopped responding to phone activity after she'd said they were going to have tea, it was fast-acting.

Who set off the alarm? Was it accidental? If not, why would anyone do that? Who turned the system on to begin with? So many questions swirled in my head. But one thing was clear. Elenore had made the tea. How could anyone else have poisoned it without her knowing? It would appear either she did it for her own reasons or at someone's instruction. Considering the professional scale of the other crimes committed, I was betting on the latter.

I needed to have a serious talk with Mack Ryan. I still didn't completely trust him. But I trusted him more than I trusted the rest of his team. If he was clean, he'd be just as interested in getting to the bottom of this as I was.

Bright sunlight spilled into the room when I jerked awake. I sat up straight and snatched my arms from the armrests. I pulled out my sanitizer and rubbed a thick layer on my hands and arms.

"You'll probably die from alcohol poisoning," Calista said. She was propped up on pillows and grinning at me.

"You're awake."

"Yes, but still a bit muddy-brained."

"How long have you been watching me sleep?"

"Just a few minutes."

"I just dozed off."

"You need to go home and get some rest."

"No, I need to stick with you. And we need to haul Mack Ryan in here and find out how his high-dollar system failed so miserably last night. Again."

"But you said the alarm went off."

"The audible alarm went off. But no one from the monitoring center responded. Something didn't work right, or Blake would've gotten a call, and one of SSI's teams would have been dispatched."

"Oh." Her eyes widened. "What were Mrs. Harper and I poisoned with?"

"Rohypnol."

"But neither of us were harmed. Why would someone knock us out just so we'd go to sleep?"

"That's one of several very good questions I don't have the answer to—yet. Have you remembered anything else?"

"No." She squared her shoulders. "Have you spoken to Jimmy, Grace, and my mother?"

My heart hurt. "Calista, there's something I haven't told you."

"What is it?" She bit her bottom lip.

"There's no easy way to say this. Jim Davis is dead. Nate and I found him in his car, parked across the street from your house just before the alarm went off."

She raised both hands to her face. "Jimmy? Why would anyone hurt Jimmy?"

"I suspect because he saw someone entering or leaving your house and could have identified him."

"Or maybe Grace killed him for spite after what happened yesterday at lunch."

"Do you suspect Grace knows how to handle a gun?"

"He was shot?"

Nate's voice came from the door of the room. "Actually, it looks like Jim committed suicide."

"What?" I said. "Do you have a time of death?"

"Preliminary estimate is between nine and eleven p.m."

I processed that. It didn't clear anyone.

"I don't believe it," said Calista.

Nate grimaced. "He left a note. It appears to be his handwriting. The gun was registered to him. The coroner won't make a final ruling until an autopsy is done, but his preliminary finding is that it's a suicide."

"What did the note say?" Calista asked.

Nate's eyes were compassionate, his voice gentle. "That he couldn't live without you anymore."

I said, "That doesn't make a lick of sense. He's lived without her for eighteen years."

Nate shrugged. "He was emotional yesterday."

"But not depressed," I said.

"I don't care what any report says. I'll never believe Jimmy killed himself," Calista said adamantly. "It just wasn't his nature. Whoever is trying to kill me killed him because he wanted to protect me."

"I think that's closer to the truth," I said.

"Let's see what the coroner's final report says," Nate said. "For right now, why don't you get some rest and let me stay with Calista a while."

Calista said, "Both of you should get some rest. No one is going to bother me here."

I shook my head. "I don't believe that for a minute. We're not leaving you alone again."

"Then you're going to need reinforcements. You have to sleep. You can't guard me twenty-four-seven."

I said, "The problem with that is the only private security company in the area with the type of personnel we need is SSI, and we can't trust them."

Nate said, "That's not exactly true. We don't trust two of them."

I nodded. "Let's get Mack Ryan in here."

Mack Ryan came quickly when Calista called, I'll give him that. Twenty minutes after she told him what had happened and where she was, he was standing in the room. He looked exactly the same as he had the day I'd met with him, right down to the black SSI logo shirt.

Calista sat quietly as Nate and I filled Mack in. When we finished, he turned to Calista. "Ms. McQueen, I'm deeply sorry. I'm sure you know this is not typical of our operation. If it were, we wouldn't stay in business long. We will provide around-the-clock personal security until this threat has been neutralized."

"I'd like that coordinated with Ms. Talbot," Calista said.

"Yes, ma'am." Mack nodded at her, then me.

"Neither Ryder Keenan nor Tim Poteat are coming anywhere near her," I said.

"They'll both be placed on administrative leave until we complete our investigation," said Mack.

"Are there any other former Charleston PD officers on your staff?" I asked.

Mack nodded. "One currently. And one that left our team a few months ago."

I said, "I'll need those names."

"Anything else?" Mack asked.

"Actually, I'd like a complete roster of all your current and prior employees. And I'd like to know Keenan and Poteat's movements last night," I said. "They were both on duty, and both inside your offices at eight-forty-five."

Mack nodded. "The motion detectors in Ms. McQueen's home did not activate the cameras. Our office did not receive an alert when the audible alarm sounded. However, we did receive a code yellow, indicating a malfunction with the equipment earlier in the evening. Keenan was dispatched to check it out at twenty-one hundred."

"He went alone?" I asked.

"Affirmative. He has a law enforcement background, but he's also technically skilled. It was efficient for him to go alone. We were aware of no threat. This left one response team and a watch supervisor available for other calls."

"Were there other calls?" I asked.

Mack wrinkled his forehead. "Affirmative. We had a call out on Kiawah Island. Motion detectors activated and a prowler was observed on camera. Team two was dispatched."

"Was Tim Poteat on team two?" Nate asked.

"No. He is Keenan's partner. He stayed at headquarters last night to serve as watch supervisor in case we needed to call in another team."

"Was anyone else called in?" I asked.

"No."

"So last night, Ryder Keenan went alone to Calista's home, and Tim Poteat never left the office?"

"That's correct," said Mack.

"What did Keenan report?"

"He checked the control panel, which is hidden and secured outside the residence so we can access it without disturbing our clients. He replaced a bad switch. He reported the perimeter secure at twenty-two thirty and came back to headquarters afterward. We were not aware anything was wrong until I received Ms. McQueen's call."

"Tell me about Ryder Keenan," I said.

"He's a family man. A straight arrow. I stand behind him one hundred percent. That said, we must follow protocol. I will make him available for questioning."

"And Tim Poteat?" I asked.

"Since Poteat didn't leave the office last night, my opinion, that clears him," said Mack. "If the local PD wants to question him as well, I'll see that he complies."

"And you're positive he couldn't have left without you knowing it?" Nate asked.

Mack grimaced. "I'm positive of very little. But technicians in the monitoring room spoke to him several times. It's highly unlikely he could have left undetected."

"How about this. I'd like headshots of your entire staff, plus the guy who left recently," I said.

"To what purpose?"

"To see if Calista recognizes any of them," I said.

Mack said, "But several of them have been to her home at various times. She is going to recognize them. What does that prove?"

"I want to know if she recognizes any of them from somewhere else." Between the first shift employees, the ones who would have been off the night before, and anyone on vacation, there were quite a few SSI employees we hadn't vetted. Not to mention the guy who recently left. Keenan might be our guy. He also might be the victim of a frame. I wasn't ready to pronounce Poteat or anyone else cleared at that point. A conspiracy among several of them was possible.

Calista said, "Mack, please give her whatever she needs."

Mack nodded once. "Very well."

TWENTY-SIX

Calista and Elenore were released just before noon on Sunday. Thankfully, Jim Davis's car had been removed by the time we arrived, sparing Calista that sight. Nate, Mack Ryan, and I searched the house together. Blake had removed the teapot and cups and taken them into evidence. Other than that, the house was undisturbed, the premises secure.

After a lengthy interview with three former Marines who'd been with Mack Ryan since he opened SSI, Nate, Calista, and I agreed they passed muster. The plan was for them to rotate shifts, with Nate and me dropping in unannounced periodically. With his reputation on the line, Mack would no doubt also be checking in. Nate and I went home and crashed.

We woke up just in time to shower, dress, and get to Mamma's house by six for Sunday dinner. Hand in hand, we walked towards the front door.

"I like your dress," Nate said.

"This old thing? I just threw something on." I'd been planning to wear that green-flowered sundress all week. It fit me just right, and the square neckline suggested things but didn't shout them. The lace around the hemline was feminine, the overall effect subtly sexy.

Nate grinned. "I'll enjoy helping you take it off later."

"Nate Andrews. When we leave here, we need to check on Calista."

"We will, Slugger. We'll tuck her in, look the Marine in the eyes, and then we can have some down time. It's been a rough weekend."

"Boy howdy." I smiled and reached for the door just as Mamma opened it.

"Liz, honey, I heard all about this incident on the ferry. Why on earth didn't you tell us what happened?" Mamma hugged me tight, then held me at arm's length and checked me over from one end to the other. "Are you all right?"

"I'm fine, Mamma. But I'm gonna kill my brother, straightaway."

"Now don't go off on Blake. He didn't tell me a thing. And I've had words with him as well. I heard all about it over at Phoebe's Day Spa." Mamma let go of me and grabbed ahold of Nate. "Darlin', it's so good to see you. I can't thank you enough for saving Liz from that horrible man."

I sighed deeply. "Mamma, how do you know I'm not the one who did the saving?"

"Well that's not what they were saying over at Phoebe's. Y'all come in the house. I'm just finishing dinner. Frank, get these children something to drink."

Daddy stirred from his chair. Chumley didn't get up, but woofed a hello.

Daddy said, "Nate, how about a Jack and Coke?"

Nate smiled. "Jack sounds good. Let's save the Coke for later."

"All right then." Daddy poured two fingers into a highball glass and handed it to Nate.

"Tutie, I've got Merlot open. Does that suit you?"

"Sounds good, Daddy."

"Your brother and sister are out in the screened porch. I can't think what for. It's hot as blazes outside." Daddy handed me a glass of wine.

"I'll see if Mamma needs help in the kitchen."

"Nate, have a seat," Daddy said.

I gave him a little smile over my shoulder and followed the smell of fried chicken into the kitchen. "If you could bottle that fragrance, you could make a billion dollars."

Mamma manned two cast iron skillets—one with chicken and one with okra. "Honey, would you slice a couple tomatoes? Grace gave me some from her garden, and they'll be good with this okra."

"Sure, Mamma." I went to the sink to wash my hands.

"So tell me about Nate."

"What about him?"

"Darlin', your makeup is perfect. I love that shade of lipstick on you, by the way. You haven't put on a dress with lace around the hem for Sunday dinner since I stopped dressing you myself. So tell me about Nate."

I smiled slyly.

Mamma looked at me and nodded. "That's what I thought. Are you sure about this? You sure had your heart set on Michael Devlin for a long time."

"I'm sure. Michael and I aren't the same people we were in college." I set to peeling and slicing tomatoes.

"You share a lot of history—a lot of common roots."

"It's just not there for us anymore, Mamma."

"The way I hear tell, that's not the way he sees it."

I tilted my head back and forth. "He'll come to see things my way."

Mamma looked at me sideways. "I just want you to be happy."

"I know, Mamma."

Mamma knocked on the window. "Merry Leigh? Come light the candles."

The back door opened and Merry and Blake stepped into the kitchen. Everybody said hey and all that. Merry went through the swinging door into the dining room.

I looked at Blake. "You get any sleep?"

"A little. You?"

"Enough."

He nodded. "I've got Ryder Keenan coming in tomorrow morning for an interview. Sonny's got eyes on him just in case."

"Seems like he would try to run if he's guilty—and I think he is," I said.

"Mack Ryan has personally vouched that Keenan will show up. I think he has people sitting on him, too. Ryan has a lot to lose."

"What time is he coming in?" I asked.

"No," Blake said.

"Give me one good reason why not?"

"Because this is an open police investigation and you are not a sworn officer. And because you'll talk all over the top of me, like you always do."

"I do no such thing."

"I will tell you everything he says. You can listen to the recording of the interview if you want to."

I was only slightly mollified.

Mamma piled the last few pieces of chicken on a platter. "Blake, take this into the dining room, would you?"

She scooped mashed potatoes into a bowl. "Liz, take these in with the tomatoes."

I followed Blake into the dining room. Mamma had outdone herself. The table was decked out in her best china, silver, and crystal. The wall sconces and chandelier were dimmed, and soft candlelight flickered from the table. An arrangement of fresh-cut hydrangeas in mixed colors spilled out of a porcelain pitcher.

Mamma was right behind me with a squash casserole and a gravy boat. "Blake, bring the biscuits. Frank, you and Nate come to dinner."

We all took our places, Mamma and Daddy at either end, Nate and me to Mamma's right, and Blake and Merry to her left. Mamma held out her hands and we all followed suit, joining hands for the blessing. Mamma returned thanks, making sure she worked in how grateful we all were that Nate and I had been spared on Friday night.

Then we all focused on passing food and piling it on our plates, which were really more the size of a typical platter. Mamma wouldn't have anyone going hungry at her table.

Nate said, "Mrs. Talbot, this looks fabulous. I can't remember the last time I had a home-cooked meal like this."

"Please call me Carolyn." Mamma smiled. "E-liz-a-beth Su-zanne Tal-bot, do you mean to tell me you haven't cooked this young man a proper dinner?"

Nate's eyes widened. His face froze in an alert expression one might see on a cornered rabbit. "Oh, yes ma'am. Liz is a great cook. But I can't talk her into frying chicken, now."

"Mamma, I save my calories for coming to your house. I cook lighter things through the week so I can splurge on your biscuits and gravy."

"Just don't be letting poor Nate go hungry because you're on some diet," Mamma cautioned. "A man has to have a good meal at the end of the day."

"Oh, I'm not going hungry." Nate bit into a piece of chicken, likely to avoid further discussion of my cooking talents.

I took pity on him. "Mamma, when are you and Daddy leaving on vacation?"

Blake chuckled and Merry grinned. I knew I'd stepped into something.

Merry said, "Napa Valley this year, right?"

Daddy grumbled under his breath.

"You can have wine shipped home. Make sure you stock up on Cabernets," Blake said.

Mamma sighed, "I've been wantin' to go to wine country for years. All of our friends have been."

"You're going for the harvest, right?" I asked.

"That was the plan," Mamma said. "I have everything arranged. I've spent hours planning our itinerary."

Daddy put down his fork. "Why do we have to chase those grapes all over California when we can sit right here and let them come to us? We can order any wine you want from the Internet. Every damn one of those wineries has a website. And I tell you something else—we can order a lot of wine for what those plane tickets cost alone."

Blake said, "Dad doesn't want to fly."

I looked at Mamma. "He always does this. You know he'll get on the plane. And he'll rave for months to everyone who'll listen about how much fun y'all had when you get back."

"*If* we get back," Daddy muttered.

"Frank, why do you insist on aggravating the fool out of me every time we plan a trip?"

I looked at her from under a raised eyebrow. Mamma well knew the answer to that question. We all did. Daddy aggravated her for sport. Apparently she enjoyed the game. She'd stayed married to him more than thirty years.

"Why don't you and the girls go out there. They'll like all those snooty restaurants you have picked out where they bring you two bites of a bunch of stuff, none of it recognizable."

"I'd like to have a nice romantic vacation with my husband." Mamma's voice dripped with icicles.

"Daddy, remember how much fun you had in Bermuda?" I asked.

"They have beaches there," Daddy said.

"For heaven's sake, Frank, we live at the beach." Mamma set down her fork.

This was going nowhere good. We needed to capture both their attention with anything else. I said, "Mamma, I meant to ask you. Do you remember Elenore Harper?"

Mamma drew back her chin. "Why, of course I remember Elenore Harper. Odd woman. Why do you ask?"

"She's working for a client of mine as a housekeeper."

"A housekeeper?" Mamma sounded incredulous. "Lauren will get a kick out of that. I hadn't heard anything about it. Last I heard of her, she'd gone back to Summerville." Lauren Harper, Warren's second wife, was in Mamma's Jazzercise class, Episcopal Church Women, Garden Club, et cetera.

"That's what Daddy said. I remembered her, but I didn't recall she'd moved back and forth so much," I said.

"She had another child with that man she was running around with, didn't she?" asked Merry. "I went to school with Jessica, Warren and Elenore's oldest child. Seems like there was a scandal."

"No," Mamma said. "What it was, they found out she had a child before she married Warren. Left him with family in Summerville. Hid him all those years. Then, when she and Warren divorced, she went back and got the little boy."

"Crazy woman screwed up four children's lives," Daddy muttered. "Blake, pass the biscuits. Where'd that gravy get to?"

Something tickled the back of my brain. The only birth records I'd found while doing Elenore's profile were hers and the ones for her three children with Warren.

Merry passed the gravy around. "So Liz, are you okay with me taking the kids camping as soon as the weather breaks?" Merry worked with at-risk teenagers. She'd asked to take them camping on the property I'd inherited from Gram.

"Of course. There's three hundred acres of woods and a beach. Use it anytime you like. Maybe I'll come roast marshmallows with you."

Blake snorted. "Merry, have you ever camped in your life?"

Merry raised her nose. "I certainly have."

"When?" Blake challenged.

"You can't count when we went to summer camp," I said. "We had cabins."

Merry said, "How hard can it be?"

We all looked at her.

Mamma said, "Blake will help you. That's what brothers do." She smiled at Blake.

Nate said, "I can help out. I know how to put up a tent."

"Thank you Nate," Merry said. "*You* are a gentleman."

"Maybe Liz and I will join you," he said.

My family burst out laughing.

Nate said, "I'm trying to help her overcome some of her phobias."

Mamma shook her head, "Bless your heart." She patted him on the hand. "Honey, you have a neurotic tiger by the tail."

"I don't think I have a grip at all."

I regarded him from under my eyebrows. "When you're all finished making fun of how I avoid germs, snakes, spiders, and mosquitoes—all things that can kill you, mind you—shall I bring in dessert?"

"What's for dessert, Carolyn?" Daddy asked.

"Chocolate cake. But you're not getting any." Mamma stood and cleared her place. She glided into the kitchen.

"Oh for heaven's sake, Carolyn. You know I'll get on the damn plane."

TWENTY-SEVEN

True to his word, Mack Ryan had a stack of photos delivered to my house bright and early Monday morning, along with a full list of all current and former SSI employees.

I sat at my desk and flipped through them while finishing my coffee. They were labeled with names, all former Charleston police officers flagged. None of the men were smiling. These headshots looked like military service photos. But nothing about Ryder Keenan, Tim Poteat, or the other two former police officers screamed, "I'm a psycho."

"I'm going to take these over to Calista's," I said. "Why don't you check in with Blake?"

"That innocent tone doesn't fool me any more than it would him. You want me to crash the party with Ryder Keenan," Nate said.

"Of course I do. Two sets of eyes, and all that."

"I'm not eager to antagonize your brother."

"Trust me. He'll be so happy *not* to see me, who he fully expects to show up contrary to his instructions, that he'll do a little dance when he sees you."

Nate looked skeptical.

"Okay, maybe not dance. But he'll get Nell to bring you coffee."

"Fine," Nate said. "But if he asks me to leave, I'm leaving."

I had a ton of work to do that morning. I wanted to comb through all the profiles I'd compiled on the case, profile the new names I'd just gotten, reread my notes, and work on a few puzzle pieces that nagged me—like Elenore's mystery child and the way several players had a Summerville connection and. But Dr. Gadsden was due at Calista's at ten, and I needed her to look at the stack of photos Mack had sent before Gadsden arrived. Also, his relationship with Calista smacked of unhealthy. I wanted to lay eyes on him.

A man roughly the size of a small mountain stood guard by the front door. In aviator sunglasses and ball cap, he might have been any one of the three Marines we'd interviewed. He nodded good morning.

Elenore was marginally more civil than usual when she let me in. "Good morning."

"Good morning, Elenore. How are you feeling?"

"Much better, thank you. Ms. Talbot, I appreciate your coming to our rescue Saturday night. I'm afraid to speculate what might have happened otherwise. Surely someone knocked us out for a reason, and you intervened before anything worse happened."

I smiled at her. "You're welcome. Have you remembered anything that happened after you and Calista had tea?" Did she know she was my number one suspect in the Rohypnol incident?

"I'm afraid not. This way, please." She led me into the great room.

Calista was curled into the corner of the white sectional, a pillow hugged to her chest. "Liz. Would you like some coffee?"

"I've had plenty, thanks. I have the photos Mack Ryan sent. I'm hoping you recognize one of these men from somewhere in your past." I handed her the folder and took a seat.

Slowly, she flipped through the pictures. "They don't look happy, do they?"

"I think it's a military thing. They encourage you to look threatening for photos."

Calista studied the last photo. "There are thirty-five of them. Somehow I imagined an army." She handed me the folder. "I don't remember any of them from before the security system was installed here."

I sighed. "Would you mind taking another look?"

"Not at all." She looked through them again, slower this time. She shrugged and handed me the folder. "If I've ever seen any of them before, I don't recognize them."

"It was worth a try." I studied her for a moment. "You're meeting with Dr. Gadsden at ten?"

Calista glanced at her watch. "Yes. He should be here any minute."

"I tried to talk to him, but his receptionist wouldn't make an appointment."

"I can talk to him and ask him to speak to you," she said.

"I'd like to try something else."

"Okay."

"I want to hear how he treats you, without him knowing."

"You want to listen on a session?"

"Exactly. I know it's an invasion of your privacy, but that's the fastest way for me to understand his intentions."

Calista stared out the window and bit her lower lip. "I guess it would be okay. How do you want to do it?"

"Where do you typically meet?"

"Sometimes outside. But on hot days like today, right here."

"Okay. When the doorbell rings, I'll call your phone. Answer it, press the home button to change the screen, and lay it on the coffee table before you answer the door. I'll wait in the guestroom, and listen through the open call."

She looked queasy.

I reached out and touched her arm. "Anytime you feel uncomfortable, pick up the phone—pretend you have a text or something—touch the green bar at the top to bring the call back up on the screen, and hang up."

"All right."

The doorbell rang.

Calista said, "Liz, there are one or two things I haven't told you."

Dread washed over me. "Really? I mean…"

"Maybe this is for the best. Some things are hard for me to talk about."

What more could there possibly be? "Calista—"

"Mrs. Harper will be showing him in any second."

Dashing towards the guest room, I tapped her name to place the call. I closed the door and stretched out on the lounge by the sliding doors. Then I popped in my earbuds so I could hear better.

"Dr. Gadsden has arrived." I imagined Elenore's surprise when she didn't see me in the room. At that moment, I was thankful she was less than chatty.

Calista said, "Good morning, Doctor Gadsden."

"Calista, dear one. Warren told me about your scare Saturday night. Naturally, we're both quite concerned."

"I guess it's a good thing I wasn't taking sleeping pills," Calista said. "The combination might have killed me."

The doctor was quiet for a moment. "Indeed."

"And poor Jimmy…. I used to think he meant to kill me, but after he stuck up for me with Grace, I don't think he was part of that at all."

"Do the police have any leads?"

"None that I'm aware of. They're saying Jimmy killed himself, but I don't believe it."

"I see you have protection posted outside. Is he one of SSI's men?"

"Yes."

"That's smart. This is a small town. Law enforcement here is not what it is in larger cities."

"And yet, the crime rate is much lower," Calista said. "Odd, isn't it?"

I smiled. I liked my client more all the time. If we both lived through the week, we might be best of friends.

"Yes, well. Err on the side of caution." The doctor cleared his throat. "Now, dear one, tell me, how are you handling Jim's death?"

"I feel bad for him and his family. I'm angry someone killed him because of me. I'm sad he's dead. But I'm not falling apart, if that's what you're asking."

"Good, good. It's tragic, of course. But you're not responsible for what happened to Jim. You understand that, right?"

"No, actually. I think it was directly because he was trying to look out for me. That's what got him killed." Calista sounded agitated.

"You don't still suspect your mother and Ms. McKee of trying to kill you on Saturday, do you?"

Silence.

Dr. Gadsden said, "Leaving everything else aside, do you suppose they're capable of the kind of planning such a thing would require? All these dog barking and pill incidents...those things would seem beyond the skill level of the women you've described to me. Frankly, I was amazed they drove across the country. Of course, I've never met them."

"Never underestimate Grace McKee. I do think mother has been her pawn. I don't think mother means me harm. But you'll never convince me Grace isn't still trying to cash in on the coincidence of my birth and looks."

I wondered briefly if Calista's looks were simply a coincidence. As far as I knew, no one had ever established to a certainty who Marilyn's father was. Wouldn't it be something if Calista was distantly related?

"Calista, you must let go of this obsession," said Dr. Gadsden. "It isn't healthy. And what's more, it's dangerous. It prevents you from being alert to very real dangers."

"Oh, I have people looking into other possibilities."

"Really?" The doctor sounded affronted. "What do you mean?"

"I mean, I hire people to take care of things. You take care of my emotional issues. Elenore takes care of the house. I have an attorney for legal matters. And I have people looking into who might want to hurt me."

"You mean SSI?"

"Yes, of course."

I wondered why Calista chose not to mention me. Was she having doubts about the good doctor?

"I wonder if I should have a talk with them on your behalf."

"Whatever for?" Calista asked.

"To save you that difficulty, of course."

"That won't be necessary." Calista's voice sounded stiff.

"Don't be silly, dear girl. Why deal with these muscle-bound mercenaries yourself? Much more suitable if I do it."

"Dr. Gadsden, really—"

"In fact, now that I've given it some thought, I think it would be best if you came and stayed with me. My wife is in New York at the moment, but the staff is in residence, so everything would be quite proper, I assure you—"

"That's kind, but no," Calista said firmly. "I'm staying right here."

"Well..." The doctor sounded petulant. "I can certainly recommend any other professional services you might need. Call me any time you need me—day or night. After all you've been through, it's important that you know you have one person you can always rely on. And I wouldn't want you to trust the wrong people."

This guy was giving me the willies. Even I knew he was overly solicitous to the point of pathology. Or perhaps criminal intent.

"Thank you, Doctor Gadsden," said Calista. "I do rely on you."

"Very good. Now, tell me, are the nightmares any better?"

I heard rustling, as if Calista were shifting on the sofa, adjusting pillows and throws. "Not really. I had a really bad one last night."

"Tell me about it."

Silence. Then, "He was here, in this house. Not the one in West Ashley."

"I see. What happened in the dream?"

"He tied me up on the bed, exactly the same way he did two years ago in West Ashley. The same way he does in every dream. The only difference is it happened here."

"And then..."

"He stole everything—electronics, jewelry, everything he could carry off."

"Did he hurt you?"

Calista's voice was tight. "No, Doctor. He didn't...molest me. Not in the dream, not two years ago. I would have told you that by now. I'm not hiding anything. But what he did was bad enough. I thought he was going to kill me. He terrorized me for hours. He taunted me without saying a word while he ransacked my house, and he left me tied to the bed. Only in the dream last night, instead of the police, it was Niles who found me."

I was frozen with shock. This was what she hadn't told me. She'd been attacked. Tied up and left for—how long?

"The yoga instructor?" asked Dr. Gadsden.

"Yes."

"Do you see him as your savior?"

"I see him as a friend. I don't have many friends."

"But he's an employee."

"That's true. But he's also a friend. Like you are."

The doctor cleared his throat. "I just want you to be careful who you rely on. You're very vulnerable right now."

"And I'm very careful, Doctor."

"Very well. When you woke up from the dream, were you able to go back to sleep?"

"No. But it was five o'clock. I got up and watched the sunrise."

"You're simply not getting enough rest. If you won't consider pills, how about an injection? I can control the dose very carefully. There's no way you could overdose."

"Absolutely not." Calista's voice rose.

"All right, dear. Calm down."

"Doctor, I'm very sorry, but I have to speak with the authorities this morning. I'm afraid we're going to have to cut this meeting short."

"I don't think that's a good idea. Can't you give your statement this afternoon?"

"No."

Silence. The doctor made a few blustery noises. "Then I think we should meet again tomorrow. What time is good for you?"

"Let's just meet again on Wednesday for our regular eleven o'clock."

"I don't recommend that."

"I'm sorry, Doctor Gadsden. I'm sure you understand. This week is going to be very busy for me. I have to arrange for Jimmy to be sent home to his mother."

"Why does that fall to you, for heaven's sake?"

"Because I volunteered to do it."

"But why—"

"Doctor Gadsden, please excuse me. I must get ready for my day."

He sighed so loud the phone picked it up. "Very well. I'll see you on Wednesday."

I heard footsteps.

After a moment, Calista said, "He's gone, Liz."

I ended the call and rejoined her in the great room.

She'd built a wall of pillows and throws around her, and she hugged the biggest pillow tightly. Tears slipped down her cheeks. "Now you know everything."

I sat beside her and pulled her in for a hug. She hooked an arm under mine and put her head on my shoulder. She cried and I let her. "I'm sorry I didn't tell you before," she said through delicate sobs. "It can't be related. It was a random burglary. I happened to be home. They never caught him. It was...horrible."

"Shh." I continued holding her until she pulled away.

She wiped her eyes. "I'm such a mess."

I couldn't help but smile, but I felt it collapse almost as quickly as it formed. "Sweetie, you're gorgeous even with red eyes."

"You're not mad at me?"

"Of course not. But do you mind if I ask you a few questions? Are you up to it?"

She shrugged. "Sure."

"When did this happen? I didn't find any record of it."

"It happened the same night Joey was killed. That's part of what makes it so awful. The police found me tied to the bed the next morning when they came to tell me Joey was dead. By then, I was worried sick because he hadn't come home, and terrified no one would find me. They knocked on the door and I screamed and screamed. The burglar left the door unlocked. They came inside and...it was the most awful day of my life."

"Did you file a report?"

"No. I couldn't. I had a funeral to plan. The police officers were very kind to me. I think they must have felt sorry for me. I refused to report the burglary or the assault. They tried to get me to, at first. Burglaries aren't a high priority, but there had been two others in the neighborhood. But I was a mess. Finally, they left me alone. I couldn't even talk about being tied up and left like that. That's when I started seeing Doctor Gadsden."

"Did you see the guy who attacked you?"

"No. He wore a ski mask."

"Was their anything familiar about his voice?"

"He never said a single word. So you see, I couldn't identify him. Why put myself through talking about it to strangers when there was no hope of catching him?"

"How did he get in?"

"He came in through the front door. He must have picked the lock because the door wasn't forced. I was in the shower. I never even heard him until he was in the bathroom with me. He pushed back the shower curtain, grabbed me and tied me to the bed. I kicked and fought. But he was too strong. He gagged me. And then started going through our things, looking for valuables. Before he left, he held a knife to my throat and stared at me for the longest time. He took the gag out and kept the knife to my throat. It's like he was warning me not to scream. It was senseless. We didn't own a thing worth all of that."

"What did he take from your house?"

"Everything he could carry. He tore the place apart. It's like he was trying to destroy what he couldn't take. He was very angry."

My brain vibrated. "Calista, was this before, or after, you claimed the lottery prize?"

"Before. *I* didn't even know about the money, so no one else did, that's certain."

"Did anyone else know the numbers Joe played?"

Calista shrugged. "It's possible, I guess."

I pondered that for a moment. As motives go, seven hundred million dollars was a humdinger. If someone had known the numbers, he might have carjacked a man to get the ticket. And once he'd killed that man, he might believe the widow owed him the jackpot. It felt like I was on to something solid.

Gently, I said, "I think maybe your burglar did know. Maybe he was looking for the lottery ticket. I'll bet you he killed Joe for that ticket. Where was it?"

Calista sat up straight, her eyes round. "It was inside his lucky cap. Normally, he kept them in his wallet. But I'd gotten him a new wallet a few days before. He'd started putting them in his ball cap for luck, he said. I thought they didn't fit in the new wallet without folding or something, but he didn't want to hurt my feelings."

"I don't think that carjacker killed Joe for eleven dollars and change or a ride in his Cadillac. I think he killed him for that lottery ticket, and when he didn't find it on Joe, he came looking for it at your house. Your address would have been on the car registration. And the burglar would've had Joe's keys."

"That's why he trashed the place. And that's why he was so angry. But why wouldn't he ask me where it was?"

"That would've been too risky."

"I don't understand."

"If he'd asked you where the ticket was, and you didn't know, and he'd let you live, you'd have known what he was after and reported it. Then there would've been a much higher probability of him getting caught. They would have tied him to Joe's murder. But, he couldn't kill you if you didn't know where it was. With you dead, he wouldn't have known what would happen to the money. If he'd found the ticket, he would've killed you. But without the ticket in his hand, he needed you alive to claim the prize so he could come back later and get the money."

"Joey was wearing the ball cap. He had the ticket. The police returned it to me with his personal effects that had no value as evidence. I found it by accident. I was wearing the cap around the house. I felt something in there. The only reason I even checked the numbers is because it was on the news that the winning ticket had been sold at the mini-mart near our house, but the prize hadn't been claimed. The first thing I did was call an attorney who specializes in lottery winners."

"That was smart."

"I can't believe it. But I do. It never made sense to me why anyone would carjack a minor league baseball coach. Why not some lawyer or banker driving a Mercedes? This makes perfect sense. He was looking for the ticket."

"Not only do I believe he was looking for that ticket, I think he's still looking for the money."

TWENTY-EIGHT

While Blake and Nate interviewed Ryder Keenan that Monday morning, the Charleston Police Department executed a search warrant on his house. They found Rohypnol, a jacket splattered with blood which was a type-match for Jim Davis, and the gun used to kill Harmony. Keenan swore it was all planted. That was all he said before he lawyered up. Sonny and Blake were convinced he was guilty. Me, not so much.

Mack Ryan was busy doing damage control. He had one team at Calista's house all Monday afternoon testing equipment, and another going through logs at SSI offices. Her round-the-clock security was still in force.

Tuesday morning, Nate and I splurged and went to the Cracked Pot for breakfast. We ran an extra three miles to make up for what I planned on eating. I might have had other motives for suggesting we go out. Moon Unit Glendawn was a great source of island information.

"Well, good morning, y'all," Moon Unit called from behind the counter. "Sit anywhere you like. I'll be right over."

"Let's snag that back booth," I said.

The bells jangled behind us, announcing more arrivals. We hustled to the only empty booth and slid in quickly. Nate picked up a menu.

"I know what I want," I said. I could already taste the red eye gravy and biscuits.

"I think I'll have what you're having. Locals always know the menu best."

I reached for his hand. "It won't take long for you to feel like a local."

His expression was unreadable.

Moon Unit appeared by the table. "Hey, sweetie. My, my, what do we have here?" She looked Nate over like she could just eat him up with a spoon.

I said, "Moon Unit, have you not met Nate?"

Nate said, "I don't believe I've had the pleasure. Nate Andrews." He offered Moon Unit a hand.

She took it and held on. "Nate *Andrews*." She looked at me.

"Yes," I said. "He's Scott's brother. They are nothing alike."

"Well, of course *not*." Moon dragged the word into three syllables. "I'm so sorry for your family's misfortune."

"Thank you," Nate said. He gave me a look that screamed *make it stop.*

I said, "Moon Unit we are starving. We ran nearly ten miles this morning. I'd like scrambled eggs with cheese, country ham, grits, and biscuits with red eye."

"Sweetie, I know what chu want for breakfast, right down to ice in your orange juice and Splenda and cream in your coffee." She turned to Nate. "What would you like, darlin'?"

"I'd like the same, except eggs over easy, please."

"Coming right up." She whirled away.

"She's energetic," Nate said.

I laughed. "That's one way to put it. She's harmless. We've been friends since high school."

Nate raised his eyebrows.

Moon Unit set down two mugs, a pot of coffee, a ramekin of sweetener packets, and a small pitcher of cream. "I can't hardly believe we've got us another dead body on our hands, can y'all?"

"It's a tragedy," I said.

"Hard to believe," Nate murmured.

Moon picked up the coffee pot and poured. She shook her head, "Mmm, mmm, mmm."

"Moon, how well do you know Elenore Harper?" I asked.

She screwed up her face. "She's an odd duck. Not well. I doubt anyone does. I can't think what possessed Warren to marry her. Him being a doctor and all. Lauren is a much better fit for him. She's just the sweetest—"

I said, "Did you ever meet Elenore's oldest child?"

"That boy? I met him a time or two. You know she kept moving back and leaving, moving back and leaving. He was a year or so older than us. What was his name? She consulted the ceiling. "It'll come to me." She rushed off to greet someone else.

Nate tilted his head at me. "Did we come here so you could pump her?"

I reached for an innocent look. "I came for country ham, biscuits, and gravy."

"Nate and Sonny are convinced they have the right guy."

"It feels too neat. I'll have to tie him to that lottery ticket before I buy it. And someone needs to explain how the Rohypnol got into the tea. What was your read on him? From the interview?"

Nate shrugged. "He didn't seem the type. My instincts would've pegged him for innocent. But my instincts aren't admissible in court, and all that evidence is."

"Did he have an alibi for Friday night?"

"By the time we got to that question, he was under arrest and had lawyered up. He's not answering any more questions."

"This smells like a frame to me," I said.

"Liz, let it go. Two jurisdictions of police departments are working this case. Calista has around the clock security. There's strong evidence against Keenan, who was one of your prime suspects just yesterday."

"I know, I know."

"Then relax. Let's go for a swim later. The temperature's down to something below broil. How about a beach day?"

I winced. I still had too many loose ends.

"After we build a sand castle, we can wash the sand off each other..." Nate smiled wickedly.

"How about a compromise?"

"And that would be?"

"After breakfast, I can work for two hours wrapping things up so I feel comfortable. Then we'll have lunch and spend the afternoon on the beach."

"And then I can wash the sand off of you?"

"Why, naturally." I offered him my sultriest smile.

"Deal."

Moon Unit delivered our breakfast. "I'm still thinking on it. Seems like he had two first names." She whirled and was gone.

I needed to figure out what to do about Dr. Gadsden. Calista remained unconvinced that his relationship with her was inappropriate. Because I worked for her, I couldn't call up whatever agency regulated therapists and file a report. My loyalty was to her, but that also meant protecting her from unscrupulous headshrinkers. I'd have to deal with him later—find a way to convince her.

I zeroed in on Ryder Keenan, digging deeper into his background. Except for the fact he was in debt over his head, there were no red flags. And a lot of people in this country had debt. I called Mack Ryan, and he told me Keenan had been off Friday night. So he could've been the guy on the ferry.

But he wasn't Elenore's love child. His family was from Summerville, but they'd lived there for several generations, and his parents were still married to each other.

I dug around for a birth certificate with Elenore's maiden name—Causby—but still couldn't find birth records for any children of hers except her three children with Warren. Her older son must've been born out of state. My databases accessed all fifty states, but the information available varied from state to state, as did the search criteria and the completeness of information. This would take more time.

Then I started fleshing out Joe Fernandez's profile, looking for any connection who might have known about the lottery numbers. But that's not the kind of information stored in databases. I searched the archives of the *Post and Courier* and read everything they'd printed about Joe's death. There was nothing about the burglary or Calista's attack. And not a word about that lottery jackpot after the one mention of the unclaimed prize. Calista's advisors had done a good job of keeping her anonymous.

I needed to talk to the staff at the mini-mart, though I realized it was unlikely the same clerks would be there several years later. That type of job was not exactly a long-term career. I was just about to shut the archive window down when a headline caught my eye: *Convenience Store Clerk Missing.*

I read the article three times.

I called Calista. "Did you know the clerk who sold Joe the winning Powerball ticket disappeared the same night Joe was killed?"

She inhaled sharply. "I had no idea. I was in sort of a state for months after Joey died and...the burglary. The law firm I hired claimed the prize for me, but that was more than a month later. They never mentioned anything about the clerk going missing. Do you think he did it? He could easily have remembered the numbers. Joe bought tickets at the same store every time."

"I don't know yet," I said. "If so, he's not acting alone. He could be in on it—part of a conspiracy. It's either that, or someone made him disappear because he knew whose numbers those were. Is your Marine on duty?"

"Yes. I've invited him in for lemonade."

"Calista, send him right back outside. I don't think we're in the clear yet. Someone needs to be on guard."

"All right."

A quick call to Sonny verified my suspicion. Roy Lee Jenkins had never been found.

Nate held me to my deal, even after I told him about Roy Lee Jenkins. He was not swayed by my concern for poor Roy Lee's mamma, who had never found out what happened to her only son.

"Liz, you can't make everything all right for everybody," Nate said. He said this to me a lot.

Finally I gave in. Nate can be very persuasive when he sets his mind to it. We spent Tuesday afternoon and evening frolicking outdoors and in. It was fun—we kept things light. Maybe too light to suit me. There was a pall over my happiness. It was unusual for Nate and me to disagree on a case. He might think this one was solved. But every instinct I possessed screamed it wasn't.

TWENTY-NINE

Early Wednesday, I headed over to West Ashley. The clerk at the Mini Mart on Sam Rittenberg was busy, so I browsed until the crowd thinned. By that time he was eying me like maybe I was casing the joint.

I approached the counter with my Diet Cheerwine slowly, smiling. His nametag labeled him as Boone. I showed Boone my PI license. That seemed to calm his nerves.

"Boone, were you working here a few years ago when someone bought that big lottery ticket?"

"No ma'am. I ain't worked here but three months."

"Do you know anyone who was working here then?"

"Prolly the manager was. His name is Mister Patel."

"Does Mister Patel come in today?"

"Yes, ma'am. He'll be in at ten. He's real prompt."

I nodded. "Good to know. Boone, if it's okay with you, I'll just pay for my Cheerwine, and wait in my car for Mister Patel."

He shrugged. "Well, sure, okay." He rang me up.

At five minutes to ten, a gentleman arrived and walked behind the counter. Boone pointed at me and was explaining all about me when I walked back into the store.

"Good morning," I said.

"Good morning," said Mr. Patel. "How may I help you?"

I asked if he had managed the store when the big lottery ticket was sold.

"Oh, yes ma'am. Very exciting. The store won a prize, too, for selling the ticket."

"Do you remember the gentleman who sold the ticket? Roy Lee Jenkins?"

"Yes, yes. I don't know what happened to him. He left work one night and disappeared. His mother reported him missing. I checked with the police several times. I don't think they ever found him."

"Was he unreliable? The type to maybe just quit and leave town and not say anything?"

"Oh, no ma'am. He was very conscientious. Came in early for his shifts. He was always available to take an extra shift if someone called in sick. Ehh...he was a little strange—very, very quiet. Hard to engage in conversation. But he was polite to the customers. He was a good employee."

For Roy Lee's sake, I'd been hoping to hear he'd wandered off before. "Mr. Patel, do you have cameras in the store?" I could clearly see that he had several.

"Yes."

"Do you tape the feeds?"

"Yes. But the tapes are reused every thirty days."

Damnation.

"Unless there's a reason to keep them." He smiled.

"Did you keep the tape from the night the big ticket was sold?"

"Yes, that one we kept."

"Did the police ever ask you for it? After Roy Lee disappeared?"

"No. I thought they might, but no one ever asked to see it. There were many crimes to solve—murders, gang activities, drugs. In a tourist town, it is important to make people feel safe. The police were very, very busy. There was no evidence Roy Lee was a victim of a crime. I suspect they thought Roy Lee simply left town. His mother made a very big disturbance with the police department. One of the police officers thought he left to get away from her."

"May I see the tape?"

He hesitated. "Are you searching for Roy Lee?"

I decided to keep things simple. "Yes."

"The man who won all the money. Did he ever get it? It was very strange. We never heard. Usually there's a big ceremony."

"The prize was claimed." I offered him my sunniest smile. "Is the tape here?"

"Well, it is a DVD. High tech. No, it's in storage. I can find it for you. It may take a day or two."

I sighed and swallowed my impatience. Pushing my luck wasn't smart. Nothing said Mr. Patel had to give me the time of day, much less a DVD. "Thank you so much." I pulled out a business card. "Would you call me when you find it?"

"Surely." He nodded several times.

"Thank you. It's very important. I really do appreciate your help."

"You are very welcome." He smiled and nodded.

I smiled and waved. "Bye now."

We continued smiling, him nodding and me waving, until I was out the door.

I had an early lunch at The Blind Tiger Pub on Broad. I had a powerful hankering for their pot roast sandwich. They put roasted tomatoes, caramelized onions, Swiss cheese, and horseradish-sour cream on it, and it was to *die* for. But I ordered the fried green tomato caprese instead, and lingered over my salad and iced tea. I had some time to kill before Dr. Gadsden would be back from his session with Calista.

I'd asked her to move it to ten on the pretext that I needed to meet with her at twelve. The good doctor rarely stayed less than two hours. Of course, I'd canceled my appointment this morning on another pretext. I felt bad about manipulating my own client, but I needed to deal with this doctor.

The protective urge I felt towards Calista struck me as odd given that, at thirty-six, she was five years older than me. I always did my best to get results for my clients. But this was the first time I'd experienced an instinct to look after one. Something about her inspired that. It occurred to me that this could be a slippery slope, and perhaps I wasn't the first to go down it.

I parked a block down from his Broad Street office and waited for him to return. He must've stopped for lunch, because it was almost two when he finally showed. I knew he was in his late fifties, and he looked his age. He was roughly five-ten, had a paunch, light brown hair, and a receding hairline. I scrambled out of the car, caught up to him, and followed him inside. He regarded me quizzically from behind square-rimmed glasses, but held the solid wood door for me.

"Thank you so much," I said.

"Do we have an appointment?" He smiled, all courteous.

By that time, we were in his elegantly appointed lobby. A man waited in a wingback by the floor-to-ceiling windows.

I leaned in close. "No," I whispered conspiratorially. "But I do need just a moment of your time. It's regarding a patient whose life I'm afraid is in grave danger." This was the truth.

He drew back and scrutinized me. "Did you try making an appointment with my receptionist?"

I glanced at her. She stood and crossed her arms.

"Yes, sir, I surely did," I whispered. "But she declined to make me one. And this is of the utmost importance. It's about Calista McQueen."

The receptionist objected to the whispering. "Doctor, is everything all right? Your two o'clock is waiting."

He squinted at me. For a moment, I was sure he was going to order me out of his office. But curiosity won the day. "I'll be just a moment," he said to the receptionist. He regarded me like a spider he was considering squashing, but thought might be poisonous and didn't want to get that close. "This way."

He walked into his private office and I followed. He sat behind his colossal desk. "What's this all about?"

I approached his desk, but remained standing. "I told you. It's about Calista McQueen."

"What about Ms. McQueen? You mentioned her life was in danger?"

"Yes, it is. And she is being protected around the clock."

"I'm happy to hear it. What can I help you with?"

"Doctor, here's the thing. I don't know what your relationship is to your other patients, and really, it's not my concern."

"I beg your—"

"But I do know, for a fact, that your relationship with Ms. McQueen has crossed several doctor-patient boundaries."

He stood, red-faced. "Get out of my office."

"Oh, believe you me, sir, I will not stay here one single second longer than absolutely necessary to make my point."

"And that would be what, exactly?"

"You've just had your last session with Calista McQueen."

"I most certainly have not. Who do you—"

"I'm so sorry to interrupt, but in the interest of not keeping your next patient, God help him, waiting, I need to cut to the chase. And really, who I think I am isn't relevant. Focus. You have an inappropriate relationship with a patient. I know it, and so do you. Cut ties with her today. Refer her elsewhere, or better yet, tell her she doesn't need more therapy."

"I think not." He oozed indignation.

"Here's how this is going to go, *Doctor*. At five o'clock, I'm going to call Calista. If she fails to mention your sudden defection, I will be back. And next time, I will bring a Charleston police detective and a warrant. And, I will talk to a reporter about your scandalous behavior. I'll report you to the South Carolina Board of Examiners. What do you think they'll have to allow about you asking Calista to come and stay at your home—with your wife out of town no less?"

He started sputtering. His red face now sported splotches of purple.

"I. Have. Evidence" I glared at him like I was trying to knock him backward via telekinesis.

He dropped into his chair.

"So. We good here?" I asked.

He looked at his desk for a long moment, then nodded.

"I'll see myself out."

THIRTY

I spent Wednesday evening and most of Thursday comforting Calista, who was distraught over Dr. Gadsden's decision to stop treatment. He'd told her they'd made great progress, but he'd done all he could for her. He did not recommend another therapist, for which I was grateful. Calista was not. She was accustomed to paying someone to listen to her talk. I was of the opinion that she needed to put more effort into relationships with people who didn't charge for that.

But hells bells, who was I to say who did or didn't need therapy? I was on shaky ground. By the time Elenore was making her bedtime tea Thursday night, Calista was calmer.

By Friday morning, I was pacing the floor of my office like a caged tiger waiting for Mr. Patel to call. I didn't want to push him. I decided to wait until Monday. If I hadn't heard from him by then, I'd go back over there. Or call. Calling would be less pushy. But I needed that DVD.

Calista called early in the afternoon. "We're still going out tonight, right?" She seemed to have recovered from her initial panic over losing Dr. Gadsden.

I'd forgotten all about girls' night. "Of course. I'm looking forward to it. You want me to pick you up?"

"Sure, that'd be swell."

I made a couple of quick calls to Merry and Moon Unit, who were all in.

Nate wasn't so thrilled. He looked up from his laptop. "Calista's a client. Doesn't this cross some sort of boundary?"

I raised my left eyebrow at him. "Since you, Blake, and Sonny think the case is closed, she's not a client anymore, is she?"

Nate sighed. "There's only one bar on this island. Will it put a damper on your female bonding ritual if I happen to be there?"

"You can come with us," I said. I tried to sound enthusiastic. But really, no one ever took their boyfriends along on girls' night out.

"No thank you. I may hang out with Blake."

"Blake and Sonny are playing at The Pirates' Den tonight."

"What's the name of their band again?"

"The Back Porch Prophets."

"I've never heard them play."

"They're really good. You should come. You don't have to sit with the girls. Sit up front. Blake'll probably put you to work doing something. You can hang with the guys between sets and during karaoke."

"Karaoke?" He made the word sound like it tasted bad.

I grinned. "Oh, yeah."

"Are you going to sing?"

"Maybe."

"For that alone, I will go."

Merry, Calista, Moon Unit, and I arrived early at the Pirates' Den and scored a table close to the stage. Before long the house was packed. I scanned the boisterous crowd for possible threats. I wanted Calista to have a good time, but I was still on my guard. We ordered a pitcher of mango margaritas and some appetizers.

Calista lifted her glass. "To my first ever girls' night out." She squealed and we all clinked glasses.

I took a small sip. "Hear, hear!"

Moon Unit whooped. "Your first? Honey, this is an *occasion*."

We toasted again. It crossed my mind that Calista didn't drink liquor. Apparently, she was making an exception for the evening. She seemed so happy. I was happy she was having fun. She needed this.

I remained unconvinced her troubles were over, but for that night she couldn't have been safer. She was surrounded by law enforcement officers with a room full of posse, private security—the Marine on duty sat at the bar sipping club soda—and Nate and me. I relaxed. I needed this, too.

Merry said, "Who all is singing karaoke?"

"We all are," I said.

Calista shook her head emphatically. "I don't do stages."

"Have another drink," Merry said.

Moon Unit eyed Calista. "I always knew you'd be gorgeous with your hair and make-up done. Has anyone ever told you that you look just like Marilyn Monroe?"

I inhaled my margarita and narrowly avoided spewing it. Calista and I laughed out loud.

"What?" Moon squished up her face.

"What's so funny?" Merry asked.

"Nothing." I washed down that last swallow with another.

"She does look like Marilyn," Merry said.

The band started playing, making further conversation difficult. We swayed and clapped to the music. And we worked our way through that first pitcher of margaritas.

Nate sat near the corner of the stage. He helped move things around and provided cold beer as needed. And he kept an eye on me.

Our waitress brought another pitcher of margaritas. Merry poured us all a fresh glass. "What shall we toast?"

"To Jose Cuervo!" I said.

We clinked glasses.

Blake and his buddies mostly played their own music. But they took requests. When they started playing "Someone Like You" by

Van Morrison, I scanned the room. Bingo. Michael Devlin had requested that song. I knew he had. That was our song. And Michael was walking towards me with purpose.

"Uh-oh," Merry said.

"What?" Moon Unit followed Merry's gaze. "Oh, my *goodnessss*."

"What's wrong?" asked Calista.

"You see that tall dark and handsome thing at ten o'clock, closing in?" asked Moon Unit.

"Oh, my yes," Calista said.

Merry said, "That's Liz's ex. Double ex."

I looked at Nate. He was watching Michael. Nate downed half a beer.

Calista asked, "Is your double-ex a gentleman?"

"Yes," I said.

"But you don't want to dance with him because it might send the wrong message and because Nate is about to have a seizure."

"Right," I said.

"Maybe I can distract him." Calista stood, finished off her margarita, and glided over to Michael. She pulled him onto the dance floor.

Michael glanced over his shoulder at me. He looked at Calista, confused. Then, ever the Southern gentleman, he put his arms around her and danced.

Merry and Moon high-fived. Nate looked at me and shook his head.

I felt just the teensiest bit cranky on account of how he seemed to think he held title to me after a romance spanning a whole week and a half.

"What's wrong?" Merry asked.

"I'm feeling pent up," I said.

"Oh boy. This is gonna be fun." She refilled my glass.

"Y'all wanna sing 'Lady Marmalade?' They have a set of karaoke after this song," I said.

Merry and Moon Unit hollered approval. That was our favorite girl's number.

I watched Michael dancing with Calista. Maybe he'd ask her out on a date. She needed some normal. Michael was nothing if not normal.

The song ended. I felt a touch on my shoulder and turned to see Nate towering above me. Michael escorted Calista back to the table. He and Nate locked eyes.

Calista said, "Thank you ever so for the dance, Michael."

"My pleasure." He smiled at her, glared at Nate, and sauntered away.

"You girls having fun?" Nate asked.

Moon whooped again. Merry howled. Calista giggled loudly.

I looked up at him, "Hell, yeah. Come on girls." Merry and Moon pulled Calista along and we climbed on stage. I nodded at Blake. He shook his head, grinned, and queued up "Lady Marmalade."

It didn't take much to get Calista comfortable onstage. The four of us channeled "four badass chicks from Moulin Rouge." Some of our dance moves might have been the teensiest bit suggestive. But the thundercloud on Nate's face was uncalled for.

Everyone else in the room applauded wildly. We took our bows and returned to our table. Nate was at the bar with Sonny. They picked up beers, and Nate grabbed an extra bottle. A third for Blake. They ambled over to the karaoke machine. Blake smiled and reached for his beer. Nate said something and Blake's smile faded as he looked my way.

I drained my glass. Merry refilled it.

"Can we sing again?" Calista asked.

"Of course we can," I said. "What do you want to sing?"

"I like country music," Calista said. "Do you think they have 'Before He Cheats,' by Carrie Underwood?"

We all laughed.

"That's our second favorite song," Merry said.

I felt like singing something mad. Why on earth did Nate Andrews think he needed to guard his territory? I was just having fun.

He wasn't any happier with our second number than our first. The rest of the audience was loving us. We went right from Carrie Underwood to Miranda Lambert. I caught a glimpse of Michael as we made our way back to our table. He looked every bit as pissed as Nate.

I was fed up with both of them. "Merry."

"Yeah."

"Tell Blake to play 'All She Wants to do is Dance.' Not the karaoke version—Don Henley."

Merry's eyes got big. "Shit."

"Do it," I said.

Merry hopped up. A minute later she came back to the table. "I made Coop ask. I'm betting Blake wouldn't play it for you."

"Why wouldn't he," asked Calista.

Moon Unit refilled our glasses, a gleam in her eye. "You'll see. Cheers, y'all!"

We all toasted and drank. On the opening drumbeat, I drained my glass and stood.

My hips swayed to the electric guitar. Somebody hollered, "Hell, yeah!"

By the time the horns kicked in, I was dancing around the table, arms above my head. The crowd parted to give me room.

"Whoo-wee." Several wolf whistles pierced the air. "That's what I'm talking about."

Halfway through the song I was dancing on the table.

Merry, Calista, and Moon danced in a circle around the table. We all belted out the song. Most of the people in The Pirate's Den were singing, which is likely the only reason my brother didn't change the song.

Then Nate had me over his shoulder. I kicked and screamed all the way out the door.

THIRTY-ONE

I had a hellacious hangover Saturday morning. I almost didn't answer the phone when it rang at nine. I brushed the hair out of my eyes and blinked at the screen. I didn't recognize the number. Then it hit me. It was a Charleston number.

I answered on the last ring. "Hello?"

"Miss Talbot?"

"Yes. Mr. Patel?" I sat up.

"Yes. I found the DVD. I'm so sorry it took me this long. It wasn't where I thought it was."

"When can I see it?" I was fully awake.

"I've made you a copy. I come in to work at seven o'clock this evening. If you don't mind coming by then, I will give it to you. I hope it helps you locate Roy Lee."

"Me, too, Mr. Patel." I was pretty sure if I located Roy Lee it would only serve to confirm his mamma's worst fears. "Thank you so much for your help."

I had twelve missed calls from Mamma. How had I slept through that? No doubt her phone had rung slap off the wall that morning.

All the clean-living folks in Stella Maris who never touched alcohol, but were nevertheless at the Pirates' Den last night after the dinner hour, would've hated having to tell her I danced on a table and had been carried out of there. I would call her later. The list of things my mamma wasn't going to have would not be a short one.

I crawled out of bed. No sign of Nate. I swallowed a couple of aspirin and climbed into the shower. The hot water helped. I needed a greasy breakfast, but didn't feel like going into the Cracked Pot. I made myself a grilled cheese sandwich with lots of butter. Then I could manage coffee. After I had two cups in me I felt human again.

Where was Nate? His car wasn't in the driveway. I'd be damned if I was going to call him. He had no right, nor any invitation, to treat me like his personal property. He'd been way out of line last night.

And I'd told him about it, all the way home. It was coming back to me.

Nate was most likely on his way back to Greenville.

I curled up on the sofa and hugged a pillow to my chest for comfort. Maybe it was for the best. I was falling in love with Nate.

I was in love with Nate.

But he'd made it clear staying in Stella Maris wasn't in his plans. And I'd lived as much of my life as I could making decisions based on what the men in my life did, or wanted, or didn't want. I needed to live my life. And my life was on Stella Maris.

Rhett sat down at my feet, tongue hanging out in a sloppy grin. "Hey, boy." I ruffled his fur and hugged my dog.

Merry called about lunchtime just to check on me. She knew without me telling her I didn't feel like talking.

Calista called early in the afternoon. "I don't have a hangover at all," she said. "That's the most fun I've ever had. I hope everything's okay with you and Nate."

"It will be," I said, though it wasn't clear to me at all what our future relationship would be. "Do you still have an SSI man out front?"

"Yes," she said. "Mack Ryan wants to continue that for at least another week. It does make me feel safer, although, I'm not worried about tonight anymore. I finally feel like I'm fully me, not some freakish reflection of Marilyn. I have you to thank for that. Confronting my past was the best thing for me. Though I'm awfully sorry about Jimmy."

"That's good," I said. "Have your mother and Grace gone back to California?"

"Grace has. I think she finally accepted the doomed nature of her scheme to make money using me as a sideshow freak. Mother is still at the bed and breakfast. I told her she can stay as long as she wants. Who knows? Maybe there's still a chance for us to have a relationship."

"That's really good. She's your family."

"Well, when you feel up to it, maybe we can have lunch sometime."

"Of course. I'd love to."

"I guess the case is pretty well solved."

"I'm still tying up a few loose ends. Nothing to worry about."

"Let me know what I owe you when you finish."

"I'll send you a final statement. But Calista..."

"Yes?"

"I'm really glad we've gotten to be friends."

"Me, too."

Appropriately, "You and Tequila Make Me Crazy," was up on the playlist in the car. I called Sonny on the way into Charleston and asked him to meet me so we could both screen the DVD. I had the photos Mack Ryan had given me, but Sonny knew the former police officers from the time when the winning ticket was drawn.

Mr. Patel gave me the DVD with a smile and best wishes. I parked a few spots down from Kudu and took the DVD and my laptop inside. Sonny waited in our usual spot in the back left corner.

"What is it you're looking for?" Sonny asked.

I opened my laptop and waited for it to power up. "Someone else in the store. Joe always played the same numbers. He didn't buy quick picks. He wasn't in a lottery pool. The numbers he played were personal. He would have either filled out a form, or, more likely, since it was just one set of numbers, called them out to the clerk."

"You think it was the clerk?"

"The clerk went missing the same night Joe was killed and Calista was burgled and attacked. He's the guy I asked you about. Roy Lee Jenkins."

"Shit," Sonny said.

"Right."

I popped the DVD in. The beginning time stamp was 7:00 p.m.

"What time was the ticket purchased?" Sonny asked.

"I don't know. Calista said Joe bought the winning ticket five weeks before the drawing. He bought ten-draw tickets."

"How would anyone remember what numbers someone else picked five weeks before?"

"I don't know. But I think the answer is on this DVD."

Sonny stood. "Better get some coffee. This could take a while. You want a mocha?"

"Thanks, yes. With soy, please."

Sonny rolled his eyes. "I'll be right back."

We were into our second cup when Joe Fernandez walked into the store. At first, I didn't recognize him. I'd only seen photos Calista had shown me, and those in the newspaper articles. The camera was pointed at an angle. Joe reached for the handle at the same time another hand entered the screen. It looked like the other person opened the door and Joe walked in. He seemed to thank him. Then both men walked to the counter, Joe in front. We couldn't see the man behind him.

Joe waved to Roy Lee. There was no sound on the DVD. It looked like they chatted for a moment, then Roy Lee handed him his ticket. Joe waved and left the store.

The man behind him stepped to the counter and smiled.

"Sonavabitch." I pressed pause.

"What the hell?" said Sonny.

I stared at him. "You know this guy? Niles Ignacio? He's the yoga instructor."

Sonny shook his head. "No. That's Tim Fuckin' Poteat."

"Oh. My. God." I turned back to the screen. "This is not the same Tim Poteat in the photo Mack Ryan sent over. Calista and I both would have recognized him instantly."

"Then someone swapped the photo. Because I'm telling you, that's Tim Poteat."

"I need to get to Calista," I said.

"This DVD is evidence in Joe Fernandez's murder and Roy Lee Jenkins's disappearance. I need to get the original, get it logged in, and get a warrant for Poteat's arrest. He still has friends in the department and the Solicitor's office. I'll have to handle this with care."

I nodded. "I'll stay with Calista until you have Poteat in custody."

"Watch your back."

"You, too."

THIRTY-TWO

I called Calista, but she didn't pick up. I called Blake and got his voicemail. Why could I never get ahold of my brother when I really needed him?

It was nine-thirty on a Saturday night. I called the station.

The phone rang through to the after-hours dispatcher at the fire station. "Good Evening, Stella Maris Public Safety Services. How may I help you?"

"This is Liz Talbot. I need to reach my brother. Do you have an emergency contact number for this evening?"

"Well, hey there, Liz! This is Mary Jo. You remember me don't you? We were in ninth grade Spanish together? How are—" She was so perky I wanted to slide through the phone and grab her throat.

"Hey, Mary Jo, I'm sorry to cut you off, but this is an emergency. Where's Blake?"

"Well, he has the night off. I can try his cell."

"I've already tried that. Can't you call him on the radio function?"

"I'll tryyyy."

"Could you do it now? Please?"

"Hold please."

She actually placed me on hold. Now she was all business. I resisted the urge to bang my head on the steering wheel. I took deep breaths. In Mary Jo's defense, it was rare for there to be an emergency on a Saturday night in Stella Maris.

She came back on the line. "I'm unable to reach him at this time. Is there a message?"

"Is Rodney on duty tonight?"

"Yes, he is."

"Please get ahold of him, Blake, or both of them, and have them call me back as soon as possible. This is urgent."

"I'll do my best," she said in a saccharine tone that suggested she'd get around to it when it suited her.

"Thank you so much Mary Jo," I said, thinking how I should've started out being nicer to her and I would've gotten further.

No use calling Nate. He was no doubt in Greenville, four hours away.

I called SSI and convinced someone on the other end of the line to get Mack Ryan to call me. I was driving off the ferry in Stella Maris when he called me back.

"Mack, who had access to that stack of photos you sent over?"

"I pulled them myself. Sent them over with someone I knew I could trust. Why?"

"Sometime in between when you pulled them and when they arrived at my house, one of them was switched."

"I don't understand."

"Tim Poteat has been moonlighting for some time as a yoga instructor. He's using the name Niles Ignacio. The real Niles Ignacio was a celebrated yoga instructor in Burlington, Vermont. I suspect he is no longer drawing breath. Calista would have recognized his photo immediately."

"Shit."

"Tell me about it. I'm on my way to Calista's now. I can't get her on the phone."

Silence.

"Mack?"

"Poteat is on guard duty at her house this evening. With Kennan in jail, I considered Poteat cleared."

"Oh, no. *No. No. No.*"

"We're on our way. ETA forty-five minutes."

I'd no sooner ended the call than the alarm on my phone screeched. Calista had pressed the emergency button on the pendant I'd given her.

THIRTY-THREE

I called Sonny and let him know where to find Tim Poteat.

"Blake with you?"

"No, I haven't been able to reach him."

"He was going out for a sunset sail, on a date. He might not be back yet. I'm headed your way. I can deal with the details later. Don't go in there alone. Wait for me."

"Sonny," I said, "you and I both know I can't wait. Calista's life may depend on it. Mack and his guys are on the way. You can't beat them. They have a head start. Get the evidence. Get the warrant."

He grumbled, but finally agreed.

I parked on Ocean Boulevard, down the street a ways, where Poteat couldn't see my approach. I called the too-perky dispatcher at the fire station.

"I gave Rodney your message," she said. "Didn't he call you back?" Her tone oozed innocence and the desire to spank Rodney for not doing as he was told. But I wasn't buying what she was selling.

Through gritted teeth, I snarled my location and told her to send Blake and Rodney PDQ on a matter of life and death. I prayed Blake's date had brought him back to shore for dinner. It was unlike him to be out of touch for long.

I skirted the perimeter of the yard and went up the steps to the pool deck. I pulled my weapon from the holster at my waistband and led with that. The house was quiet.

The door to the pool house was ajar. Where was Elenore? Was she a victim, or part of the threat? I crossed the pool deck and parted the curtains. Elenore was in bed, under the covers. I approached the bed with caution, shook her gently. No response. I felt for a pulse. She was alive, and dressed for bed, as if she'd simply turned in early. I shook her harder. She was unresponsive. Drugged again.

It was just me and Poteat.

I scanned the windows and doors of the house for any sign of movement and found none. Was he even still here? I crossed the patio in a crouching run. The door to the great room was unlocked. No one was in the main part of the house. I eased the door sideways on its track and stepped inside. I left it wide open in case I needed to make a quick exit.

Water was running in Calista's bathroom. I slid through the kitchen and down the short hallway. I slipped Sig in the waistband of my capris, reached inside my pocket and tapped voice memo and record on my iPhone. I slid the phone back in my pocket, microphone up, and retrieved my weapon. If things went sideways, Blake would know to check my phone. I continued down the hall.

The bedroom door was halfway ajar. I moved to the left side, flattened myself against the wall, and then peered inside. Calista was undressed and tied, wrists together and ankles together. Her wrists were anchored to a thick chain that wrapped between the mattress and the headboard. Her ankles were attached to the other end of the chain near the footboard. She wasn't gagged. She struggled against the thick, padded bindings.

When she saw me, her eyes widened She shook her head, as if warning me to run.

I showed her my gun.

She nodded, closed her eyes a moment. Her chest rose, as if she drew a deep breath. "You'll never get away with this, Niles."

His voice came from the bathroom. It still had that soothing, yoga-speak quality that called to mind Mr. Rogers and got on my last nerve. "Of course I will, dear heart. Once you go to sleep, I'll have all the time I need to find your bank account passwords and transfer all that lovely money—my money—wherever I like. Then, I'll get on a plane and disappear." The water stopped running.

"You'll never guess the passwords," she said. "They aren't written down anywhere."

"Well, no wonder I've had such a hard time finding them. You'll have to tell me, then, before you go to sleep. In fact, now that I think about it, we should just get all that tedious transferring out of the way first. I'll get your laptop as soon as I finish mixing your cocktail."

Oh, dear heaven, what was he doing in the bathroom.

"I'll never give you the passwords to my accounts. You can't execute a wire transfer without the account numbers, the passwords, and my security codes. You don't even know which banks the money is in."

"Why, of course I do. I've had plenty of time to gather nearly everything I need from your files. Some nights, after you were asleep, I'd slip in here and disable the alarm so I could search. I know exactly where the blind spots are in the cameras."

"You're the one who drugged our tea, aren't you?" Calista said.

Poteat laughed. "The Rohypnol is ground up in your loose tea—the chamomile. Thank you for reminding me. I need to take that with me. You've been drinking it most nights, just like I suggested. I couldn't have you waking up and finding me going through your things, now could I? Happily, the old lady's been drinking it, too. Every night she slept here. Put two birds to sleep with one cup of tea. Well, usually just one apiece."

"Did you kill Jimmy?" Calista asked. "Tell me. You owe me that much."

"I hadn't planned on it. Is it my fault he was parked outside mooning over you like a lovesick teenager? He saw me coming in. He had to go. I'm sorry."

"No, you're not. Don't you dare say that. You're not one bit sorry."

He sighed. "You're right. I'm not. It had to be done. And then your little detective showed up with her boyfriend in their Scooby-Doo van. I had to set off the alarm to distract them so I could leave. I was parked not far down from your ex-husband. They'd have noticed my car in another minute. What a waste. I could have searched for a good hour before I had to get back to work. You ladies were out cold. Had an extra cup of tea, did you? And of course, the wine. Tsk, tsk. I had to tuck you in. That was fun."

Calista closed her eyes and swallowed hard. She looked like she was fighting nausea. "Why were you here to begin with?"

"I was just going to have some more fun with you. You know, run the barking dog tape. Move some of your things around after you went to sleep. I was never going to kill you until tonight. You were so attached to all that symmetry. It worked for me."

"Ooooohhh!" Calista was almost as angry as she was scared.

"Now. All I need are the passwords." He appeared at the side of the bed and caressed her head. "And you're going to give them to me. I don't want to hurt you. I've grown fond of you."

"You can go to hell."

"Or, we can have some fun before you drink your Nembutal and Mountain Dew and I fill you full of chloral hydrate." The Mr. Rogers voice was gone, the one that replaced it cruel. "Like we should have two years ago, when we first met. You remember our one night together, don't you, Calista? I had to wear a mask that night, and I couldn't talk to you. This will be so much better. I can tell you everything I'm going to do first."

She screamed.

I pivoted, planted both feet, and raised my weapon. "Untie her. Now."

"Well, well," Tim said. "Nancy Drew to the rescue. Where's Nate? Oh, wait, yes, he's gone back to Greenville, hasn't he? And your brother, deputy dog, I'm sorry, he and his Charleston buddy are busy congratulating themselves on locking up Ryder Keenan. I'm so happy you've come alone. Did you come to hold Calista's hand on the anniversary of Marilyn's death so she wouldn't be afraid?"

"Untie. Her. Now. You have no idea how bad I want to shoot you."

"Likewise, bitch."

"Calista, meet Tim Poteat, ex-Charleston police officer, current SSI employee, and part-time yoga instructor. Tell me, Timmy, was Ryder involved at all? Or was he just a convenient scapegoat?"

"Not that it's any of your business, but I work alone. I won't be splitting the money I've waited two years to collect with anyone else."

"About that..." I tilted my head and gave him my dumb-blonde look. "You went to work for SSI in two thousand ten. Was that before, or after you killed Joe Fernandez trying to find that lottery ticket?"

He laughed harshly. "I left the police force not long after Joe and I took a ride. I stayed around long enough to make sure no one looked for Roy Lee Jenkins very hard."

I asked, "What did you do? Talk to your buddies? Cast doubt on a few statements, make him look like a drugged-up drifter no one cared about but his mamma?"

"Something like that."

"Is that *your* mamma in the pool house?"

Evil and disgust flickered in his eyes. "Of course not. My mother's somewhere in Florida. An unmarked grave in the Everglades, if you want specifics. What would make you think that cow was my mother?"

"Loose ends," I said. "I hate to leave a puzzle with just a few missing pieces."

He shrugged. "Makes no difference to me. You won't live to tell. After I'm gone, they'll never find either of us. And they'll think Elenore killed Norma Jeane here."

"Why would they think that? If she isn't your mother—your accomplice—why would she kill Calista?" I asked.

His eyes glittered like a snake's. "She's Roy Lee's mother."

Roy Lee. The one person I hadn't profiled. Damnation. "I can see why Elenore would want to kill *you*. Where did you bury Roy Lee? Since I'm gonna be dead soon and all. Wow me with how smart you are."

His cold, smug little smile told me he was a true believer in his own brilliance. "Roy Lee isn't buried anywhere. He spent some time in a freezer in a storage building in Mt. Pleasant. There may be a piece or two of him still there. It's hard to tell, really. The yoga instructor from Vermont was in there, too. Every now and then, I feed a hand or a chunk of leg to an alligator. In different parts of the county, of course. The freezer is almost empty now."

Bile rose in my throat. I focused on keeping my voice calm. I squinched my face with doubt. "Elenore as Calista's killer? That doesn't play." I resisted the urge to tell him Sonny and Mack already knew all about him. It worked in my favor that he thought I'd come by and caught him by accident. He had no idea backup was on the way.

He shrugged. "The way I see it, the theory will be she holds Calista responsible. Calista got all that money. Her son has disappeared to—who knows where? Calista had that crazy Marilyn obsession. Hell, the old woman's crazy, too. That's what I would think, anyway. Based on the evidence they'll find. She did buy the enema bag, after all. Come to think of it, they may think she killed me, too and somehow did away with me. If I have time, after I deal with the two of you, I'll leave some breadcrumbs in that direction. I must say, brainstorming with you is quite productive."

Calista said, "*You* put that horrid thing on my shopping list!"

"Of course I did," Poteat said. "Who else?"

Calista oozed wrath. "And you set poor Elenore up to take the fall for you from the very beginning—you're the one who introduced me to her. You suggested I hire her. You killed her son and did horrid things to him and now you're making her out to be a killer for no more reason than it's convenient."

I tried to keep my voice casual. "Does Elenore have any idea she's here as a pawn in your twisted plot?"

"Nope. She's just cleaning house. Grateful for the work. She doesn't know a thing."

My whole body itched to lunge at him. "It's such a shame you didn't think to get rid of the Mini Mart's security footage. You might have gotten away with all of this." The minute the words were out of my mouth, I wanted to call them back. I needed him to keep feeling confident for a few more minutes.

He scowled. "Roy Lee screwed me over on that. He was supposed to bring me the DVD. Told him I'd pay him a hundred thousand dollars. I couldn't ask the store manager for it. There was no case at that point—Roy Lee was still alive. Besides, I was undercover narcotics."

"You killed him because he didn't bring you the DVD?" I asked.

"I would've killed him anyway. He saw me in the store the night Joe bought the winning ticket. I was a regular. He didn't know I was an undercover cop. He was a loose end. I don't like them either."

I focused on keeping my expression one of rapt attention and hoped he'd keep on talking.

He said, "Roy Lee and that DVD needed to disappear. I thought he had it, just didn't bring it with him. Maybe he thought he'd jack up the price. But he'd had an attack of conscience. Stupid of him to meet me, that being the case, but there you go. I figured I'd find it in his apartment after I killed him. But it wasn't there. I would've bet Elenore had it, but didn't even know. That's why I arranged to make her acquaintance. Are you saying Patel still has it?"

I tried to look defeated. "He'll find it soon enough." I willed him to believe it was missing.

He smiled. "No one knows where it is, do they? That means the cow has it after all. Probably in a box of things she collected from Roy Lee's apartment."

"So, Calista coming back here, hiring SSI—that was just a happy coincidence for you?"

He laughed again, shook his head. "It was convenient. But I've been planning how to get my money back ever since Calista left town. I've followed her—electronically of course—everywhere she's been. I waited for her to settle somewhere. If she hadn't come back to the lowcountry, I could've transferred or gotten work with another security company wherever she landed. I just bided my time, built my resume. Then, when she started building her house, I got a friend at Dixon Hughes Goodman to recommend SSI."

I nodded, tried to look impressed. "And you took up yoga as well?"

His body shook with a silent chuckle. "It's great exercise. The one thing she did, everywhere she went was find a yoga instructor. So, I found one who looked like me and had no family to speak of, and became him. Of course, he relocated from Vermont—you know, to that freezer I mentioned. And then he—I—went to work in Mt. Pleasant. The rest was easy. She needed a friend."

"You are one more piece of work," I said. "But you missed your true calling. You'd have made a great actor. You sure played a gay yoga instructor convincingly. Must've been all that undercover work."

He sneered. He held his hands at hip height. He had a gun. He was ready to draw. I was going to have to shoot him. Part of me really did want to. I'd rarely met a man who was more in need of shooting. But the better part of me loathed the idea of taking a life. I didn't know if I had that in me.

His eyes held mine.

He would be fast.

Could he get a shot off?

A rustling noise came from down the hall. And the sound of...hoofs on tile? Grunting? What in this world?

Poteat narrowed his eyes.

Something was coming fast.

I pivoted back out of the doorway and against the wall just in time to avoid being trampled by three wild hogs. They knocked the door wide open. I risked a peek.

The pigs charged Poteat. "What the bloody hell?"

He fired twice. Wood splinted. Fragments of doorframe flew. A piece caught me in the arm.

I crouched low. One of the swine knocked Poteat sideways.

He fired a round at the hogs, then two at me. Missed. He was still off balance. I couldn't count on that lasting.

I braced and fired at Poteat. Three shots. He jerked and went down.

Things went fuzzy. I stared at him, numb.

The hogs sniffed him and poked at him with their snouts. He didn't move.

His gun had slid outside the ring of swine. I grabbed it and laid it with mine on the bed. Then I untied Calista. She sobbed hysterically.

"Shh...shh. You're safe. It's over."

When I had her untied, she curled into a ball.

"Where's your robe?"

"Hook. Bathroom door." She shivered, her teeth chattering.

I picked up both guns, gave the hogs a wide berth, and stepped into the bathroom. The "cocktail" Poteat had been preparing for Calista had been in a big pink enema bag. Three empty vials labeled chloral hydrate were on the side of the sink. I shuddered, grabbed the robe and went back to Calista.

"Here, let's get you into this. Help is on the way."

Calista's sobbing subsided. She stared at the pigs, who still poked at Poteat. "I don't think we need any help now."

"Nevertheless—"

"*Liz,*" Blake shouted from the back door.

"In here." I sat down on the bed beside Calista and hugged her tight.

Blake and Rodney came in, guns drawn.

They stopped and stared at Poteat and the hogs.

"I had to shoot him, Blake. He would have killed us both."

He cocked his head at me. "And the hogs?"

I shrugged. "They acted on their own recognizance."

And then twelve pissed off Marines landed.

THIRTY-FOUR

I slept in Sunday. I treated myself to eggs benedict with a mimosa for brunch. The heat wave had broken. It was still plenty hot, but with the breeze off the ocean, it was comfortable enough under the shade of the jasmine-covered pergola to eat on the deck. Colleen joined me.

"Are you okay?" she asked. "You've never taken a life before."

I pondered for a moment. "I did what I had to do. It was him, or me and Calista. Niles, Poteat, whatever his name was—he was pure evil. But there's a piece of me that feels wounded, like maybe something with big teeth took a bite out of me. I'm afraid that might not heal. Maybe it shouldn't. Killing shouldn't come easy."

Colleen's eyes looked troubled. "I wish I could have spared you that."

"You sent the hogs, didn't you?" I asked.

"Well, there is precedent."

"I'm sorry. What?"

"Swine have been used to cast out demons before. The story's in three of the four Gospels."

I threw back my head and laughed. "Are you quoting scripture now? Is there a deeper message?"

"No. I just used what was handy. I could hardly do the roman candle thing in Calista's house. I'd have burnt up everything inside the concrete shell. We needed a distraction."

"Thank you."

"I'm glad I could be there."

"I guess I'll have to revise my position on the hog issue."

"I'm sure they'd appreciate any pull you might have on town council in their favor. They're really harmless, except to demons, of course."

I sipped my mimosa.

"You're in love with Nate, aren't you?"

"I'm afraid I am."

"It's the real thing."

Behind my Wayfarers, my eyes watered. "For me, it is."

"I so want you to be happy. But you need to stay here."

"I have no intentions of leaving."

"You say that now, but most people will do anything for true love."

"Most of the people I love are right here."

"And we will always love you, regardless," she said. "It will be easy to justify leaving. But I can see alternate scenarios."

"What do you mean?"

"I can see what happens if you leave and someone else takes your town council seat. It will go to election. Your replacement will advocate limited development. After a few years, he'll wear folks down, talk them into it. There'll be a lot of money on the table. After the first two resorts, there will be a bridge. Things will never be the same here."

"Colleen, I promise, I'm not leaving. But I have to wonder, what is so special about Stella Maris that you've been sent here to protect it? I mean, I know why it's special to *me*. But there are so many awful things going on in the world..."

"And there are legions of guardian spirits at work. Some with more success than others. They don't send newbies to the Middle East. Even spirits with eons of experience can't change human hearts. Our success depends on motivating humans. That's not always easy."

"Is Stella Maris sacred ground?"

"The whole earth is sacred ground, the moon, the stars, galaxies you've never dreamed of." She faded away.

The door opened behind me and Nate walked out onto the deck. "Mind if I join you?"

I gestured to a chair. "Would you like some brunch?"

"No, thanks. I ate breakfast on the road." He settled into the chair to my left, and turned it slightly to face the beach. "Blake filled me in on last night. Are you okay?"

"I will be."

"He also told me they got the final coroner's report on Jim Davis. No news there. He was murdered, the suicide staged. Ryder Keenan's been released. That recording you made no doubt expedited that. They found Poteat's storage unit."

I shuddered.

Waves tumbled over each other and raced to shore. A flock of sea gulls flew by.

I sipped my mimosa and waited. After a while, I grew impatient with waiting.

"You didn't drive all the way from Greenville to tell me what Blake told you," I said. "Was there something you came to say?"

"Yeah. I'm just working out how to say it."

"Are you about done yet?"

"Not quite."

"I'm going to fix another mimosa. Are you sure you don't want one?"

"Best I keep a clear head."

I shrugged and went into the kitchen. When I returned, he was standing at the edge of the deck, hands in the pockets of his khaki shorts. I set down my glass and arranged myself in my chair. His long, suntanned legs were quite a distraction.

Finally, he spoke. But I couldn't make out what he was saying. He was talking into the wind.

I squared my shoulders, stood, and walked over to stand by him at the rail. "I'm sorry. I didn't hear what you said."

He turned towards me and wrapped an arm around my waist. He tipped my chin up, swiped my sunglasses, and tucked my hair behind my ear.

I searched deep pools of blue for answers.

He took a deep breath. "I said, 'I love you, Liz.'"

I smiled and shook my head slowly. Tears brimmed in my eyes. I reached up and held his face with my hands. "I love you, too. Why was that so hard?"

"Because I've never said those words to a woman before. I've never felt this way. Honestly, I always believed I never would. I just didn't think I had it in me. You make me...irrational. I don't like feeling irrational."

I laughed. "I hope you're not expecting me to apologize."

He grinned. "No. I'm not complaining. I'm just trying to explain. I'm accustomed to being in control of my emotions. Friday night..."

"I'm not apologizing for that either, just so you know."

He scowled at me.

"Well, I'm not apologizing for having a good time, anyway. I am very sorry for some of the things I said to you on the way home. I don't even remember everything I said to you."

"Probably best we both forget it. You had a lot of tequila in you, and you were mad as fire. That's a bad combination."

I hugged him close. "Forgive me?"

"If you forgive me."

"Done," I said.

He let go of me with one hand and ran it through his hair.

I pulled back. "What's wrong?"

"I don't want to be your back-up plan."

"Nate, that's crazy. You know you're not my back-up plan. It's painfully obvious to the casual observer that I'm not in love with Michael Devlin. If I wanted him, I'd be with him right now."

His forehead wrinkled. "Logically, I know that's true. But I also know that you stayed in Greenville for Scott. You stayed away from here because of Michael. Your feelings for the two of them were powerful enough that you changed your life for them."

"And that's something I never should have done."

He shrugged. "But you did. And I can't help feeling that means your feelings for them were stronger. That scares me."

"Nate, it's not that at all. I think it just took me a long time to grow up. Marrying Scott—I probably did that in part because Michael hurt my heart so bad. I did love Michael once, but it was not the same thing at all. What I felt for him, that wasn't grown-up love. And it was all knotted up with loving this salty piece of ground. I didn't even know who I was yet when I was with Michael. It was so long ago."

He nodded. "I know that in my head. But, like I said, you make me irrational. I want to haul you back to Greenville just like I hauled you out of The Pirates' Den Friday night."

Things inside me twisted like wrung out laundry. "This is my home. It's my place in the world."

He nodded. "I know. But I feel like Greenville is *my* place. Being here...it feels like I'm wearing someone else's clothes."

Tears slid down my face. "I don't know how we resolve this."

"No, no, no...please don't cry, Slugger." He pulled me to him. For a long time we held onto each other. "All I know for sure is that I love you."

I pulled back to look at him. "I love you, too. So much."

"Then we'll figure the rest out as we go."

"All right," I said. "We'll think of something tomorrow."

"Do you have any more of that champagne?"

"I surely do."

"Why don't we take it upstairs?"

I gave him my best come-hither smile and we went inside.

Readers' Discussion Guide
or
Things to Chat about While Sipping a Refreshing Beverage if You're so Inclined

1. Do you believe in Doppelgangers? Have you ever met someone who was the spitting image of you or someone you know?

2. Do you think it's possible Marilyn actually has distant family members somewhere, perhaps unaware of the connection, who resemble her?

3. Calista is emotionally isolated because of her background, but also because of her wealth. She comments to Liz that "...everyone thinks they want to win the lottery. ... If you have great wealth, you have to spend your whole life guarding it from all the people who want to take it away from you. ... Almost anyone can be bought for the right price." Do you think she's right?

4. Do you think Liz made the right choice in pursuing a relationship with Nate? Do you think there's trouble ahead for them because they work together?

5. Liz is very organized and methodical. But, like most of us, she has a lot of distractions. Family is very important to her. Nate, on the other hand, is not close to his family. Do you see this as a potential problem for them?

6. Would you have done what Liz did on the ferry boat?

7. Liz has a strong sense of place and doesn't intend to leave Stella Maris. Nate feels that he belongs in Greenville. How important is a sense of place to you? Do you see this as a problem for them?

8. Michael makes a strong case that he and Liz have shared roots in Stella Maris, and want the same things in life. But he has a real problem with her career. How would you respond to a man who wanted you to change careers because he feared for your safety?

9. Liz and Nate occasionally break the law in investigating their cases. Does this bother you, or does the end justify the means? Is it okay because they are trying to save a life?

10. What do you think drives people like Donna Clark aka Grace McKee? Do you think Gwen/Gladys Monroe was as much her victim as was Calista?

11. Who did you suspect all along was behind the strange gaslight incidents at Calista's home? Did you believe her life was really in danger, or did you think she had emotional problems which made her believe this was the case?

12. Do you think it's possible there are guardian spirits like Colleen at work here on earth? How about guardian angels?

Susan M. Boyer

Susan loves three things best: her family, books, and beaches. She's grateful to have been blessed with a vivid imagination, allowing her to write her own books centered around family, beaches, and solving puzzles wherein someone is murdered. Susan lives in Greenville, SC, and runs away to the coast as often as she can.

Her debut novel, *Lowcountry Boil*, won the Agatha Award for Best First Novel, the Daphne du Maurier Award for Excellence in Mystery/Suspense, was an RWA Golden Heart® finalist, and hit the USA TODAY bestseller list. Susan's short fiction has appeared in *moonShine Review*, *Spinetingler* Magazine, and *Relief Journal* among others. Visit Susan at www.susanmboyerbooks.com.

Henery Press Mystery Books

And finally, before you go...
Here are a few other mysteries
you might enjoy:

BOARD STIFF

Kendel Lynn

An Elliott Lisbon Mystery (#1)

As director of the Ballantyne Foundation on Sea Pine Island, SC, Elliott Lisbon scratches her detective itch by performing discreet inquiries for Foundation donors. Usually nothing more serious than retrieving a pilfered Pomeranian. Until Jane Hatting, Ballantyne board chair, is accused of murder. The Ballantyne's reputation tanks, Jane's headed to a jail cell, and Elliott's sexy ex is the new lieutenant in town.

Armed with moxie and her Mini Coop, Elliott uncovers a trail of blackmail schemes, gambling debts, illicit affairs, and investment scams. But the deeper she digs to clear Jane's name, the guiltier Jane looks. The closer she gets to the truth, the more treacherous her investigation becomes. With victims piling up faster than shells at a clambake, Elliott realizes she's next on the killer's list.

Available at booksellers nationwide and online

Visit www.henerypress.com for details

ARTIFACT
Gigi Pandian

A Jaya Jones Treasure Hunt Mystery (#1)

Historian Jaya Jones discovers the secrets of a lost Indian treasure may be hidden in a Scottish legend from the days of the British Raj. But she's not the only one on the trail...

From San Francisco to London to the Highlands of Scotland, Jaya must evade a shadowy stalker as she follows hints from the hastily scrawled note of her dead lover to a remote archaeological dig. Helping her decipher the cryptic clues are her magician best friend, a devastatingly handsome art historian with something to hide, and a charming archaeologist running for his life.

Available at booksellers nationwide and online

Visit www.henerypress.com for details

THE AMBITIOUS CARD
John Gaspard

An Eli Marks Mystery (#1)

The life of a magician isn't all kiddie shows and card tricks. Sometimes it's murder. Especially when magician Eli Marks very publicly debunks a famed psychic, and said psychic ends up dead. The evidence, including a bloody King of Diamonds playing card (one from Eli's own Ambitious Card routine), directs the police right to Eli.

As more psychics are slain, and more King cards rise to the top, Eli can't escape suspicion. Things get really complicated when romance blooms with a beautiful psychic, and Eli discovers she's the next target for murder, and he's scheduled to die with her. Now Eli must use every trick he knows to keep them both alive and reveal the true killer.

Available at booksellers nationwide and online

Visit www.henerypress.com for details

CIRCLE OF INFLUENCE

Annette Dashofy

A Zoe Chambers Mystery (#1)

Zoe Chambers, paramedic and deputy coroner in rural Pennsylvania's tight-knit Vance Township, has been privy to a number of local secrets over the years, some of them her own. But secrets become explosive when a dead body is found in the Township Board President's abandoned car.

As a January blizzard rages, Zoe and Police Chief Pete Adams launch a desperate search for the killer, even if it means uncovering secrets that could not only destroy Zoe and Pete, but also those closest to them.

Available at booksellers nationwide and online

Visit www.henerypress.com for details

FINDING SKY

Susan O'Brien

A Nicki Valentine Mystery

Suburban widow and P.I. in training Nicki Valentine can barely keep track of her two kids, never mind anyone else. But when her best friend's adoption plan is jeopardized by the young birth mother's disappearance, Nicki is persuaded to help. Nearly everyone else believes the teenager ran away, but Nicki trusts her BFF's judgment, and the feeling is mutual.

The case leads where few moms go (teen parties, gang shootings) and places they can't avoid (preschool parties, OB-GYNs' offices). Nicki has everything to lose and much to gain — including the attention of her unnervingly hot P.I. instructor. Thankfully, Nicki is armed with her pesky conscience, occasional babysitters, a fully stocked minivan, and nature's best defense system: women's intuition.

Available at booksellers nationwide and online

Visit www.henerypress.com for details

From the Henery Press Chick Lit Collection

BET YOUR BOTTOM DOLLAR

Karin Gillespie

The Bottom Dollar Series (#1)

Welcome to the Bottom Dollar Emporium in Cayboo Creek, South
Carolina, where everything from coconut mallow cookies to Clabber
Girl Baking Powder costs a dollar but the coffee and gossip are free.
For the Bottom Dollar gals, work time is sisterhood time.

When news gets out that a corporate dollar store is coming to town,
the women are thrown into a tizzy, hoping to save their beloved
store as well their friendships. Meanwhile the manager is canoo-
dling with the town's wealthiest bachelor and their romance un-
earths some startling family secrets.

The first in a series, *Bet Your Bottom Dollar* serves up a heaping
portion of small town Southern life and introduces readers to a cast
of eccentric characters. Pull up a wicker chair, set out a tall glass of
Cheer Wine, and immerse yourself in the adventures of a group of
women who the *Atlanta Journal Constitution* calls, "... the kind of
steel magnolias who would make Scarlett O'Hara envious."

Available at booksellers nationwide and online

Visit www.henerypress.com for details

From the Henery Press Humor Collection

THE BREAKUP DOCTOR
Phoebe Fox

The Breakup Doctor Series (#1)

Call Brook Ogden a matchmaker-in-reverse. Let others bring people together; Brook, licensed mental health counselor, picks up the pieces after things come apart. When her own therapy practice collapses, she maintains perfect control: landing on her feet with a weekly advice-to-the-lovelorn column and a successful consulting service as the Breakup Doctor: on call to help you shape up after you breakup.

Then her relationship suddenly crumbles and Brook finds herself engaging in almost every bad-breakup behavior she preaches against. And worse, she starts a rebound relationship with the most inappropriate of men: a dangerously sexy bartender with anger-management issues—who also happens to be a former patient.

As her increasingly out-of-control behavior lands her at rock-bottom, Brook realizes you can't always handle a messy breakup neatly—and that sometimes you can't pull yourself together until you let yourself fall apart.

Available at booksellers nationwide and online

Visit www.henerypress.com for details